I0745502

IN THE DEFENDANT'S CHAIR

LYNN YVONNE MOON

In the Defendant's Chair
An Agency Book
by Lynn Yvonne Moon

© Copyright 2014 Lynn Yvonne Moon

ISBN 978-1-953278-00-5 SB
ISBN 978-1-953278-01-2 Eb

Published by

Indignor House

*This book is dedicated
to those wrongly accused.*

PROLOGUE

THE STORM RAGED against the icy rain falling ruthlessly from the cold and dark clouds. Frozen pellets bounced off the windows as loud howling cries of unforgiving wind echoed through the house. The small wooden frame vibrated with each angry gust.

"It's going to be an ugly night," Alex commented picking up the small child's jacket from the back of the sofa. He dropped the miniature item onto the coat rack and smiled at his wife who stood at the kitchen door, arms folded against her chest. A loud bang exploded and she jumped as an eerie chill ran up her spine.

"What was that?" she asked.

"Probably just a branch from an old tree," he replied glancing out the window. "I'm sure I'll have a mess to clean up tomorrow."

"Well, since it's nasty outside," Early said taunting him with her swaying hips. "I'll get your fire going if you start a real one. I'm going to check on the kids."

"Mmmm," he mumbled. "You have a deal."

Early ran her fingers through her fine golden brown hair and grinned. There was nothing better than making love by a warm fire on a cold winter's night. The wind continued to howl with such force the house trembled with each freezing wave.

I love winter, she thought walking down the hallway.

Early turned twenty-seven a week ago, a young woman just entering her prime. It felt cozy as her bare feet hit the soft hallway carpet. She could only think of her anxiously awaiting husband in the other room.

Early opened Daren's door first and prayed the child was asleep. Daren's a healthy, rambunctious seven-year-old who would rather have his teeth pulled than go to bed. As she approached him, Early had to laugh. Daren was on his back with his head on the floor and his butt and legs on his bed, sound asleep.

"Oh my," Early sighed as she lifted him back into his bed. She covered him and kissed his forehead. Before leaving, she whispered, "I love you baby."

After Daren it was time to check on the twins, Nevada and Dakota, beautiful three-year-olds she devoted her life to. She tiptoed into their room and could not help but smile. As usual, they were not in their beds but curled up together on the floor between layers upon layers of blankets and pillows.

"Well," she whispered with a twinkle in her eye, "I'm sure glad I bought those heavy-duty pajamas." Leaving them to their slumber, she closed their door.

Early began to undress in the hallway. By the time she reached the living room, her bare skin tingled from the cool air.

"Wonderful," Alex stated not removing his eyes from his striking wife of nine years.

She swayed into his arms. After a long and wanting kiss, Early stepped back and unbuttoned his shirt. Alex handed her a glass of wine as he took a small sip of his, she followed his moves and took several small drinks. He kissed her sitting both glasses on the mantel. He touched and caressed her body, his fingers reaching every place he could find to excite her. They dropped to the floor, their legs entwined. Each slowly becoming more a part of the other as their thoughts and desires merged.

Early slid down between Alex's legs and his desire swelled. She engulfed his warmth with slow rhythmic movement. She could tell he wanted to explode between her lips. But before he could reach his limit, Early withdrew and gazed up at him. She smiled and he smiled back with a tear in his eye.

"Tell me what you want baby," he begged. "You want to ride?"

Without responding, Early straddled his waist and slowly

guided him into her. He reached up and fondled her firm breasts and excited nipples. As the movement of her thighs and hips increased, his fingers squeezed more firmly against her. She pulled him in deeper rubbing her secret place against his as fast and hard as her hip muscles would allow. Early felt a sudden release of love and longing as she squeezed against his hardened love. Her back arched and she moaned. Alex was next. He exploded inside her as his hands gripped her hips in the heat of the excitement. He moved her back and forth until his strength was gone.

She fell with exhaustion onto his chest and absorbed his love. The rise and fall of his breathing filled her with devotion. Early raised her head until their breaths met. As he exhaled, she inhaled. They were now one with each other.

"I love you, Alex," Early whispered into his rising and lowering chest.

Gasping for another breath, Alex whispered, "I love you, baby, and don't you ever forget it."

They lay together as one until sleep engulfed them. Early slept peacefully next to her husband. She loved him more than life itself; there was nothing Early would not do for him. That night, Early's dreams were peaceful and serene. She was happy with her life, the only life Early knew.

Chapter 1

APRIL 7TH - 9:37 A.M.

Early heard everything being said, but she couldn't understand a word. Her mind started spinning.

Are they speaking English? Yes... yes, she tells herself, they are, but the language is different—foreign. Sounds are echoing in my ears; oh the pain! The sound hurts... It must be the level of the noise that's confusing... my vision is blurred; I see nothing. Vagueness... haze... no wait, the room is exactly as it's supposed to be. But where am I?

Early reached up and rubbed the side of her face. She could hardly feel her hand against her skin. *Am I dreaming? Yes, that must be it. What's the last thing I remember? Think, Early... think. Oh yes, making love with Alex. But when did we go to bed?* Early could not remember going to bed after making love that night. Perhaps Alex carried her into the bedroom? No, she wouldn't have slept through that; she's too light of a sleeper.

Early heard a booming noise that startled her.

"Objection!" The deep male voice echoed through her ears. Her stomach began to tighten, then everything was dark again, peaceful and quiet.

April 14th - 10:02 a.m.

Early startled awake, again to another booming voice.

"Order... I demand order in my court. Both attorneys approach the bench, now!"

It's a man's voice, but it isn't Alex speaking, Early tells herself. Whose voice is it? It sounds familiar, perhaps the tele-

vision, did someone leave it on all night? What's wrong with me? My children, why haven't they asked for breakfast? Headache, my God how my head hurts.

Pain envelops her and then, again, a strange but peaceful quiet engulfs her and everything fades far, far away into the distant darkness.

May 21st - 2:21 p.m.

Early's darkness yielded to light. Muffled noises became sharper.

There's brightness all around me, it must be morning. Did Alex oversleep again? I really must get moving or Daren will be late for school... I just hate to be rushed. My God my head hurts.

"Your Honor, please," a voice boomed, jarring Early from her private thoughts. "We all know how long this will take if we cannot get through at least one question without this constant interruption."

I'm not dreaming, Early thought. *That is real....*

Early glanced down and saw her hands; they were shaking. She was not in her bed. She wasn't in her house. *Where am I?* Glancing around as best she could, Early realized it was not her television making the loud noise. The sound was coming from all around—front, back, and from her sides. The tips of her fingers tingled. She frantically rubbed them together, desperate to stop the strange crawling sensation running up her arms. She reached out for her warm blankets. Early wanted—needed—to feel safe and secure. But her blankets were not there. She had to be dreaming, she just had to be.

The room began to spin and a gnawing sensation nagged deep within her jaws. Floating and twirling around the room, Early felt confused and sick. *This had to be a dream.* There could be no other explanation. She reached out again for her bed covers but felt something hard instead of soft.

The dresser? Am I touching my dresser? What's it doing way over here?

The more she groped around at her surroundings, the more she realized she was not in bed. She was confused and it terrorized her, sickening her even more. She couldn't think. Her hands reached up to scratch her head, but instead she pressed her palms against her eyes to try to stop the wild spinning. The noise, muffled words... shuffling shoes... *stop... please stop!*

I'm sitting in a chair. Get a hold of yourself, Early.

Hard wooden-arms hugged her. But Early doesn't own any chairs with wooden arms.

I'm in a chair, a real hard chair.

Fear was rising from deep within and spreading throughout her veins attacking the farthest points of her sanity.

"Your Honor, that wasn't a question," a voice huffed. "It's clear he's leading the witness. I object."

Early exhaled a deep breath slowly. After blinking several times, her eyes began to focus. She skimmed the room for something familiar—anything. She had never seen this room before. *But how could that possibly be? No, something is terribly wrong. A table, a wooden table is in front of me. It's not my kitchen table.* Next to her sat a man in a dark suit wearing a bright red tie, arguing with the man standing in the middle of... of the...

"COURTROOM!" Early screamed.

Gradually the voices around her rose to the level of complete chaos before the judge slammed his gavel against his desk and commanded, "ORDER! Order in my court. Bailiff!"

"She spoke!" someone sitting behind Early shrieked.

The man sitting next to Early grabbed her arm. "My God," he whispered. "Early? Can you hear me?"

"What's going on? Where am I?" Early cried. "Who are you? Where am I?"

Early jerked her arm and backed as far away as she could. The bailiff hurried toward them. Early's fear was growing faster than her mind could comprehend.

"What's happening?" she screamed.

"My God," the stranger repeated.

"Order... I demand order!" the judge yelled as the other voices continued to get louder.

The people behind her were moving about and talking out of sync with each other. The confusion and disorder was growing as every second passed. The judge sat stunned, trying to compose himself and bring calm to the chaos. The woman, *the defendant,* who had been silent for the last several months was suddenly talking. The crazy, evil and comatose woman who slashed her children into tiny unrecognizable pieces while they slept, and who stabbed her husband over a hundred times, was suddenly awake and speaking. Early grabbed her ears and screamed for her husband to help her. "Alex... Alex, where are you?"

Chapter 2

"DOC, ANY IDEA of what's going on?"

"None whatsoever," Dr. Timothy Barnes answered while scratching the top of his balding head. "It's the strangest thing I've ever seen. She has no memory of the last several months."

"I knew something wasn't right, I just knew it," Drake Anderson surmised.

Since passing the bar exam only a few months ago, Drake was a rookie trial lawyer fresh out of law school. This would be a tough baptism, but he would give it his all, hoping at least he would be admired for a tough fight. Ever since he first met Early Sutton, Drake knew something seemed a little odd about his client. Although she answered some of his questions, her answers were always short and vague, almost to be the point of cryptic. Some of her answers didn't make sense, nor did they have any relationship to the questions being asked. Then when their sessions were over, she would zone out and sit comatose. Even when the gruesome enlarged pictures of her slaughtered family were plastered throughout the courtroom, only the accused, Early Sutton, remained calm and seemingly oblivious. When the judge asked if she knew why she was in court, Early simply stated in a low whisper, *"I can't go too?"*

He immediately called a recess, cleared the courtroom and ordered a medical evaluation. Was she, or was she not, awake and cognizant of her surroundings and circumstances?

* * * * * *

"Can I speak with her?" Drake asked, after the medical exam.

Doc nodded his head but frowned. "Make it short. She's upset. If I were you, I'd ask for a continuance so you can figure out what's going on with that little lady of yours. If she's faking it, she did her homework."

"Believe me when I say," Drake warned grabbing the man's arm. "She didn't do it, and, I'm going to prove it."

"I wish you luck, my boy," the Doc said yanking his arm from Drake's grip. "But remember, the whole world has already tried and convicted her. Your ambitions are honorable, but what you are hoping to accomplish may not be within your reach."

"Since when am I not up to a challenge?" Drake shot back.

The doctor stood silently as the young lawyer walked down the dark corridor. Doc shivered as a cold chill embraced him. The case against Early Sutton was an eerie mess.

"Is it true?" a young guard asked, yanking the Doc from his private thoughts. "Is it true she just woke up in there?"

"Something like that," he replied, not wanting to give credence to the information that could be ammunition in the trial.

"But she has to be faking it right? I mean who'd..."

"Not necessarily," the doctor replied leaving the guard with his unanswered questions.

Chapter 3

"PUSH BABY, PUSH."

"I'm pushing!" the woman yelled. "Will you just shut up?"

"Okay, Marty, all I need is one good one and she'll be here," the doctor urged.

Marty lay back down and took a deep breath, but as she did she gave her husband an evil glare. This was their third child, and it was going to be a difficult birth.

"Come on, baby," her husband coached again.

"One more, Marty, just one more," the doctor repeated.

With one last, deep breath, Marty gave it all she had. As she pushed, she screamed as the flesh between her legs tore. A nurse gasped as blood drained from Marty's already strained and weakened body.

"My God!" the nurse yelled. "What's happening? Something's wrong."

"Marty," the doctor said. "I need you to quit pushing. Stop pushing, Marty."

"What's wrong?" Marty screamed. "What's going on?"

Her husband stared at her. The doctor's eyes grew wide as the baby's head crowned.

"Marty, stop pushing," the doctor demanded.

From somewhere in the room another nurse gasped as the baby's head emerged. But it was much larger than anyone expected.

"My God," the doctor whispered. "My God..."

"What is it, David?" Marty asked. "Is our baby all right?"

The doctor guided the baby out of the mother's torn and bloody body. The nurse wrapped the baby in a warm blanket.

"The baby's fine," the doctor said, but her hands were shaking.

"I don't hear any crying," Marty yelled. "The baby's not crying."

"She's breathing," the doctor said.

"David," Marty cried. "I want to see our baby. Please don't let our baby die."

The nurse held the small bundle in her arms and gazed into the child's face. The baby whined a high-pitch shrill and reached out her tiny hands as though searching for her mother. The father stood speechless and stared at the doctor. "I want my baby," Marty demanded.

The doctor glanced up at the father who nodded slowly. Tears spilled as he watched the nurse walk around the bed. The doctor worked hard to repair the damage caused from the larger than expected baby.

"Give me my baby!" Marty yelled reaching out.

The nurse placed the small bundle in the mother's arms and stepped back. Marty pulled back the soft blanket. The tiny yellow-haired girl stared up into her mother's eyes and reached out her hand. Marty gazed into the small round pink and yellow face and screamed. The nurse seized the small bundle and rushed to the neo-natal intensive care.

The doctor ordered a sedative for Marty and asked a nurse to take the father into another room. As she continued to work on the severely ripped and bleeding mother, the doctor's eyes filled with tears. Never in her seventeen-year career had she seen such a deformity. If the child survived it would be a miracle. She knew the child was the result of in-vitro fertilization, but that should not have caused such an abnormality. She would have to run tests to be sure, but she was positive nothing could or would explain what she had just witnessed.

Chapter 4

"HELLO EARLY, I'M Dr. Derrier and I've been assigned to your case. What an interesting and lovely name, Early. I don't believe I've ever known anyone with that name."

Early sat on the bed ignoring the doctor and stared blankly out the window. She was hoping silently to herself the dark would engulf her again, take her away, or kill her. Although she heard everything the woman was saying, it seemed as though she heard nothing. If Early spoke a word now, it would only make her nightmare become real.

"Early?" Derrier asked as she pulled up a chair. "I'm here to help you. Honest. But you'll need to trust me. I can't help if you don't trust me."

Early glanced into the woman's eyes. She was young, maybe about mid-twenties or so. Dark hair that when untied probably fell down her back to her waist. She had a nice figure, neither heavy nor slim. The hand with a silver wedding band also held a writing pen. Obviously she's left-handed, which means she's more creative than scientific. A butterfly pendant hung from the woman's neck on a gold chain. She isn't much for matching. A silver wedding band should be complimented by a silver chain. Early turned to stare out the window again, hoping to fade back into the dark and quiet.

"Early, please," Derrier pleaded. "Please talk to me."

Early didn't smile; she couldn't smile, but she couldn't frown either. She simply gazed more deeply into the young doctor's eyes. The pain that transferred from one woman to the other was immense and Derrier shuttered. As the doctor rubbed the sides of her arms, Early turned back to the bleakness of the window to stare into nothing.

"My God," Derrier whispered. "Who did this to you?"

Chapter 5

"GOOD MORNING, MR. and Mrs. Starling, I'm Eugene Spangleholtz. How are you doing today?"

"Doing?" David huffed. "How can *we* be doing anything?" David fell to the floor and cried into his hands as Marty lay quietly in bed. Shock was splattered all over her face. Her eyes were red and swollen. Spangleholtz studied the young couple to decide exactly how he should approach their problem.

Spangleholtz cleared his throat and asked, "I noticed you haven't named your little girl yet. Did you decide on a name?"

"Name?" David screeched from the floor. "How do you name a monster?"

"Your little girl is not a monster, Mr. Starling," Spangleholtz said. "She has a few medical issues I'll agree, but I can guarantee you she is *no* monster."

David raised his head and gave the doctor a venomous look. The doctor returned the man's outlandish views by ignoring him. A nurse knocked at the door and entered carrying a small bundle.

"Thank you, Susan," the doctor said reaching out to take the baby.

Spangleholtz smiled as he noticed the parents were watching when he took custody of the little girl.

"Now, do you still want to tell me you don't want to name your precious baby?" he asked with a smile.

David started to cry again into his hands. But Marty spoke

slowly, stumbling over her words. "Marie Elizabeth," she stuttered. "Her name is Marie Elizabeth."

"Oh no you don't!" David scolded, struggling to get to his feet. "That name is for *my* daughter, and that... that... thing is *not my daughter*."

The doctor placed the little bundle in Marty's arms. A tear ran down her face as she pulled back the blanket to get a better view of the little girl. She was not small by any means. Marie Elizabeth weighed in at a little over twelve pounds and was almost thirty-one inches long. A light yellow fuzz tickled the top of her head with a beautiful lock of white and gold hair trailing down her back. She had the most beautiful green eyes Spangleholtz had ever seen. The more the mother held her daughter, the better chance he had of Marty loving her.

"David, she's beautiful," Marty sighed. "She's so long. No wonder I was hurting so much." Marty giggled as she gazed at her daughter.

"Beautiful? That *thing* is anything but beautiful!"

"Shhhh," Marty whispered. "You'll frighten her. Hi baby, I'm your mommy."

"Well I'm not her god damn daddy," David protested as he stormed angrily out of the room.

"She is fully functional, Mrs. Starling," Spangleholtz said. "We did have to insert a tube to help her breathe. A slight defect within her sinus cavities from what the X-rays show. Surgery will fix that when she's a little older. But for now we'll teach you how to feed her. Other than that, she's perfectly healthy. And believe me when I tell you she *is* your daughter."

"What caused this?" Marty asked. "What will she look like when she's older?"

"We're not sure yet," he answered. "But she'll be beautiful in her own way."

Two nurses arrived to teach Marty how to feed and care for her daughter's special needs. Spangleholtz excused himself and left the hospital wing to stand in the fresh air on the balcony, which was a favorite gathering place for hospital visitors and staff. Spangleholtz saw David there pacing nervously from one end of the balcony to the other. The man looked agitated and irritated, clutching his forehead and mumbling to himself. The doctor calmly tapped on his cell phone and spoke clearly.

"Dr. Spangleholtz here. I must speak with Zarek... thank you... Zarek... yes the delivery went fine, just fine... no, he didn't take it well at all, would you? Yes I believe he *will* be a problem... yes, yes, but... she's doing very well and I believe she's bonding with the child... yes... a transport would be good about this time... no we're making sure they remain isolated... yes... don't blame me, damn it, I still can't believe you allowed them to travel this far into the pregnancy, such a risk... I've done all I can here... yes I can do that... no that will not be a problem... this evening would be fine... thank you... goodbye."

Spangleholtz left the windy balcony and walked past two men sipping on coffee just inside the door. As he passed, he nodded ever so slightly then headed to the elevator to make arrangements for the immediate transportation of the mother and baby to a specialty hospital in upper Washington state.

As Spangleholtz waited for the elevator, chaos erupted on the balcony behind him. There were gasps as staff and visitors leaned over the balcony rail to look below. Splayed on the ground was a man, facedown in a pool of blood.

Several doctors and nurses rushed to the scene and worked desperately to revive the now deceased father of little Marie Elizabeth Starling. Apparently he jumped to his early demise. It seemed he just couldn't handle the anguish of having a deformed child. A little girl with an extraordinarily large head, and a slightly protruding sinus cavity and jaw bone. A little girl with thick beautiful lips and cheeks—hard, not soft. Tiny golden pointed ears resting against a large but well-shaped head. Baby soft white and gold hair trailing down her back all the way to her blonde little tail. She had all ten fingers. Her hands were perfect, but it was her feet... they looked more like tiny hooves.

Chapter 6

"TAKE THIS," TYLER said holding two cups of hot coffee in her hands.

"Thanks," Caiden mumbled taking a sip.

Tyler Brighten sat her cup down next to her wireless mouse to stretch her arms. "Is it always this quiet around here?"

"Yes," Caiden snickered but then smiled. "So, how do you like it here so far?"

"It's okay, just very quiet." Tyler took another sip as she studied her computer screen. "This is really a cool job."

"Yes it is. I never imagined I'd have a job like this. Did you?" Caiden asked with his eyes glued to his screen. "I mean while you were in college?"

"Nope. In fact I never thought my career would be sitting in front of a huge computer all day either," Tyler added. "All my time used to be spent in the bio lab at college. But now..."

The DNA string Tyler and Caiden were studying in 3-D slowly rotated. Several keys allowed them to zoom in or out and spin the string in any direction. Even though she'd only worked at the Barker Institute for a little over six months, Tyler was still having a hard time believing she was actually paid to be here. The work was fun and fascinating. Every day was more like an adventure than a job, and Tyler could hardly wait to get there each morning.

"Wait a minute," Tyler whispered as she zoomed in closer on the one strand of the DNA.

"What is it?" Caiden asked.

"The alignments are overlapping," Tyler declared.

"That's impossible," Caiden surmised. "What quadrant are you looking at?"

"I'm in eighty-six." Tyler kept her eyes locked tightly to the screen.

Caiden became flustered when he couldn't find the same place on his screen. After rolling his chair across the room to look over her shoulder, he whispered into her ear. "Wow that is definitely an overlap."

"But..." Tyler whispered. "If such an overlap is present, then the sequence assembly algorithm should have detected it. This has to be a false cut."

"No, it's definitely an overlap," Caiden whispered.

Tyler rubbed her eyes and sat back in her chair. "Let me think for a minute."

"Why are we whispering?" Caiden asked in a low voice.

"I have no idea," Tyler replied with a giggle.

The two sat in silence watching as the mutated DNA wobbled eerily on the computer screen glittering with exuberant colors as though it was mocking them to figure it out. They both scratched their heads as they contemplated the situation. Their questions to each other seemed more like they were reconfirming their strange conclusions than actually expecting an answer. Something wasn't adding up and she couldn't figure out what that was. Tyler tried hard to remember her college lectures. DNA was normally stable and predictive. After a few minutes, it came to her.

"The validation algorithm for ordered restriction maps. That's it, because it serves to establish the quality of an assembled DNA sequence by comparing it with an ordered restriction map," Tyler stated. "This isn't right... there's no correlation here... none."

"What's your doctorate in?" Caiden asked.

"Molecular DNA," Tyler replied. "Why do you ask?"

"Because the answer is so obvious and you're not seeing it."

"And you do?"

"I'm not quite sure exactly what I'm seeing, but it's the only explanation," Caiden answered. "And if my conclusions are correct, we have a major issue."

With a frown planted firmly upon her face, Tyler leaned in closer to the computer screen. After squinting for a few seconds, she saw exactly what Caiden was talking about. She shouted out before she realized what she had said, "*Oh my God*. This DNA has been tinkered with, and it's mutating!"

"Yes, you got it," Caiden replied with his finger pointing to the screen. "But what exactly was it tinkered with?"

"No, the real question is," Tyler said, now with a serious edge in her voice, "*Who* owns this DNA and *when* was it spliced?"

Chapter 7

THE EXPLOSION ROCKED an area of about five hundred miles and left behind a crater more than ten miles wide and half as deep. What was once pristine wilderness now resembled a rocky desert basin similar to the ones found on any deserted moon or dead planet. Lewis studied the strange pictures scattered across his desk. He burped and acid rose in his throat. He slapped his chest several times.

"Might want to watch what you eat these days," Dr. Allen Greghardt mused as he entered the large but comfortable room. "I've always loved these big windows," he added, walking towards them to admire the view.

Lewis left the eerie pictures on his desk and followed Greghardt. Lewis also knew this was a clue he wanted to talk and bounce ideas between them. The sun was almost at its full height and a light breeze tickled the trees as they swayed in the rhythm of the day.

"This is nice," Greghardt remarked. "Real nice."

Lewis nodded his head as he marveled at the scenery below. It seemed every year the plants and flowers surprised them with ever larger blooms and brighter colors.

Greghardt turned from the windows and said, "I need a drink. Join me?"

"It's still a little early don't you think?"

Picking up a glass Greghardt turned toward Lewis and added, "Not today my friend... not today."

"Fine," Lewis sighed at his boss. "Pour me one too."

They sat on opposing sofas staring blankly at each other. After a couple gulps of the precious golden liquid, Greghardt said. "Well, is it a secret?"

"Is what a secret?" Lewis answered sipping his drink.

"Your list of travelers."

"Oh, not at all. I've decided to send Agents Brighten, Clarke and Harris. They'll play the part of nosey tourists. Just there to check things out...the usual."

"Very laid back attitude don't you think? Is that what you're aiming for?" Greghardt asked.

* * * * * *

You're watching Another Day and I'm Jackie Peters live from Prestonia, West Virginia. A quaint little spot in the county of Webster. This place was a bustling mining town from 1907 until in the 1920s when the coal ran out. We're not sure of the exact population, but we're told it's about five thousand. As you can see from the devastation behind me, the blast must have been massive..."

The television displayed pictures of the recent destruction as the woman tried to ignore them and concentrate on her duties as president of the United States.

"Yes, Madam President?" The voice from the intercom acknowledged someone was still alive and attending her needs.

"Tina, my nerves are growing short, very short."

"I'll be right there, Madam President."

And before Vivian Strickland could put the phone back onto its holder, Tina entered the room ready for just about anything.

"Madam President?" Tina asked, afraid as to what was going to be asked of her this time.

"Please, Tina, I need you to make this happen. Call my cabinet together at once, but not everyone. Let's see... I definitely want David, Homeland Security," Strickland counted on her fingers as she spoke, "And Katrina, Department of Agriculture... and Colonel Jenkins, Department of Defense... oh, and my chief of staff, and the vice president...." She sighed and stared at Tina with a forlorn look of *help me* in her eyes.

Tina had seen this look many times before, a look that only

meant one thing—Strickland believed she was in way over her head. But today seemed different; she looked even more frightened and worse, alone.

"Madam President, how about I just gather *everyone* for a special session," Tina suggested.

Strickland had a vague expression but nodded in agreement.

"Why don't you take a rest and maybe half a tranquilizer? It'll take some time to get them here even if I send personal jets. You'll need a clear mind for this. Get some rest."

"Thanks, Tina," Strickland replied as she walked toward her private quarters.

"I'll come get you about an hour before the meeting so you can be ready."

"Thank you so much, Tina." Strickland stopped at the door and asked in almost a whisper, "What in the hell is going on out there?"

"I don't know, Madam President, but you'll get to the bottom of it—you always do."

"Thank you again and don't forget Dr. Greghardt."

"Never do. I had no plans on leaving him out."

As the door shut behind Strickland, Tina stood in front of the television and watched in horror as the devastation in West Virginia unfolded before her eyes.

"How long have you lived here?" the newscaster asked an elderly woman in ragged clothes.

"I ben 'ere about 'ifty years now. I was born in deese 'ills and I'll die in deese 'ills."

"What is your name, ma'am?" the newscaster asked, shoving the microphone into the woman's face.

"You don needs stick that thin in me face... me nam's Etta Mae Hanna... me family settled in deese 'ills 'ears before I came into dis 'urld."

"Did you see the explosion Ms. Hanna?"

"See... felt... taste... I knew me days were a ending, I knew dat fer sur!"

"About how far away were you from the blast?"

"One ridge away and it 'till set our trees on fire. See!" The woman pulled on her hair to show the singed edges. "It burnt me 'air too."

"What used to be there? What do you think could have caused such an explosion?"

"'Ere 'as strange thins going on o'er dare I tell yah. Strange."

"What do you mean by strange?"

"Funny peeple live dere. At first we tot it's a 'ospital of some kin, cuz only dokters wood cum an go. Da patients... da peeple dat lived dare... now dare the strange lookin... scary... I'm glad it's gone. Beddar dat way. Day ain't God-like I tell yah, it just ain't right."

"Tell me about how these people looked..."

Tina shut off the television and stared out the window into the beautiful day on Capitol Hill. All was calm and peaceful. People were busily going about their business as though everything was normal. But the day was anything but ordinary. With a deep breath and a sigh, Tina thought she felt a little better. She had a job to do and didn't have any more time to waste. As she glanced around the room, she felt proud to be the president's assistant. But again, she sometimes wished she had a normal job in a normal office building.

"Sometimes *knowing* is the worst," she whispered to herself. "What if what they say is true and it was a meteor after all? Would there be more to come? Would they be larger than the first?"

Chapter 8

"EARLY? I'M DR. BARNES. Do you remember me?"

Early sat staring into her hands. She didn't move nor did she speak.

"Early, it's okay if you talk to this doctor," Drake said.

Early refused.

After what felt like many minutes, Barnes finally said, "I'll order some stronger sedatives so she can get some sleep. Maybe when she has a chance to clear her mind she'll be able to talk to us." He excused himself and motioned for Drake to join him outside the room.

"So, what's the diagnosis, Doc?" Drake asked.

"Anterograde amnesia," Barnes explained. "It's a form of memory loss, where new events are not transferred to the long-term memory of the brain. In other words, the sufferer is not able to recall anything that occurs during a current period in time."

"I don't get it," Drake said. He was suddenly feeling very stupid.

"Drake..." the doctor said. "After we finish this conversation, you will remember most of what we said. Or at least you'll remember having a conversation with me, correct?"

"Well, yes," Drake replied.

"Anterograde amnesia victims remember nothing about an event. What this means to Early is that everything she experienced in that courtroom she forgot as soon as it happened.

Nothing was retained."

Drake stared at the doctor. "Then what in the hell made her forget and is able to last this long?"

"We're not sure yet," Barnes answered. "But we did find something very curious in her blood work. We detected Gamma-Aminobutyric Acid or more commonly known as GABA. The only type of drug I know of that produces these symptoms. But its effects are not long lasting. Someone must have fed it to her and when they stopped, the drug wore off. Thus she began to store experiences in her long-term memory again and she woke up."

"Someone was feeding drugs to my client?" Drake yelled. "While under *my* care?"

"Please, Drake," Barnes said. "Let's not draw too much attention to this just yet."

"Sorry," Drake added, realizing his outburst was probably not appropriate. "But you're saying that someone slipped her that drug while she was in her cell?"

"I guess I am. And if so then whoever did must have strong connections," Barnes added. "We need to tread lightly or we could be their next victims."

"Terrific," Drake whispered taking another sip of his drink. Pausing, he studied his glass. He looked up at the doctor and said, "I guess it really wouldn't be difficult now would it? Thank you, Doc."

Drake entered Early's room and closed the door. He sat on the old rickety chair in front of her and lowered his head. He took in a deep breath and let it out slowly. Then he thought in a sorrowful and regretful manner, *This is my first real case and I'm going to screw it up*. Moments later he felt a light touch on his arm and glanced up to find Early staring at him through saddened eyes.

"I'm afraid," Early whispered.

"I am too," Drake replied. Now he had her somewhat talking, he knew he had to keep her talking. It was important he completely understood what happened to her that horrible night that changed her life forever.

"I have to know what happened," Drake whispered. "Even if it's painful for you."

Early's eyes fell back to her lap and Drake felt his heart stop beating. If she clammed up now, he may never get her to talk again. Did he just mess it all up by asking her that awful question too soon? *What a dumb shit I am.*

After several long and agonizing minutes of a painful and eerie quiet, Early finally whispered to him in a meek and frightened voice, "I honestly don't know what happened. Can you help me find my husband, and where my children are? I don't understand why I'm here. Those pictures you showed me are not real. Who'd do that to my family?"

Drake held Early's hands and rubbed them gently as he spoke. "You *have* to trust me, sweetheart. I'm here for *you* and I'll do everything it takes to get you out of trouble. But you *must* talk to me."

"I don't know anything," she replied tearfully.

A loud bang echoed through the room from some far off place. For a brief moment they both froze awaiting the evil to overtake them. But nothing happened and all became quiet again.

"Okay then," Drake said, pulling them from their thoughts. "Let's go back in time and examine everything that you do remember minute by minute, second by second." He let go of her hands and stood up. He paced the floor while asking the questions, but he was cautious to ask only the ones that would not throw her back into her deep and silent world.

"What's the last thing you remember?"

Drake prayed Early needed to talk to someone. She held herself as she rocked back and forth on her cot. He knew she was afraid and in pain.

"I checked on the babies, and they were asleep. Alex and I... well... we made love in front of the fire. I love fires." Early paused and Drake almost panicked believing he had lost her again, but she yelled instead. "Why... why would anyone..."

"Okay, that's a start," he interrupted, trying to keep her focused. "Then what happened?"

"I woke up next to you," Early screamed between sobs. "I woke up next to you."

"No... no... sweetie," Drake whispered kneeling next to her. "Don't cry, we'll get through this. You and me, we'll do it together, okay?"

Early looked into Drake's eyes. "Help me find them... please."

"I will help you, I will... I promise you, Early, I promise. But we can't find..."

"They're not dead!" Early screamed. "They're *not* dead."

Drake continued to kneel next to Early and hold her hands for what seemed like hours before he dared to ask, "Did you have anything to drink that night? Wine? Soda?"

That question stopped the panic and tears as she thought before answering. "We both had a glass of wine. Why?"

"Great, great. We're getting there."

"Time's up," the guard ordered from the hall. "Let's go. Now."

Drake gave the guard an ugly look, then turned and smiled warmly at his client. "Early, don't give up. I'll be back... real soon."

Drake stood up reluctantly and glanced around at the filthy cell. He knew he had to get her out of there before they could actually get anywhere. But how would he accomplish it? Leaving her cell, his heart broke to see the fragile woman gaze aimlessly out the tiny slant of a window into the sinking sunset.

Chapter 9

"GOOD MORNING, LADIES," Lewis said with a huge smile to his small and obviously bored audience. After clearing his voice when he didn't get any type of a response, he added, "You may or may not know each other so I'll just introduce everyone. I'm Dr. Jeff Lewis, head of The Agency and here to my right we have Agent Skyler Brighten," Lewis waved his hand toward Skyler. "Agent Carrie Clarke to my left and Agent Lacey Harris at the other end of the table." Each time he pointed to one of the young ladies they nodded. "Believe it or not, each of you have a lot in common."

The three women glanced back and forth at each other with fake smiles.

"Agent Brighten," Lewis continued.

"Yes?" Sitting more upright in her chair.

"You are smart, inquisitive and eager to solve problems. Not to mention you're an expert in explosives and how they affect the human body..."

"Yeah," Skyler smirked. "They blow them apart... oh, and can make a good day turn into an ugly one real fast."

"Funny, Agent Brighten," Lewis scolded. "Real funny... Agent Clarke, you are one of my best agents."

Carrie frowned and lowered her eyes.

"There's never been a challenge you could not overcome. You almost lost a leg on your last assignment, but you never gave up. You're not afraid to do what's needed to get the job done."

"Yeah, right," Carrie answered, rolling her eyes. "Whatever you say."

"Agent Harris," Lewis announced with a wave of his hand. "We welcome you."

Lacey nodded her head.

"Agent Harris is an oldie to this Agency but one of our newest Agents. She's been around and has experienced things I wouldn't wish on my worst enemies. Although her right arm doesn't work quite as well as her left," he paused winking at her, "she refuses to let anything stop her. Oh no, not Agent Harris. She has determination and an eagerness to prove herself. Welcome, Agent Harris."

"Thank you," Lacey responded with her cheeks turning red as she smiled.

Carrie leaned over to Skyler and said, "Fresh meat you mean."

Ignoring Carrie's sly remark and giving her a quick look of non-approval, Lewis continued his short speech. "Well, let's get down to business shall we? You three are being assigned to the recent mishap in West Virginia..."

"Mishap?" Carrie mimicked. "The whole state's almost gone in a cloud of dirt and dust and no one knows why, and you call it a mishap?"

"I'm trying to put it lightly, Carrie," Lewis added with a frown on his face.

"Jeff, just get to the point will yah?" Skyler said. "Is it a meteor or not?"

Carrie also spoke up. "Yeah, the point would be nice about now."

"Yes... well, I'll get to the point then," Lewis replied feeling somewhat shifted and off guard. He had to smile to himself though. These three women were some of the toughest, but at the same time some of the most innocent agents he had the pleasure to work with. They could either brush you off or shoot you, made no difference to them one way or the other. But you would not want to get in their way unless you wanted a bullet between the eyes or a blade between the shoulders.

"As you may know, last Thursday afternoon there was an explosion just outside the small town of Prestonia, West Virginia.

The blast was strong enough to leave a crater over ten miles wide and about five miles deep," Lewis said.

"If it wasn't a meteor, then what was it?" Carrie asked. "A bomb? Maybe someone needed to get rid of something fast?"

"We need you three to find out what that big, ugly and embarrassing something is... or was. We were able to determine it was not a meteor or other large object that fell from the sky. Because, we know the explosion came from below—not from above. However," Lewis opened up his eyes to hush the girls before they could say anything. "Don't get your hopes up because it wasn't volcanic either. And as always, you'll have the full support of The Agency during your mission. You'll be disguised as tourists. So don't push yourselves around too much. Be sweet... kind... gentle. We need to know everything, not just what the local law or news reporters know. Got it? And as far as the press is concerned, it still has not been determined whether it was or was not a meteor. I don't need any unnecessary rumors. Not until we know for sure what's going on. And that's where you three come in."

All three nodded at the same time but remained silent.

"So get to know each other, pack your things, but be on your way by morning. Remember, you're on holiday not a mercenary killing spree. Make up any stories you want as to why you're there, but at least try and make it credible. And Carrie, please don't kill anyone."

Chapter 10

MARTY CUDDLED LITTLE Lizzie in her arms and sang softly. Lizzie's white and golden hair grew longer every day.

"Hello, Marty," Spangleholtz said entering her room. "How are you doing today?"

"Hello," Marty answered not removing her eyes from her little girl. "I'm fine. Isn't she beautiful?"

"Yes she is, Marty," he replied approaching her bed. "I'm afraid I have some bad news for you and for your daughter. Your husband... he's been in an accident, Marty."

"I know," Marty said, gently stroking her daughter's hair and allowing it to fall through her fingers. "It almost feels like corn silk straight from the cob. Don't you think?"

"She's beautiful. But, how did you know about your husband?" Spangleholtz asked.

"Lizzie told me silly."

"I see. And what else has Lizzie told you?"

"She tells me lots of things, and she says she loves me and I love her and everything will be fine—just fine."

"Now we all know Lizzie can't talk, she's only a baby," Spangleholtz said, but something was bothering him from deep inside. "She's just a baby."

"But she's *my* baby and I *can* hear her," Marty stated. Her voice rose but then softened. "When can we go home?"

"We have a new home for you waiting in Washington. It's a special place where no one will ever bother you."

"But I want to show her off to my children and all my friends. Her sisters will want to see her and she has many aunts and uncles and…"

"I'm sorry Marty, but Lizzie is too special to share with just anyone. I've sent for your girls, and they will meet you at your new home. Everything will work out, you'll see."

"Lizzie won't like Washington, it gets cold there," Marty replied. "She just told me so."

The doctor watched as Lizzie's little fuzzy hand stroked her mother's cheek.

With an air of caution, he added, "As I said, all of you will be fine. You'll have your own house and a big yard for Lizzie and her sisters to play in."

Marty stared into her little girl's eyes. Little Lizzie reached up and it looked as though she was rubbing the side of her mother's face. But how could that be? Lizzie is a newborn. The bond seemed to be very strong between the two, which was beginning to make Spangleholtz nervous.

"Will she be able to speak one day?" Marty asked, then added in a strange way, "She wants to know."

The doctor stared at the mother and child, and wondered whether or not the mother was losing her mind, or was there something else happening—something he needed to worry about.

"We won't know until she's much older," he said. "She has vocal cords, but well we'll just have to wait and see how they work with her jaw line. If nothing else, she can learn sign language. She'll be able to communicate with you in one form or another."

Tears fell from Marty's eyes as she sighed. She snuggled her baby even closer to her chest before saying, "We communicate just fine, doctor. Just fine." Marty looked up at Spangleholtz with a wickedness that frightened him.

As the doctor turned to leave the room, he could hear Marty whispering to her daughter, "What should I do now, Lizzie?"

Chapter 11

"SO, WHY DID you want to meet for dinner way out here?" Tyler asked as she placed her napkin in her lap.

Caiden glanced around then leaned toward her. "We're in trouble, Tyler."

"Trouble? For what?"

"For knowing too much...They're watching us."

Tyler leaned over the table and said, "Okay, I'll fall for it. And the *They* are who?"

"You're mocking me," Caiden replied, lowering his eyes. "I wouldn't have asked you out here if I wasn't concerned about telling you the truth."

Tyler giggled. "Oh well, I thought you asked me here 'cause you liked me or something like that."

Caiden shook his head then blinked his eyes several times. "Why is it every time a guy has something important to tell a woman, they always think it's some kind of a come-on?"

Tyler twitched her nose and sat back. "Okay fine; then you *don't* like me."

"I didn't say that... I mean..." Caiden sighed.

"Will you make up your mind?" Tyler giggled, staring at him for an answer.

Tyler knew Caiden was in a lose-lose situation. No matter what he said now, he was in deep trouble.

"Okay, if we get through the next few weeks alive we'll go out for real, but for right now just listen to me."

Tyler leaned forward again and smiled. He covered himself good on that one. "Just giving you a hard time. So spill."

Caiden shook his head and glanced around the room before he began. "The extra research we conducted on that weird DNA has gotten a lot of attention... and it's not the kind that gets you promoted either. It's the kind that gets you dead."

"Good evening, have you been to Ambrosia before?" The waiter smiled down at them with his hands folded precariously across his chest.

Both Tyler and Caiden almost fell out of their chairs as their hearts jumped through their throats.

"I'm sorry," the waiter said. "I startled you. May I bring you some drinks to start off the evening?"

Caiden answered for the both of them after catching his breath. "Yes, we'll have sweetened iced tea." When the waiter left, they both laughed. "He scared me to death."

Wanting to get back to their conversation before the interruption, Tyler asked between giggles, "Okay go on, you have my attention now."

Caiden kept glancing around as though he felt someone was watching them. "I found out where that DNA sample came from."

Tyler was now excited and frightened. "Where?"

"You know that old hospital that's just over the mountain toward the east?"

"You mean the old Berryview place?" she whispered. "I thought that place closed a long time ago."

"So did I," Caiden said softly, peeking around the menu. "But I discovered that it never really closed. It only seemed to close, or to look like it closed."

"Here you go," the waiter said, sitting two glasses of newly brewed and chilled iced tea in front of them. A small mint leaf rested on each glass rim along with a slice of lemon. "Are we ready to order?"

"We'll both have the baked stew in the bread bowl," Caiden replied looking over at Tyler for approval. She nodded and after the waiter walked away Caiden added, "I did some snooping and that old hospital quit taking patients about twenty years ago. I was told it switched from sick people to *weird* people."

"What's a *weird* people?" Tyler asked sipping on her drink with a strange feeling rippling through her body.

"Like extra arms and legs, or half-human, half-rat type people."

"*Right*... and I suppose *Elvis Presley* lives there too? Come on, give me a break Caiden," Tyler laughed as she took another drink. "You're talking stupid now."

"Stupid or not, Tyler. I'm telling you the truth. We're in big trouble."

Suddenly an eerie feeling of being watched blew over Tyler's body. As she sipped, a feeling she didn't like was slowly consuming her.

Chapter 12

THE ROOM WAS barren and echoed with every sound, such as a clank of a cup on a table, the screech of a chair on the floor, or a simple cough. Cool air radiated with a strong aroma of disinfectant, which created a sterile sensation that discouraged any soul brave enough to enter. Ceiling fans circulated the arid air, which formed a heavier and more confusing stench.

"I don't like it here," Early said with tears in her eyes.

"Neither do I," Drake replied. "I've got to get you out of here. Even a mental hospital would be better than this stinking place."

The sounds of Drake's feet pacing the room echoed against the barren walls.

"Sit down, that noise is creepy," she snapped.

"Early, you have to talk to me. Do you understand?" Drake gazed into Early's eyes, begging for understanding.

"What do you want from me?" she cried as tears rolled down her cheeks.

"I'm saying you have to talk to me. I can't help you if I don't know what happened."

"Okay, but what exactly am I supposed to tell you?" she yelled. "I don't know anything. You know more than I do."

"Start at the beginning; just start talking, Early. You probably know more than you think you do," Drake said, clicking on the recorder. "My name is Drake Anderson, lawyer for Early Sutton." Drake nodded and she nodded back.

"My name is Early Rize Sutton. I'm twenty-seven years old."

Early looked up at Drake and sighed. Drake nodded his head to say *go on*.

After a short pause and another deep breath, she continued. "I was born on January 7th. My mother is Margaret Rize-Hampton and my father is Bruce Eagleton Hampton."

Early became suddenly quiet, which frightened Drake. "What is it?" he asked desperate to keep her talking now that she started.

"I haven't been allowed to see my parents," she cried into her hands.

"Early, you're on trial for murder," Drake said. "This is no country club. You'll not be allowed any visitors until after the trial. That's the law. Now continue... please."

Early's tears ran down her face as she talked. "My father's a surgeon and my mother was a nurse. After I was born she stayed home...she doesn't believe in daycare. I have four sisters and one brother, all younger. I was born and raised in Dallas, where my parents still live... in the same house. I love it there, I was happy."

"That's good Early, just keep telling your story," Drake urged.

"After high school, I went to Texas Women's University. I majored in music therapy. It's a great major. I studied dance, visual arts, physiology, and music. If I had to choose what I like best about my life, I'd have to say my college days were some of the best ever. Aside from my life with my children and husband of course." Her eyes lowered and her voice softened. "Because that's where I met Alex... during my junior year."

Early paused, and Drake prayed she would continue. After a few seconds she began again, "He was attending the Texas Medical School. His goal was to become a surgeon but he ended up in research. He likes his profession... I think, yes... he likes it a lot."

"Was there a specific area of concentration for Alex?" Drake asked, wondering why she hesitated in her answer.

"Actually yes. He's especially interested in skeletal deformities. He believes there's a way to cure the problem before a child's born."

"Really?" Drake asked, now curious. "Such as? Can you give me an example?" Drake scooted his chair closer to Early.

"Spina-Bifida for one. Alex learned if the spinal opening was surgically closed before birth, then the child had a better chance of developing normally. Alex loves children and feels especially strong about those who have medical conditions. He's dedicated his life to his research. That's what made me fall in love with him. I met him in February and we married a year and a half later. It was September fourteenth. We had such a beautiful wedding. I became pregnant right away and nine months later we had Daren. Then we tried for another but I just couldn't get pregnant. So we decided on in-vitro, and it was successful on the first try. It was just three years ago I gave birth to our twins, Nevada and Dakota. When I became pregnant with the girls we bought our house. It's not far from the hospital where Alex works. Then all this..."

"How was your love life with Alex?" Drake asked.

"Excuse me?" Early gazed eerily up at Drake.

Drake sighed but then urged, "Just go with it, Early. I promise I'm taking this somewhere."

Early frowned. "We love each other very much. It is good, okay?"

"Your children, anything about them, anything at all?"

"No, they're perfect," Early yelled. "My babies are perfect and I want them back."

"Okay, Early, let's get back on track to what we're talking about. Why don't you tell me about your average day?"

It took several minutes before Early could speak calmly again without crying. "I stay home to take care of our children," she said protectively. "I'm a housewife and I love it."

"Did you ever work outside the home?" Drake asked.

"No, I work *in* our home. I make sure the house is clean and dirty clothes don't pile up. I cook and plan our dinners...I just do what every other housewife does every day. I love and care for my family."

"Okay, okay. Now tell me about your husband."

"Well, Alex is a doctor at the hospital. He conducts research."

"Do you know what he researches?"

Early shook her head as the tears continued to fall. "I'm sorry, but he never talks about his work. He keeps it pretty much to himself—patient confidentiality. But it must have something to do with the bones; like I said it was his concentration at med school."

"Hmm," Drake was now wondering what could be so confidential about his work. "He's in research?"

"Yes," Early replied. "But he also has patients."

"Did you ever meet any of these patients?"

"Only one... her name's Marty... Marty Starling. She's pregnant and my husband's her doctor."

"Her doctor? Is Alex a gynecologist too?" Drake asked, thinking of things faster than he could write, forgetting all about the recorder.

"No, he works with bones and bone marrow. *I told you that.*"

"Then why would a pregnant woman go to him?" Drake asked.

"I don't know," Early answered, shaking her head looking confused. "Maybe her baby has a problem other doctors can't fix."

"Just a couple more questions," Drake said. "Did he ever go on trips?"

"Sometimes. There's an annual meeting in Washington."

"DC?" Drake asked.

Early smiled. "No, state... Washington state. Then there's other conferences he attends from time to time. They're all over the world. We went to Rome once. It was wonderful."

Drake sighed and knew he had to ask one more question no matter how much it hurt her. He took in a deep breath and reached for her hand. Then he said, "Tell me what happened the last night you were with your family."

With this question, Early's sobs became uncontrollable. Her face echoed a remorse and sadness Drake had never seen before. "We had to stay indoors all day," she cried between sobs. "The weather was so bad. The children wanted to bake cookies, so we did. I put a chicken on to roast about three-thirty and we ate about six. Then I bathed the children and cleaned the kitchen."

"What was Alex doing during this time?"

Drake studied Early's face and it looked as though she was trying hard to remember everything exactly as it was. "I don't believe he was doing much of anything. He was on the computer for a while, then he was on the phone, and then he made a fire to warm the living room."

"Did you have anything to drink before you two made love?" Drake asked, studying her reaction.

"Yes, Alex poured us some wine... why?"

"Did you see him pour the wine," Drake asked.

Early paused a moment before answering, "No, he'd already poured the wine before I came into the room. I went to make sure the children were asleep and tuck them into their beds. When I came back, Alex had the glasses in his hands." Early paused for a few seconds then added, "We made love in front of the fire. Are you saying he put something in my wine?" Her sobs became louder and stronger.

"What's your next memory, Early?"

"Hearing voices and sitting next to you in the courtroom," she cried looking lost and confused.

"Nothing at all between making love and the courtroom? Like using a bathroom or climbing into bed? Anything?"

"No... nothing," she yelled.

"Okay, Early, that's all for now," Drake said turning off the recorder. He noticed his scribbled notes and slapped himself on the forehead. He was losing it faster than she was, and he's not on trial. "I want you to rest. The doctor wrote you a prescription for a sedative so you can sleep." Drake put his hand on top of Early's that were resting on the table and smiled. "You take care, I'll get to the bottom of this... okay?"

"Okay," Early replied as another tear rolled down her cheek.

Chapter 13

THE RAIN PELTED Tyler as she darted for her front door. Not even an umbrella could keep her dry on this kind of a night. Prince, her hefty Golden Retriever, excitedly greeted her as she shook off the rain.

"Hey dude," she said as Prince danced breathlessly around the room. "Ready to go out?"

Prince gave Tyler a look of *are you nuts*.

"Well, maybe it'll stop raining in a little while," Tyler laughed. She glanced over at the chocolate cake sitting all alone on the kitchen counter. After the strange dinner with Caiden, Tyler felt a little comfort food would ease her mood. With Prince sleeping peacefully on the hearth rug near the fire, and a large piece of chocolate cake paired with a glass of milk, Tyler plopped down on the couch next to her Mickey Mouse phone. She punched in the well memorized number and waited as the rings echoed in her ear.

"Who diss?" the wonderful familiar voice sang through the phone.

"Aunt Mad?" Tyler whined.

"Hi sweetie, how's my little TyTy doing?" Mad's voice instantly calmed her yearning heart.

"Aunt Mad, I really need to talk. Are you busy? Did I call at a bad time?"

"Never am I too busy for my TyTy, and it's *never* a bad time, sweetie, you know that. Now, what's up? Is it the new job?"

Tyler knew her aunt could tell something was bothering her. But Maddie's past experiences was something Tyler knew she could rely on to guide her through this crazy maze Caiden stuck her in.

Tyler is an identical twin. Skyler and Tyler were Maddie's younger brother's and he was devoted to them while she *spoiled* them. They were always at her house and she was active in their life just as much as their father and mother. Their cousin, Toby, and the girls were always together, Christmas, weekends, vacations; they even went to the same private school. Toby graduated several years ahead of the girls, but they remain close. Toby left college after his master's degree to work for the FBI, but the girls decided to stay in college and work on their doctorates instead of entering the workforce.

Skyler went to work for The Agency right after graduation, but Tyler accepted a position with a bio-medical research facility just outside Granite Falls, Washington. Her position not only paid a hefty salary, but also offered her the chance to work on her internship toward an additional medical degree. Unfortunately, the position took her a long way from home, which bothered everyone in the family. But it gave the girls a chance to become their own person instead of a mirror image of each other. This was the first time the girls lived apart and being alone for the first time is always hard, but for a twin it can be especially difficult.

"Well, remember all the stories you told us as children, Aunt Mad?" Tyler asked.

When the girls spoke of their past it was never *me* or *I*, it was always *us* or *we*. It's only recently they've started identifying themselves as individuals.

"Well one in particular keeps nagging at the back of my head," Tyler added.

"And which one is that?" Maddie asked.

"Well, it's not a story exactly," Tyler hesitated. "But a situation."

"Okay, spill the beans, kiddo, what's wrong."

Tyler was a levelheaded young woman and never jumped to simple conclusions. So, for her to be stuck on a past memory meant something was definitely wrong. Tyler knew she had to explain carefully.

"You know where I work, well the other day a co-worker and I did a little... *side job*... and the sample gave a strange reading. It's almost like... like we were not only analyzing human DNA, but also fish DNA... at the same time."

"Excuse me?" Maddie asked.

"I know it sounds crazy, Aunt Mad... but what really bothers me... well, Caiden, my co-worker, and I spent hours playing with that sample. And tonight... well tonight he said we're in trouble because of our extra research. Aunt Mad, can you check on my company and make sure everything's on the up and up?"

"No problem, baby. I'll get right on it. In the meantime young lady, if anything weird happens, anything at all, you come straight home. You understand? Home to Oklahoma."

"Okay, I understand. I feel safer just knowing you're aware of some of these things."

"You want us to come up for a few days for a visit, kiddo?" Maddie suggested. "Nothing strange about an aunt and uncle coming to visit their niece now is there?"

"That would be wonderful, but I..."

"Look, your safety and security comes first. Let me do a little research and I'll check on flights. See you in a few days, my sweet. Be safe, and TyTy, I love you very much."

"I love you too, Aunt Mad. Bye."

* * * * * *

After hanging up, Maddie looked over at her husband, Nate, and frowned.

"What's up?" he asked.

"We need to do some snooping on TyTy's company. Make sure they're the real deal and not into something they shouldn't be."

Maddie told Nate what Tyler told her and he too thought something sounded odd. They decided perhaps it wouldn't be a bad idea if Nate also stopped by Lewis's office in the morning for a brief chat.

Chapter 14

SPANGLEHOLTZ STARED ADMIRINGLY at little Lizzie. She was beautiful in her own way. His hand shook as he touched her. A light layer of golden blonde hair covered her small body and felt soft to the touch.

"Fur?" he asked softly. "I wonder how long it will grow."

Spangleholtz pulled out his wallet and flipped through the photos until he found the one he was looking for. The quarter horse was a blonde beauty. He held it up to the light and compared it to little Miss Marie Elizabeth. The color was almost the same, so was the shade. He chuckled then stood back and smiled. This little experiment was a success and the salvation of the human race was close at hand. All his plans, his hard work, the cost, the lives, everything had been worth it—even the failures.

"Next time we need to be a little more particular on which strands we merge. I believe you got a few more of the characteristics than we'd planned, but we'll see, huh Lizzie? You're a beautiful little girl, a real beauty. I believe you'll find it was all worth it."

It was time to leave, time to leave little Lizzie alone. He walked through the nursery admiring the other newborns when he noticed a nurse watching him.

"How's it going?" he asked.

"Fine, but that new baby makes me nervous," she replied staring away from the child.

"And why is that?"

"I don't know why; she just does. What's wrong with her anyway?"

"What's wrong with you?" he asked. "She's just a baby. A baby with special needs, yes, but a baby nevertheless. And it's your job to care for her. Are you saying you're incapable of performing your duties at this hospital's neonatal intensive care unit?"

The head nurse heard the heated discussion and jumped into action.

"Excuse me," she whispered. "But we *do* have babies sleeping. Can we keep it down or take it somewhere else?"

"Nurse...?"

"Thembleson... Doctor. Nurse Thembleson," the head nurse whispered.

"Well, Nurse Thembleson," Spangleholtz whispered. "It seems *this* nurse doesn't have what it takes to care for a special-needs baby. That makes me nervous, very nervous."

"Explain, Paula, please?" the head nurse asked now facing the frightened girl.

"I... I just said she made me nervous, that's all. I don't want to hurt her and I'm afraid I will if I pick her up or try to feed her. He took it the wrong way... honest."

"I see," Spangleholtz interjected. "Will you change her diaper please? I'd like to watch."

Paula hesitated for a second but when the head nurse nodded her approval of the doctor's request, Paula turned around then paused as though in thought. She glanced back at Spangleholtz then walked into the room with the special incubator. She cautiously picked up the baby. As she gazed into little Lizzie's eyes, Paula smiled.

"She's beautiful," Paula said to Spangleholtz and the head nurse who were now standing just behind her.

"Yes she *is*," he replied.

"Can she suck? Will I hurt her if I give her a bottle?" Paula asked.

"I'm glad to hear you ask these types of questions. It means you're willing to learn. We must use a special bottle for her. Her mouth protrudes."

"Almost like a horse?" Paula surmised.

Spangleholtz chuckled, "Yes, almost like a horse. So we must use a flat-tipped nipple instead of a regular one. These are longer and easier for her to grasp on to. Here give it a try."

Nurse Thembleson handed Paula a special bottle and little Lizzie began sucking. She opened her eyes and stared at the woman who was holding her. Paula smiled and glanced at the doctor, who patted Paula on the shoulder.

"See, nothing to be afraid of, she's just another baby but with special needs. That's all."

"Yes, doctor, thank you. But doctor?" Paula asked.

"Yes?"

"What about the tail?"

Chapter 15

DRAKE READ THROUGH the names for Starling, but without the husband's first name he was stuck.

"What's up?" Shelby asked as she gathered her things for the night.

"Can you help me before you leave?" Drake asked.

"Can you help me before you leave?" Shelby mocked. She dropped her purse and sweater in a chair and said, "Okay, what's up?"

"I need to find a Marty Starling, but I don't know her husband's first name. Any ideas?" he asked.

"With that doggy please help me look splattered all over your face? How could I possibly refuse? Tell me something about this woman."

"All I know is she's pregnant."

"Well, that definitely narrows it down doesn't it?" Shelby laughed. Drake ignored her so she added, "Did you check the recent births? Or do you know her doctor's name?"

Drake hit himself on his head. "I'm so stupid."

"I could have told you that and it wouldn't have been so painful," she laughed.

"No... I mean.... dag gone it Shelby, I know the doctor's name."

"I'll tell you what. Email me what you *do* know and when I get home tonight I'll see what I can find out. Okay? I'll have it for you in the morning. No reason for the both of us to be up all night."

"I really appreciate this Shelby," he said smiling at her. "I also need you to contact the detectives. I want to know if there were any wine glasses in the kitchen sink or in the living room of the Sutton place. Or in the whole house for that matter."

"Anytime, boss, anytime."

Chapter 16

CARRIE, SKYLER AND Lacey checked into a small hotel in Centralia, West Virginia just off the major highway. After unpacking their clothes, they decided they would head out to the blast site deep in the hills of Prestonia. As they passed through the lobby, Lacey decided to check a few things out for herself.

"Hello," she said to the clerk behind the desk.

"Hi," he answered.

"How far is Prestonia?"

"Why you want t' go out there fer?" he asked with a deep accent.

"We came to see the new hole in the ground like everybody else."

He shook his head and said, "It's about an hour ride, but no one goes there, and there's no road for yer car." Lacey looked confused so the clerk added, "Yah take the train."

"Where?" Lacey asked.

"The station's just down the street to yer right. You'll see it," he winked at her, which made Lacey squirm and feel somewhat nasty inside.

"Thanks," she replied looking out the window for a glimpse of a train station.

* * * * * *

The girls fell onto the beds exhausted. It has been a long day and they were dirty, tired and hungry.

"Let's order a pizza," Skyler suggested.

"Yeah," Lacey agreed. "Great idea. I'll call."

"So what did we get out of today?" Carrie asked. "Anything at all, or did we ride that stupid train all the way there and back for nothing? I wish we had the time to stay and see the hole."

"Who ever heard of a town with no roads anyway?" Skyler asked. "I'm hitting the shower before the pizza gets here."

"I'm next," Carrie hollered.

Lacey tossed the phone book onto the desk after dialing the number. "I guess I'm last."

After they all showered and ate as much pizza and soda as their stomachs could hold, each girl was about to fall asleep when Lacey sat straight up in bed.

"Is it just me or did anyone else notice there wasn't any clean up going on out there today?"

"No, I noticed it too," Carrie mumbled almost asleep. She sighed then added, "It did seem odd there was only us around, no police, no nothing. It almost looked as if it'd already been sterilized or something."

"Or something," Skyler moaned barely lifting her head off her pillow. "Just keep those thoughts until the morning okay? I'm bushed."

With the lights off and only strange shadows reflecting off the walls, each girl slept dreaming about the huge crater that laid quiet and abandoned in the middle of a large forest only a few miles away.

Chapter 17

"... IS THE SIXTH case this year where the mother mutilated her family and claims to have no memory. Tammy Brooksfield woke from a trance today in court, just like Early Sutton and the other four women. The only difference between their stories is the mileage. Sutton lives in Pennsylvania, Brooksfield in California, and the others in New Mexico, Washington, Montana, and Florida..."

As the newscaster continued to talk, Drake dropped his coffee, which splattered across the floor.

"Damn it, Drake," Vickie yelled. "I just cleaned this place yesterday."

"What in the..."

"Hello? Drake... anybody home?" Vickie hollered from her knees wiping up the coffee.

"Oh sorry Hon, but did you hear what that lady just said?" Drake asked running for the remote to turn up the volume.

"How can I *not* hear? The TV's too loud," she screamed over the now blaring television.

"...the judge has ordered a continuance but everyone involved is suspicious for each woman's story is exactly the same. Their husbands are doctors and they all have young children between the ages of..."

"Is she saying there's other cases like mine?"

"Where have you been? Mars?" she asked, shaking her head.

"And turn that damn thing down will yah? Maybe you'll be able to hear *me* better."

Drake hit the mute button and turned to his wife. "Honey, I'm sorry. I guess I've had my head up my ass lately with this case and all. But I haven't had the chance to watch the news or read the papers in months, what's going on?"

Vickie stood up holding the dripping coffee-soaked rag in front of her. "How do you expect to *win* a case if you don't come up for air once in a while? Yes, there's been several other mummies just like yours—Baby-Killers. But I think yours is the first."

"Explain please?" Drake urged.

Vickie dropped the dripping rag into the sink and grabbed a handful of paper towels as she handed her husband another cup of coffee. "Come and sit down before you drop this one too."

His wife continued to explain and clean the floor as he sat at the small kitchen table numb.

"I don't know what's going on exactly, but each of those women killed their families and then several weeks later they suddenly *wake up*." Vickie sat up and flailed her arms over her head as if to pretend she was floating in the air then added, "... they claim to know *nothing*... nothing at all. Can you honestly believe that? Well, I can't." Drake sat in silence realizing something more evil and sinister was unfolding. Five other women suddenly waking up in a courtroom, each having no memories of the last several weeks or months. *This just can't be a coincidence,* he thought. *What in the world is going on?* Drake jumped up and accidently knocked over his hot cup of coffee as he grabbed his car keys from the table.

The coffee dripped down in front of Vickie and she screamed. "Drake. What is the matter with you? And where do you think you're going?"

"I've got to get in touch with one of those other lawyers," he yelled as the front door slammed behind him.

Vickie sat in silence, watching as the coffee dripped from the table onto the recently cleaned floor. Then she looked over at the sleeping dog by the fireplace.

"I don't imagine you'd like to slurp this up would yah, Henry?"

The dog looked up, yawned, then lay back down.

"Didn't think so..."

Chapter 18

THE THREE GIRLS admired the view from the deck at the train station that overlooked a deep drop into the valley below. They were waiting for the *seven at seven* to arrive. All three held hot coffee and shivered as a cool breeze seeped through their sweatshirts. The sun rose from behind the distant mountain range but didn't warm them.

"I didn't know it's so cold up here in May," Lacey said shivering.

"With the mountains so high the heat doesn't show up 'til about ten thirty or so. It'll warm up a little, but don't count on much," Carrie stated admiring the view.

"You're pretty sure about that?" Skyler asked.

"Well when your significant other is a member of a native tribe, you eventually end up in the mountains once in a while," Carrie smiled as she spoke. "And spring is rather cool. Late summer and fall are the killers."

The distant whistle of a train announced it was close to seven, so the girls blew faster on their drinks to get a few more sips before boarding. Their view was spectacular. The rolling ranges with their various trees and rocks mirrored their vivacious colors as the dew reflected the morning sun. Fresh mountain springs and newly bloomed wild flowers filled the air with a sparkling newness full of life and innocence.

"It's beautiful up here," Skyler exclaimed turning around to see how close the train might be. "Wow, when did all these people get here?"

Lacey and Carrie turned only to be surprised by a rather large group of people now waiting for the train.

"They were not here a few minutes ago," Carrie said with a weird look on her face. "Nor were they here yesterday afternoon. Let's get in line before we lose a seat."

Skyler and Lacey followed Carrie down the stairs to the rather large group of people waiting silently for the train. Skyler, in her mid twenties, had inherited her long blonde-reddish hair and freckles from her fraternal grandmother and her height from her mother. She was just over five eight and an exact copy of her sister Tyler. Skyler studied Human Psychosis Prediction for her PhD, which delves into the inner mind and how humans react to a sudden and life-threatening event. Tyler, however, stayed in the field of biology with the goal of becoming a physician. Although carbon copies of each other, both girls were complete opposites when it came to their wants and desires.

Lacey was younger than the others and like Skyler just recently joined The Agency. Her uncle had worked for The Agency for as long as Lacey could remember. As a young child, Lacey was involved in a NASA conspiracy and almost lost her right arm in South America. Although a little weaker than her left, the only lasting effect was a nasty scar that ran the length of her inner arm. Her mother urged her to have plastic surgery, but Lacey refused. The scar was a reminder of what could happen. Lacey favored more her father than her mother. She had long wavy brown hair and was of average height. For medical reasons, Lacey spent many years at The Agency after her terrible childhood experience and soon became so comfortable she decided early on she would dedicate her life to her country.

Carrie was just Carrie, blonde, blue eyes and sharp as a whip. Carrie, now in her late twenties, was already an accomplished professional. Her cases ranged from the most dangerous to the most bizarre. In her early days at the FBI, Carrie's first assignment was to track down the famous Senator Killer... Maddie Edwards. Although Maddie was an Agent for the Agency, it wasn't until years later Carrie got to know her personally.

Carrie also knew Skyler was Maddie's niece and therefore was dedicated in making sure Skyler returned home safe. Carrie's last assignment almost took her leg and life. Carrie blamed herself for running madly into a dark basement and falling down the stairs. Carrie was so anxious to save her client she failed to notice several steps had been deliberately removed. When her foot hit the missing stair and sunk into the abyss, she fell forward snapping her shin bone. Not only did she almost bleed to death, she also put her partner's safety in jeopardy. She promised herself she would never again put herself, or anyone else, in that kind of danger. Carrie also discovered what a few months in rehab could do to a person's mind, body and spirit. Isolation does strange things to a person when they're left to their own justifications.

The three stood in line as the train crept to a stop. As they waited, Carrie just couldn't hold it in any longer. "Okay, I give up, where did all you people come from? I've been here for the last half hour and when I first got here there was no one but us. So where did all of you come from?"

Some passengers turned and looked at Carrie but then, without saying a word, turned back around. Others completely ignored her altogether. One woman, who looked to be in her mid-thirties glanced over at her and said, *"Home."*

That was all she needed; Carrie took the bait. "What is this place anyway? *Twilight Zone* USA? Hello? Are we alive here or are we all the walking dead?"

Again, no one paid her any attention. Carrie gulped the rest of her coffee and tossed the paper cup into a nearby trash bin. She then looked over at her companions and shook her head.

"Maybe they don't speak-a-da English. Maybe they only speak Western Virginia. CAN ANYONE HERE TRANSLATE FOR ME?" Carrie yelled.

Skyler and Lacey both gave each other a glaring stare as they walked right past Carrie and boarded the train. Carrie stood back and watched as the passengers ignored her and boarded. Not one person spoke to another. It was a weird sensation and Carrie didn't like the feeling one little bit. Not to mention the woman who had talked earlier was now also ignoring her. It was as if Carrie wasn't there; perhaps no one could see her anymore.

"Drats," Carrie said to no one in particular. "If I can talk to a ghost, I'm sure I can talk to someone from West Virginia."

Carrie turned to a woman wearing a business suit and asked, "Ma'am, are you going out to the blast site?"

The woman stared at Carrie and without any change in facial expressions said, "And why would I want to go there?"

Carrie sighed and crammed her hands deep into her sweatshirt's pockets. She studied each person who boarded the train and deliberately made sure she was the last one. As she walked down the cramped aisle, she paid close attention to each individual and what they were doing, which wasn't much. After a few seconds, Carrie plopped herself between Skyler and Lacey.

"Well, are you done making a fool of yourself?" Lacey asked. "Nothing like trying to start something so soon."

"Just checking," Carrie answered.

"Checking for what?" Skyler asked.

"Oh just checking to see which movie we just dropped into, you know, *Silent Hill*, *Blair Witch*, or maybe *The Body Snatchers*." Carrie grinned.

Skyler sighed and turned to stare out the window. But Lacey, not having a window, just stared down the aisle.

"Now you resemble one of them," Carrie whispered into Lacey's ear.

"Will you give it a break?" Lacey whispered, pushing Carrie away.

"Fine," Carrie replied as she pulled out her cell phone to check for messages.

Chapter 19

SPANGLEHOLTZ CHECKED HIS ticket and frowned when he realized he had some spare time before his flight. *Get here several hours early... huh?* He said to himself. *What a joke.*

He found an empty seating area and selected a chair next to a window. Spangleholtz preferred solitude, prying and meddlesome people bothered him. After pulling out his tablet, he looked around to make sure he was alone. When his email popped up from the secure line, he scrolled through the long list searching for a certain message. He found it and read a few lines before he hit reply. He spoke slowly into the small device:

Mother and children need not be eliminated. But must be removed to a secured place. They have too many relatives and friends. TOO RISKY! Make sure their deaths look natural and leave replacements in normal body positions. I'd wait until mother returns home from hospital to make swap. A house fire would be a good front. Let me know as soon as they arrive. Take special care, baby has difficulty eating and breathing. We want nothing to happen to our new member. And I mean nothing. Father out of picture, labeled as suicide. Good job. But get going. I can't believe we allowed a delivery in a regular hospital. Someone will answer to this. We need to cover our tracks before the press gets a hold of it.

Spangleholtz read over the message before hitting the send button. He then checked through a few other emails, but when nothing important jumped out he decided to walk around the terminal. After tucking his tablet back into his jacket pocket, he stood and stretched. A plane was landing in the distance and he watched as it made a smooth touchdown. His stomach growled announcing that a quick breakfast before departure wouldn't be such a bad idea. As he passed a newsstand the front page of the *New York Times* hit him like a Mack Truck from out of nowhere.

HUMAN HORSE CROSSBREED WEIGHS IN AT A LITTLE OVER TWELVE POUNDS AT MERCY MEDICAL CENTER

"What the..." he almost said before he stopped himself. There it was right in front of him, little Lizzie's picture as plain as the nose on his face and in full color. He grabbed the paper from the stand and read the article. With his blood pressure rising, he wasn't sure if he could hold back his anger. After throwing down a five-dollar bill on the counter, Spangleholtz walked away with the paper and yanked out his cell phone. This had to be squelched immediately before it went any further. *How in the hell did this get out?* Someone was going to pay and pay dearly, and it wouldn't be with money.

Chapter 20

DRAKE WAS IN such a hurry to get into his office he stumbled through the door. As usual, Shelby was waiting for him smiling proudly from her desk.

"Hey cowboy," she smirked. "Just left the saloon?"

"Very funny. Did you find anything?"

"Yep. All five of them," she replied, waving a piece of paper in the air. "Seems they all want media attention—unlike *you*."

"Look I told you, the less press the better for my client," Drake defended.

"Well, I don't think you can keep her in the dark any longer my friend," she replied. "The press will be all over her now there's others just like her."

"Terrific, just terrific."

Drake read down the list and realized most were on the other side of the country from him. The only one he would be able to reach this morning would be the one in Florida. He dialed the number and was happy to discover the attorney was in his office.

"Look," the attorney demanded, "if you're with the tabloids or something I'm not interested. My client's a real person and I'm..."

"I'm sorry, Mr. Kranton, but I represent Early Sutton."

"Holy shit, for real? I've been trying to find you. Seems like your number's classified information."

"I'm right here, I'm not exactly hiding," Drake interjected.

"I would love to meet with you if that would be all right. I'm having a hell of a time with my case and yours isn't helping."

"What would my case have to do with yours?" Drake asked.

"Copycat," Kranton explained. "Everyone is saying *copycat* murders."

"I don't believe that for one second," Drake added.

"Me either. I'm telling you, something very strange is going on and I want to get to the bottom of it."

"I plan on contacting the lawyers involved in the other cases, would you be interested in a meeting of the minds?" Drake asked.

"Absolutely. The more the better. I'm sure a group meeting would be beneficial to everyone. When... where?"

"That's exactly what I'm thinking. Let me see if I can get a hold of the others and I'll schedule a mutual time and place. This is exciting," Drake said with his hands shaking. "Hold on, I'll transfer you to my assistant and she'll take your availability."

"Hey man, I really appreciate this. I'm telling you, my little lady could not have done what they're claiming she did. My God, there's nothing left of her family. Nothing."

"No problem," Drake replied. "Believe me... I know the feeling. Hold on, I'll transfer you now."

* * * * * *

Drake stared at the dark phone number on the stark white paper. It required more than his courage to dial. Although a long shot, he knew he had no other choice. As the tone rang through his ears, Drake's whole body shook with anticipation.

"Hello?" a young voice echoed.

"Yes, may I speak with Ms. Paula Cornwell please," he asked.

"Speaking."

Now what should he say? In all honesty, Drake did not believe anyone would answer.

"Ma'am, my name's Drake Anderson. I'm Ms. Early Sutton's attorney."

"Okay and you're calling because?" the young woman replied.

"Yes ma'am. I understand you work at the hospital where Ms. Starling gave birth and I was given your name. I need some information on Marty Starling and her baby. She was a patient of Ms. Sutton's husband."

"I don't wish to talk about it." Suddenly the woman's voice became aloof and distant. It was obvious she had no intention of continuing the conversation. "I need to go."

"No please," Drake pleaded. "I beg you."

"How do I know you're who you say you are?" she asked.

"You can come to my office if you wish. Or you can call me back," he suggested.

"What do you want?"

"I need to find her."

"You're too late, she's dead. They're all dead," the woman said before the connection was cut.

Chapter 21

THE TRAIN PULLED away leaving the three standing alone at a deserted station in Prestonia, West Virginia. The slight breeze and the rustling of trees was the only sound.

"That was weird," Carrie said as she looked around. "Let's just pretend we're the only ones onboard and check out that hole."

Carrie walked away toward the dirt road just past the small deserted train station.

"Whatever," Skyler and Lacey said at the same time.

"Jinks," Carrie yelled from up ahead. "Okay, it's a hole."

"Yep, it's a hole," Skyler added.

"A big hole," Lacey mumbled.

The three stood in front of the crater that was so large they could not see the other side. It was vast and the trees for miles laid flat to the ground.

"Well, it only took half a day to get out here, so now what?" Skyler asked.

"Lunch," Carrie declared as she dropped her backpack onto the ground.

The three chose a semi-clean spot and sat on some logs to eat and drink and revive themselves. It was obvious the hot sun was not going to give them any breaks, and they sweated as they rested in the sunlight. With all the trees either gone or down, shade was not an option.

"I think a night here might be a little more informative," Carrie stated between bites.

"A what?" Skyler asked with a mouth full of peanut butter and bread.

"How can you eat that stuff?" Carrie asked.

"What does that have to do with anything?" Skyler defended. "Let's go back to the night thing."

"Well, as you can see, all's quiet. Except for us three sightseers and those photographers up there. So obviously nothing is going on during the day." Carrie took a drink from her water and stuffed the wrappers from her sandwich back into her pack.

"What photographers?" Lacey asked.

"Behind you," Carrie said as she pulled out some cookies.

Lacey and Skyler froze in place. They thought they were the only ones stupid enough to be out here.

"Hello," Carrie yelled with a wave.

"Don't do that," Skyler said with soda dripping down her chin.

"You're leaking," Carrie laughed.

"Shhhh," Lacey whispered.

Carrie smiled and continued to wave. "Too late," Carrie sang.

CHAPTER 22

EARLY PACED BACK and forth across her cell not once raising her head. It had been a couple of days since she heard from her lawyer and now she was getting nervous.

Where is he?

"Hey Baby Killer," a voice echoed from down the corridor.

"We don't like people who *kill* babies," another voice yelled from the other direction.

Early's pacing increased. Back and forth from the wall to the bars, from the bars to the wall.

"Hey baby killer we have a surprise for you."

"Come down here you coward."

"Yeah, come down here."

I didn't do it. Early cried. *I didn't do it.*

"B-A-B-Y *killer,*" someone sang. "We have a *present* for you..."

I didn't do it. I didn't do it. I didn't do it.

The ranting continued as the speed in Early's stride increased. She was bouncing off the wall and then, off the bars. Blood was running down her face from where she was hitting the cell's parameters. But still the chanting continued from outside, *Baby killer! Baby killer! Baby killer!*

"I DIDN'T DO IT... I DIDN'T DO IT!" Early yelled as loud as she could over and over again. "I DIDN'T DO IT!"

But the chanting continued. Now someone was dragging something along the bars and the noise was even louder.

Screams, rants and raves, and banging were chaotic and uncontrollable. But through it all Early continued to proclaim her innocence.

"ENOUGH!" a woman's voice echoed from up the corridor.

All became quiet except for Early's screaming declarations of innocence.

"I said that was ENOUGH!" the guard ordered as she headed for Early's cell.

"Yeah, you tell baby killer that," a voice yelled from above.

"Martha, I'm warning you. SHUT UP," the guard ordered.

As the guard approached Early's cell she saw the blood on the bars first, then she pulled out her walkie-talkie. "EMERGENCY IN CELL 142, EMERGENCY... CELL 142."

"Emergency Cell 142," a high-pitched voice mocked from a few cells down. "Baby killers have *NO* emergencies."

"ENOUGH," the guard yelled again. "SHUT UP!"

Early continued to bounce off the cell's wall and scream out her innocence. The blood was everywhere, down her face, her shirt, on the wall, the bars...

"Ahh SHIT," the guard yelled as she swiped her badge against the locking device.

There was a large clank as the doors on Early's cell slid opened. Other help was just entering the lockdown as the woman guard grabbed Early and pulled her to the floor. Early continued to scream although her voice was almost gone.

"Ah, Sweetie, calm down," the guard said.

"Ah sweetie," the high-pitched mocking echoed from outside. The back-up guards pulled out their sticks and banged on the cells.

"That is quite enough," a deep voice demanded and everything went dead. "What in the hell is going on in here!"

"Sir, she's hurt," the guard pleaded.

"No shit Sherlock. Call the medics," he ordered. "And shut these others up."

"I didn't do it," Early whispered over and over again. "I didn't do it."

Chapter 23

STRICKLAND'S PALMS WERE sweaty as she looked at her overly quiet cabinet members. She wiped them on her hips before she picked up her notes. For some strange reason her hands sweated absurdly when she was under pressure. It was the only thing she hated about her body. "Good afternoon," Strickland began.

Jumping from vice president to president during the first year of her first term was scandalous enough, but when she won the election three years later on her own, the tabloids had a field day.

She had served as vice president to Alfred Lloyd, an entrepreneur who made millions in the health insurance and scientific research business. He and his female running mate ran as reform candidates, promising to advance medical research and fix the broken healthcare system. But news journalists linked him to companies committing healthcare fraud and discovered prior to his election he took kickbacks for helping private research companies secure government grants.

The vice president publically admonished Lloyd and even pushed Congress to investigate. She had committed political treason and was condemned by her party and political pundits as a traitor. She quickly turned to hero when the truth about Lloyd and his connections and kickbacks emerged.

Lloyd was impeached and, under threat of indictment, he resigned. Now president, Strickland was seen as the true reformer and easily won her own term in office.

Acknowledging heads nodded as Strickland stood in front of her audience. With a strong grasp of her notes in her left hand, she used her right hand to steady herself against the podium.

"As you should know, there was a rather large explosion in a small town in West Virginia. I asked for Dr. Greghardt, our Subject Matter Expert, to discuss any details he may have concerning this explosion. Dr. Greghardt?"

Strickland stood aside and held out her hand as a signal for Greghardt to take over. As he passed, he patted Strickland on her shoulder.

"Good afternoon," Greghardt said. "I have satellite surveillance of before and after the incident."

The first picture that flashed up on the screen was of a heavily wooded area. He clicked the remote and a view of a massive crater displayed.

"I know that was a little fast, but please study the two pictures as I continue to alternate between them."

After a few seconds he paused, then flashed up another picture of a heavily wooded area. "This photo was taken about ten years ago. I would like for you to concentrate between this photo and the one just before the explosion."

After about two minutes, Katrina from the Department of Agriculture pointed her finger at the large pictures.

"You see something, Kate?" Strickland asked.
Kate had a bewildering look on her face as she spoke, "There! There in the middle of the screen," she was talking excitedly. "A building or something's in one picture but not in the other."

"You are exactly right, very good... very good indeed," Greghardt praised.

"I don't see anything," David from Homeland Security snapped.

"Let me zoom into the area of the picture Kate's referring to." Greghardt winked at Kate before he turned his attention back to the pictures.

The trees became crisper as he zoomed in. It was then the green metal roof of a large structure gradually emerged before their eyes. Although the trees seemed to grow strategically over the roof to conceal most of it, there was still just enough open space to make out an enormous-sized building.

"What is that?" Colonel Jenkins asked studying the screen.
"Now that is the one question we have no answer for and were hoping someone in here would," Strickland replied, rubbing her hands against the sides of her pants.

Chapter 24

THE GIRLS NERVOUSLY sat as the two men approached from the tree line. One man was short and could not have been much over five foot. His red ball cap covered the top of his long dark hair that was pulled into a ponytail. The other man was not much taller than the first, perhaps five four standing perfectly straight. He wore a long sleeved, bright red T-shirt and faded jeans. His quilted black vest and black boots reminded Carrie of an L.L.Bean catalogue. Both men toted several cameras hung from their necks as well as a large bulky bag that probably housed their zoom lenses and other needed supplies. The second man had blonde hair and a bushy blonde beard. Carrie smiled as they approached, but her two comrades remained fixed and rigid.

"Good day to you," the short man greeted with a Whales accent. "My name is Mick Yorkshire and this is my partner Zack Lankensmith. We work for National Geographic."

"Nice to meet you. I'm Carrie and these are my friends, Skyler and Lacey. We just wanted to see the big hole."

"And it's a hole," Lacey laughed.

Skyler simply nodded.

"Mind if we shoot a couple pictures of you three eating lunch in front of the crater? It would make a great black-and-white," Zack added.

"Sure," Carrie replied smiling. "Why not?"

Skyler and Lacey gave Carrie an exasperated gaze as they continued to sit rather oddly on their fallen logs.

"This is pretty weird isn't it?" Mick asked looking at the large crater.

Carrie stared into the vastness with him. "It sure is. I wonder what caused it."

Zack backed up and began snapping away at the small group standing in front of the rather large void.

"I could have sworn this is where the old hospital was," Mick added. "I had a cousin that grew up not far from here and I remember the talks about the crazies. I could have sworn it was right here."

"Crazies?" Carrie asked.

"Yeah, when I was a kid I remember coming here with my uncle to fish just over that ridge. With only a train and no roads, we had to hike to the lake. Our walk took us right by the large hospital. He said the people who lived there were crazies and they had weird things wrong with them."

"Really?" Carrie asked still staring out over the large abyss. "Interesting story."

Mick shook his head before adding, "But whatever was here is definitely not here anymore. I mean, talk about sterilization. It will take decades before anything looks normal again. I wouldn't doubt if this crater becomes a lake someday. The water table's pretty high in these mountains and there's already some at the bottom."

As Mick walked back to join his partner, Carrie's mind began to churn. Then it hit her. She suddenly knew what had been bothering her this whole time, and she wanted to kick herself for not seeing it before.

"Well, thanks for the shots. I really appreciate it," Zack added, showing Carrie and the girls a digital picture of their backs sitting on the logs in front of the huge crater. "If they want these in the magazine they'll contact you. You want a copy? I can email it. Right now. Skyler gave me all your contact information."

"Nah," Carrie replied. "Be more exciting to see it in the magazine. Send us one if we ever make the centerfold."

"Okay, thanks." Mick laughed. The two left and walked down the sloping side of the crater toward the bottom.

"Damn," Carrie stated as she stood next to the other girls. "I can't believe I hadn't thought of this before."

"What?" Skyler asked.

"Come on, I'll explain." Carrie turned and headed back to the train station.

"Wait Carrie," Lacey yelled. "Why did you tell them we didn't need a copy of the picture? I want one."

Chapter 25

SHADOWS FROM THE ambient light created an ominous aura around the room. The room was exceptionally quiet as the small group sat patiently around the oval mahogany table. Lewis entered from the back with a stench of authority. The walls echoed his black silhouette as if recording the event for some future unknown reason. Footsteps were the only sounds, but even those were muffled by the heavily carpeted floor and soundproof brick walls.

"Let's get started," Lewis demanded heading for the podium. "We received an urgent but unsettling message with photos this morning on the secured line."

Lewis nodded to the excited but quiet agents sitting at the oval table.

"I'm not going to sugar coat this." As he spoke the words, a photo flashed on the screen behind him. "As you can see, these are bones of what looks like an animal. However, if you look closer you'll see they resemble humans more. The local authorities sent us these fragments for analysis. What came back was horrifying. I received the results this morning."

Lewis pushed a small button on the podium and the screen changed to another picture of an unusual skeleton laid out on a metal table.

"The results, people, are these bones are indeed both human and... animal," Lewis stated turning to also look at the screen.

"So, a human and an animal were buried together?" One

of the female agents asked from the back of the table. "We can plainly see for ourselves the skull is... or *looks* feline... perhaps a cat?"

"Agent Schuster?" Lewis asked.

"Yes," Schuster replied. "Hybridologist, sir."

"Expert in the field of cross-breeding if I remember my briefing correctly," Lewis interjected. He started to walk toward her but then stopped short. "Some things may not be as they appear, Doctor."

"But no human head could possibly resemble that," she stated. "The human skull is unique and mimics no other. But the animal kingdom has several species that resemble the same skull shape and size."

"Thank you, Agent Schuster," Lewis added clicking another upsetting display onto the screen. "But do animal skulls contain human DNA? Do animals wear clothing?" he asked raising an eyebrow.

"Are you saying those bloody clothes were around those bones?" another agent asked.

"Agent Abuline?" Lewis asked. "Your specialty is Forensic Analysis correct?"

"Yes sir," Abuline replied.

Lewis added, "We'll need each of your specialties on this case. We have samples in the lab for you to examine."

"Samples?" A petite woman who didn't look much over sixteen lowered her eyes as she spoke.

"Ah, Agent Bonneville, how nice to see you," Lewis smiled and winked. "Our DNA expert."

All heads turned and stared at the young-looking woman who smiled innocently back at them.

"To answer your concerns, the bones are missing," Lewis replied. "They were stolen from the morgue shortly after the samples were sent to us. It's been reported they were not to have been taken until the following day. However the doctor in charge had a special meeting planned so he prepared the samples personally that evening instead. Whoever took the bones and the clothing was not aware the samples were already locked away in a freezer."

"It's still impossible for those to be human," Dr. Tabatha

Schuster demanded with an odd look written all over her face.

Lewis handed each agent a file folder then stood back. "Examine the results for yourself. You'll also have access to the samples in our lab. Once you've talked yourself into it, let me know. We have a lot to cover."

"What do you want from us?" Agent Bonneville asked.

"This is your next case," Lewis replied. "Highly classified, as all our assignment are of course, but this one is unique. I want nothing, absolutely nothing to leave your lips. You discuss this only inside the secure rooms. Nothing and I mean nothing, leaves this building. Not even you."

"Sir?" Agent Abuline asked.

"You are being sequestered until your research is finished. Once you've completed your initial reports you will be visiting the site where these bones were found. You will conduct a full investigation, but I don't want anyone to know who you are or why you are there. Understand?"

The agents nodded.

"I knew I could count on you," Lewis added. "It is imperative The Agency knows what these bones are and who they belonged to. Also, the age and perhaps time of death. We are not sure if these are of a recent or ancient individual. We also need to know how this individual died."

"Yes sir," the agents said at once.

"The only others who know, or think they know, are the original doctor and a few police officers in the small town where the remains were discovered," Lewis explained.

"But sir," a small man said who had not spoken before. "If this is a human, then it could only mean…"

"I know what it might mean," Lewis almost yelled. "But we will *not* speak of it. Not until we are sure. Understand, Agent Mirada? You keep your conclusions for your classified reports."

The other agents stared at the miniature Agent Mirada who had a look of horror on his face. His eyes were wide and his mouth gaped open. Lewis gave him a look that left nothing to the imagination. He understood Mirada knew immediately he was not allowed to speak a word of his suspicions, but it was those few unspoken words that scared the life out of the other agents.

Chapter 26

THE ATTORNEYS SAT around a small table in a small room at a rather large and unimpressive hotel. Each one held the same agenda and the same purpose, to gather information that would acquit their clients. After several minutes of silence, Drake swallowed and loosened his tie. He knew at a glance he was the youngest and least experienced attorney at the table, and he also knew they all expected *him* to lead the meeting. Staring at the stern faces, he thought of Early's expression when she realized where she was. Her fear was so strong he could feel it, and that disturbed him to the point of realizing he was all she had. It was at that point Drake knew she was innocent, and she honestly knew nothing about how or why her family died.

"Uh... uh..." Drake cleared his throat as he rubbed his hands together. He felt inferior around these other great lawyers. Some were famous for their past cases they had won, others were just well known because of who they are. "Uh, I'm Drake Anderson and I'm so," Drake had to clear his throat again, "glad you could come."

"I've come to the conclusion there's more here than I've been led to believe," Darrell Westmore from California stated when Drake paused. "The crime scene was just too over-staged from my point of view."

"Exactly what I thought about my case." Justin Combs from New Mexico added in excitedly.

Judy Stonebridge shifted in her chair then said firmly, "My

client weighs in at just over a hundred pounds. It's physically impossible for her to have done what the authorities claim. There's just no way."

"My client is very caring and loving. If someone sneezes she'll jump to find a tissue," Kelly Starks from Montana explained. "It would have taken more than courage to kill her family. I understand there *are* mothers out there who kill their children. But my client only gives and never takes. These actions are simply not a part of her personality."

The room became quiet. Drake glanced around and realized Ash Kranton from Florida had not yet said a word. "Mr. Kranton? You're very quiet over there. What's going through your mind?"

Ash took in a deep breath then coughed. He shifted in his chair then righted himself. "I keep asking myself if this could be some kind of a scheme from a rather unique serial killer. But the killings are too widespread to be from one person. So then I must ask myself, what in the hell is going on? These children are slaughtered beyond recognition to the point of mutilation. The husbands as well."

"Oh my," Kelly popped up.

"What?" Drake asked.

"If our clients didn't do it, then we must ask ourselves who did?"

"Okay," Drake said wondering where she was taking this idea.

"So, why the mutilation? To shock? No, simply killing the whole family would be shock enough," Kelly stated, then she lowered her voice as she concluded. "We mutilate to hide... to cover up."

"Hey," Darrell Westmore added. "What if the remains are not our real victims?"

"Bait and switch?" Drake asked.

"But for what purpose?" Ash Kranton added.

Drake suddenly felt equal and declared, "Who the hell cares at this point. Let's get some DNA tests ordered."

Drake was certain, more so than before, of his client's innocence. He felt revived, but at the same time overwhelming grief for this innocent, confused woman he represented.

Drake's cell phone rang from his pocket.

"Drake! It's Shelby. Early's been taken to the hospital."

* * * * * *

Drake stood next to Early's bed. Her face was badly bruised and the bandages barely covered the stitches.

"I'm so sorry, Early," Drake whispered to the sleeping woman. "I am so sorry."

Drake picked up Early's hand and kissed it. He turned and motioned for his wife, Vickie, to join him. Vickie walked up to her husband and placed her hands on his back. She glanced down at Early and closed her eyes.

"This is the baby killer?" Vickie whispered.

"Supposedly."

"But she doesn't look like a baby killer," Vickie surmised.

"I don't believe she is one. This is why I wanted you to come with me."

"But the news makes her out to be such a bad ass."

"I know," Drake replied putting his arm around his wife. "That's why I don't watch the news."

"I don't understand," she said with her heart breaking.

"Neither do I," Drake answered. "Neither do I."

Chapter 27

IT WAS COLD and the rain was winning the small battle. Charlotte shivered as she pulled more of her socks from the drawer and shoved them around the old window. She rubbed her hands vigorously together as she blew her warm breath over her cold and aching fingers. The strong wind rattled the glass pane and frightened her. All she needed now was a broken or cracked window to complete the freezing process. It was cold enough in her room already. She did not wish for the wind to blow directly through her room too.

"Darn!" she whispered as she turned and glanced around her small and tidy space. "There has to be something better."

Giggles echoed from across the hall and a song blared from a radio in the adjoining room. Charlotte tightened her robe about her waist and opened her door. The dark hall was long and narrow. For some strange reason, it seemed even colder out here than in her room. *But how could that be possible*? Sounds of scuffles from her slippers against the shiny wooden floor echoed off the walls as she hurried toward the stairs. Dancing candlelight followed her from along the walls as she skipped. She loved how the aroma from the fireplace several floors below drifted all the way up here to her room. But at this moment she would prefer the heat instead. At the banister, Charlotte leaned out between the slats to see if anyone else was awake besides her. But all she could see was the reflection of the fire dancing against the dark stone walls beckoning her to come and warm herself.

She cautiously descended the stairs while being extra careful not to slip or make any noise. Her foot still ached from her last little mishap. The freshly cleaned stairs can be quite slippery and dangerous if one wore only socks or fluffy slippers. But she was not about to take off her warm pink pig slippers now that her feet were so cold. Besides, she was also wearing socks which would make slipping even more possible. As she descended the rounding stairs, Charlotte was careful to stay away from the large stone walls that emanated the cold from the outside. Living in a large castle, as she called it, did not have the greatest means for keeping everyone in the house comfortable.

When she reached the main hall, Charlotte adjusted her robe. With no one in sight, she hurried to enjoy the heat from the large fireplace. The stone hearth was taller than any of the adults in the castle. Large sculptured lion heads adorned each side. During the warm summer months when the fireplace was not in use, Charlotte would play within the deep recesses pretending the lion's heads were her guardians and she was their princess. Together, they would hold long conversations that would help to pass the long boring days. Although it was almost spring, a sudden and unexpected cold front brought a severe snowstorm that required the continuous burning in the large fireplace in order to warm the extra large house.

"Chilly missy?" The unexpected voice from the large red-velvet chair startled her.

Charlotte forgot to check the furniture before dashing through the room.

"Sorry sir," she curtsied and then turned to run back upstairs. To be out of bed at this time would bring a strong punishment and she didn't need any more trouble today. She was already on restriction for trying to glide across the small lake that reflected the beauty of the large house that lay just beyond the tree line.

"Come here, missy," the deep voice stated.

Now she knew she was in trouble and there was nothing she could do. The Master of the house had caught her red-handed. Charlotte walked meekly to the large over-stuffed chair and rested her hands on the smooth velvet arm. She loved to rub her hands over the soft velvet—the nap is smooth in one direction and rough in the other.

"Now, either you are not sleepy…" he began, "or, you are cold. Which is it?"

"Cold sir," Charlotte said so softly he could barely hear her.

"Come to me," he said opening his arms.

Charlotte climbed into his lap as he cuddled her in a warm embrace. It was wonderful resting in his strong arms. She could smell the lingering aroma of pipe tobacco on his clothes, which always made her feel safe and secure. Charlotte cuddled up a little closer.

Parting her hair with his hands, he kissed her head and whispered, "You know you are not supposed to be out of bed."

"I know, but it's so cold up there," she pleaded, "in my room."

"I see. But you have the feather bed and all those heavy warm blankets. You should be as warm and snug as a bug in a rug," he chuckled.

"But the snow," she whispered.

"What about the snow?"

"It comes in under my window."

He paused for a moment then held her a little tighter.

"I see," he replied. "That will have to be fixed now won't it?"

He stood up and laid her gently in the large chair. He pulled the small knitted throw over her body and tucked her in. After stretching out his back, he pulled the cord that dangled near one of the lion's heads. Within seconds, a man in uniform stood at the double glass doors by the hallway.

"Would you summon Bart for me please?" the man with the pipe asked.

"But it's late, sir," the man in uniform replied.

"I don't care what time it is. One of my ladies is having a problem with her window. Now where's Bart?"

"Yes sir, I will fetch him at once."

"Okay young lady," Steward said with a smile to the little bundle in the big chair. "If he can't fix your window tonight, we'll find some place warm for you to sleep."

Charlotte smiled and yawned. "Thank you, sir."

It was hard for her to keep her eyes open. The day had been long and she was quite tired. As she watched the flames dance, Charlotte closed her eyes for only a few seconds, but was soon fast asleep and as warm as ever.

Steward watched as the small child slept peacefully and shook his head in disbelief. She was so frail and tiny. At only a little over two feet, Charlotte could not weight much more than twenty pounds. But she was adorable at the sweet age of six and she was his favorite.

"Sir?" Bart's voice echoed through the room.

"It seems Ms. Charlotte's window needed attending. But this is probably impossible tonight. Would you please set up a cot in my room for her? Close to the fire, but not too close."

"Yes sir," Bart's voice reverberated with concern. "I'll fix that window first thing in the morn. I'll put in a new seal and that'll fix her right up."

"Thank you, Bart," Doctor Steward said staring at his pipe in his hand. "Also double check and see how much heat is coming through her vents. I want her room warm. She's too small to depend on her own heat."

Bart nodded and left. Doctor Steward enjoyed his last pipe of the day and with the last puff, a young woman entered the room.

"I'll take her to bed sir," she said. "It's all ready."

"Take care not to disturb her wings. They are very delicate and she has major arteries flowing through them. Any break and she'd bleed to death in minutes."

"Yes I know. I've cared for her before," she said smiling. "She's so light I'm amazed her bones don't break like her sister's did."

"Yes, it is wonderful she's so much stronger than Marlow," he replied tapping his pipe against the side of the hearth. "She was always in such pain." His voice lowered as he mouthed his last words.

"Sir," the young woman said as she picked up the little girl. "She's not in pain any longer."

"Perhaps," he acknowledged, "but it should never have happened. Not today, not with what we know."

"I'll put her to bed now." But before the woman left, she turned and stared sympathetically at the elderly man standing alone in thought next to the warm fire. Her heart ached for him.

* * * * * *

Charlotte picked up the small green fairy doll and tossed it gently onto her bed.

"So," Charlotte whispered. "Where are the others?"

As she glanced around the room to find her other dolls, her heart longed to be released. Her intense feelings of entrapment were almost more than she could handle. Her small slender fingers grasped firmly around the red fairy doll's body. As she squeezed, Charlotte felt a sudden urge to escape. Stretching her small frame, she slowly released her wings. It always felt good to allow them to spread out freely in the air instead of having to constantly bind them behind her back. Charlotte looked out her window and studied the treetops. They seemed to be beckoning her, taunting her to fly to them.

"Charlotte!" A voice yelled from her door. "You'd better hide your wings or else I'm telling."

"I don't care," Charlotte yelled back. "I'm in my own room. Get out!"

"I'm telling." The little girl from across the hall yelled.

Everyone knew Charlotte's wings were not to be released into the air.

"I don't care anymore," Charlotte whispered into the glass window. Her breath left a foggy impression as Charlotte wrote a message to no one in particular on the glass window pane with her small slender finger. *Help me.*

Chapter 28

"OKAY," LACEY WHISPERED. "It's dark and cold and damp and I'm miserable. So will you please remind me why we are here?"

"Shhhh," Carrie hushed as she studied the area through her infrared binoculars.

Lacey sighed and decided it was time for some hot cocoa. With only a slight glance back at Carrie, she walked into the tree line and headed to camp. But after only a couple of steps, Lacey knew she was in trouble. Without a flashlight or a campfire, everything looked and felt the same. Without hesitation, Lacey turned around to try and spot Carrie again. But the more steps she took toward what she thought was Carrie, the more she feared she was lost.

"Damn," Lacey shouted. "Carrie?"

She knew there were only two things she could do. She could either continue to yell for the girls, or just stand and wait and hope they would come looking for her. Lacey decided to stand and wait. She didn't need Carrie scolding her again.

The layers of dew were rising and the night's chill was seeping through her jacket and chilling her bones. Her legs ached and she wanted a warm bed more than anything right now. But minutes slowly ticked away and felt more like hours. Tears formed in her eyes as memories of her terrible ordeal as a child became hauntingly real again.

Her thoughts drifted off to her cousins, Melissa and Banner, who were held hostage with her when they were just children. To this very day, Lacey could still recall the scent of Melissa's blood. As memory became all too real, the recollection of Banner's urine-soaked pajamas stung her left arm and the odor of Melissa's blood-soaked hair filled her nose. For twelve long, dark hours, Lacey clung dearly to both of them trying hard to maintain her sanity. She jumped, as a swift breeze stirred and pulled her from her thoughts.

"Shit!" Lacey screamed.

"Lost?" a young voice sprang up from behind her. As she whipped around, Lacey came face to face with a sweet young boy who was about twelve years old.

"Umm," Lacey stumbled. "I'm afraid I am."

"So why don't you just yell out or something? Your camp is just over there." The boy pointed over Lacey's right shoulder. "I've been watching you stand here and was wondering if you were going to squat and pee or something. But you're just standing here. Kind of frozen."

Lacey sighed and gave the young boy a strange look. "Okay, which way to my camp?"

"Come on, before you really do get lost." He shrugged his shoulders and walked off in a direction Lacey just knew was the wrong way. But after only a few steps, she was standing next to their large dark tent.

"How in the world did you—" Lacey began to ask but suddenly changed her thoughts. "And were you going to watch me pee or something?"

"Don't ask," he answered before Lacey could finish her question. "On both accounts."

Carrie emerged from the tent smiling. "Found a new friend I see."

"Got lost," Lacey declared before darting into the tent.

"Thank you," Carrie said nodding to the young man. "Appreciate your help. I knew exactly where she was, just wanted to see what she would do."

"That wasn't very nice. She was cold and scared."

"Just trying to toughen her up a little."

"What are you doing way out here anyway?" the boy asked glancing around at their strange and almost empty and dark camp site. "And where's your fire?"

"Don't need one, got a heater inside." Carrie sipped on her drink and studied the boy. "You from around here?"

"Yeah, not far," he said shoving his hands into his pockets.

"Wanna come in and visit for awhile?" Carrie asked. "We're safe, we're not a bunch of crazies or nothing."

"Sure," the boy said following Carrie. "I'm always up for talk."

With his arrival, she concluded they must not be the only campers on such a cold night.

Skyler gave Carrie an *evil eye* after everyone settled down on the warm blankets and drinking hot cocoa. The boy was of a typical size for a twelve-year-old. Light brown hair cut just below the ears gave him an innocent look. But it was his eyes that caught her attention. Huge eyes with a yellow hue and extra large dark pupils. Carrie couldn't keep her eyes off them.

"So, where's your camp?" Skyler asked, taking a sip.

"Don't have one. We live just down the ridge. So, what're you guys looking for? There's nothing left after they blew it up."

The girls glanced at each other then back at the young boy.

"Want a cookie?" Skyler asked, holding the package out toward him.

"Sure, why not." He took several from the bag and began dunking them into his hot cocoa.

"You always wander around at night alone?" Carrie asked.

"Yeah, the sun hurts my eyes. So I go out at night."

"What's wrong with your eyes?" Lacey asked.

"Nothing, just sensitive. I see better in the dark," he said.

Carrie smiled and knew she had to question this kid. But at the same time she didn't want to frighten him off either.

"So..." Carrie began innocently. "Who blew up what?"

"Don't know the *who*, but it *was* a hospital," he answered, dipping another cookie.

"Hmmm, really?" Lacey added to coach the boy to say more. "Way up here?"

"What kind of hospital?" Skyler added.

"What do you mean?" he replied.

"Well, where's all the patients?" Lacey asked.

"They took 'em away months ago," he said with cocoa-soaked

cookies in his mouth. "Then they boarded the place up. Put up a huge fence and had military people guarding it. Then last week... KA-BOOM. The whole place went up."

After sitting his cup on the tent floor, the boy threw his hands over his head almost kicking over his drink. "Oh, I have lost my manners. I'm so sorry. Allow me to introduce myself. I'm Jonathan Gable Huntington. My friends call me Gabe."

"Lost your manners? Well it's nice to meet you, Gabe," Carrie said with a smile. She held out her hand and he shook it. "I'm Carrie, and that's Lacey... who you rescued... and that's Skyler."

"Nice to meet you." He nodded his head.

"You go to school around here?" Carrie asked.

"No, home school," he said, going back to dunking another cookie into his cocoa.

"You live with your parents?" Lacey asked.

"It's just me and my mom. I don't have a dad... that I know of."

"Shit happens," Carrie added.

"Carrie!" Lacey and Skyler shouted together.

"He's just a kid!" Lacey declared.

"I'm old enough to know what *shit happens* means and it does happen. I may be just a kid, but I'm not stupid."

Their talk continued. It didn't take long before the girls discovered his mother had worked at the hospital as a surgical nurse. He was home schooled and didn't have any friends other than the children from the hospital, and now that the hospital was gone, the critters in the forest were his only companions. The more they talked, the more Carrie wanted to meet his mother. He continued to explain that his mother was offered a job at another hospital, but she didn't want to leave their home. There was no explanation or discussions, she simply told him they were not going to leave, and that was that.

"Well," Carrie finally said. "It's late and you'd better be getting home. How about if we come and visit tomorrow?"

"How about if I come back here and get you once the sun goes down? I'll introduce you to my mom," he said with his eyes wide and a huge smile.

"Sounds cool to me," Lacey beamed.

After a few more goodbye words, the boy was gone and

their campsite was quiet again. Carrie pulled out her laptop and emailed a short note to Devon, her boyfriend. She wanted to know everything and anything about a boy named Jonathan Gable Huntington who had extraordinary and intriguing eyes.

Chapter 29

THE LARGE BLACK limousine pulled to a stop in front of Stonefield Castle Hotel that stands high on the Kintyre peninsula, Scotland. Immediately, three butlers ran to cater to the inhabitant's needs. The driver who was wearing military apparel stood at rigid attention after opening the black shiny door. A highly decorated US Navy military doctor exited with his aide following suit. The driver saluted the doctor as the two butlers hustled to retrieve the luggage. The third butler stood stiffly with his hands clasped together. The dirt crunched beneath the doctor's feet as he walked toward the old gray and black marble stairs.

"May I show you to your room, sir," the butler asked without blinking or moving a muscle.

The doctor nodded and they followed the man indoors. Three new butlers ran to service the white limousine that pulled up behind the first. A US Army general emerged this time with a harsh face and a very tired body. As she stood, she used her hands to help stretch out her back.

"Ma'am," the butler said opening her car door. "May I show you to your room?"

"Actually, I'd much rather be shown the way to the bar and my bags taken to my room if you don't mind." She winked at the butler as she climbed the steps. After closing the car door, the butler smiled.

The same scenario continued for the remainder the day with

various government and military doctors from around the world arriving one by one. The financial world was also represented by several of the world's richest men. The global capitalist elite were present for this highly secret and secluded meeting of the Order of the Skull and Bones. Even a select few of the world's leaders, past and present, arrived with their assistants and documents in tow. In all, more than sixty representatives from various businesses and governments arrived to represent their company, their country or themselves.

With the liquor warming her veins, Lee enjoyed a hot shower and a change of clothes. She had no idea why she was here other than she was a replacement for someone who couldn't make it. The view from her room was a spectacular panorama overlooking Loch Fyne, a sea cove on the west coast of Scotland. Lee had never experienced a more breathtaking sight. White jagged rocks peaked through the trees and the waters beyond were a dark reflective blue. Glancing around her room she spotted what she was looking for, the hotel brochure. As she scanned through the pages, Lee discovered the castle was built in 1837 on sixty acres of woodland and was once the family home of the Campbell's. But now, it was a thirty-three room hotel offering all that was the best in Scottish hospitality. Lee tossed the book onto her bed and glanced out the window again.

"Where is my itinerary?" she said as she pawed through her briefcase. "Ahh, here it is."

After reading through the lines, Lee was happy she was free until dinner at six. There was a meeting scheduled tomorrow at one in the afternoon. But, a note at the bottom urged the guests to mingle and get to know one another.

"Who cares," she said as she glanced in the mirror. "I'm Lady Campbell today and I don't mingle." Lee laughed as she danced around her room. "I only wished," she said as she ran back to the window, "I only wished."

Chapter 30

MADDIE AND NATE waited patiently while the person at the ticket counter examined the names and the identifications before boarding.

"This was much easier before they started putting pictures on tickets," Maddie said as they waited their turn.

"Maybe, but it wasn't as safe," Nate added.

"Tickets please?"

"Here you go." Maddie handed hers and Nate's to the woman.

The tickets sucked one at a time into a slot and one at a time their faces displayed on the screen along with their names.

"Thank you Mr. and Mrs. Sce—Sce—I'm sorry."

"That's okay, it's Scelestus, pronounced Sel-ed-tus," Maddie said with a grin. "It's hard to figure it out if you're reading it."

"Where's it from?" the airline employee asked.

The dictionary, Maddie wanted to scream, but knew better.

"My grandparents were from Greece," Nate answered.

"Well have a great flight Mr. and Mrs. Scelestus."

"Thank you," Maddie replied.

Nate and Maddie laughed as they walked hand in hand down the ramp to board the plane to Washington state.

* * * * * *

"Aunt Maddie, Uncle Nate," Tyler yelled as she ran down her front steps.

Maddie held tight to her young niece and kissed her on the side of the head.

"You're looking wonderful," Nate said with a smile.

"Oh Unc," Tyler laughed. "You always know how to flatter. Come on, I have the spare room all ready for you."

Nate pulled the luggage behind him following the hugging women into the house.

"It's great to be off the plane," Maddie stated.

"It's great to have you here," Tyler almost yelled and giggled at the same time. "I have missed everyone way too much."

"I bet you have, sweetie," Maddie added.

Nate headed for the back bedroom as Tyler and Maddie sat down at the kitchen table to catch up on family gossip. Sitting the luggage down next to the closet, he heard a rustling from outside the bedroom window followed by a pounding or hard knock. He pulled aside the drapes and watched as a shadow of a man ran through the backyard and hopped over the fence.

"Wonderful," he said letting the drape fall back into place. "Just wonderful."

* * * * * *

The doorbell rang. Tyler giggled and shoved the bowl of butter into the oven and the hot potatoes into the refrigerator.

"Well, I can see Caiden is more than just a coworker." Maddie laughed as she pulled the steaming potatoes from the refrigerator and switched them with the butter.

"Why would you say such a thing?" Tyler asked as she put the dishrag into the microwave and shut the door.

"Before you burn down the house, why don't you go say hello to Caiden and introduce him to your uncle? I'll finish in here," Maddie said shaking her head holding back a laugh.

"But..." Tyler protested and Maddie pushed her out of the kitchen. Maddie laughed as she put the kitchen back into some order.

It seemed introductions were not necessary when Tyler reached the living room. Caiden and Nate were already deep in conversation. She glanced over at the hallway mirror to make sure she was good, and after a few adjustments strolled toward the talking men.

"Hey," Tyler said.

"Hi." Caiden jumped up to greet her.

When Tyler walked toward him, Caiden took her hand and planted a soft kiss on her cheek. "How's it going, Sweets?"

Tyler smiled and took his arm. "Uncle Nate, how do you like my friend and co-worker, Caiden?"

"He is a very nice young man," Nate said. "I'll check on dinner and let you two talk."

"I like your Uncle," Caiden said as the two sat down. "He's easy to talk to, not like my dad."

"Yeah, he's pretty cool," Tyler replied. "Sweets... is that my new name?"

"When we're alone," he winked. "If that's okay with you. I did some thinking after dinner the other night and it was wrong for me to say what I did. It was a date. I was anxious to be with you. I hope you don't mind."

"But..."

"Listen, I do like you and I do enjoy being with you. I'm probably going outside my bounds here but... even though we work together I still want to see you... if you're okay with it."

"I'm okay with it," Tyler said giggling.

Caiden smiled then kissed her gently on the lips. It was a wonderful first-time kiss for Tyler and she wanted nothing more than to melt. Her heart pounded and suddenly she wasn't hungry any longer.

After clearing her throat, Tyler looked into his eyes and knew she had fallen in love. "Shall we go see what's happening in the kitchen?"

"Sure."

But as they stood, Prince jumped up from the fireplace and started to growl.

"Prince, this is Caiden. You know him, what's the matter boy?"

Prince ran to the back door and jumped up on the small window. He began barking and pawing at the door.

"I guess he wants out," Tyler said.

Caiden opened the door and Prince ran into the yard and darted for the shed. He was barking and growling and jumping up and down.

"What's up?" Nate asked rushing into the room.

"I don't know," Tyler answered.

Nate grabbed the flashlight he had left on the hallway table. He flipped on the outside light and ran into the darkening afternoon.

"Well," Maddie said drying her hands. "I've almost got dinner ready."

Caiden ran out the door following Nate. With all the noise, it was obvious the dog trapped something or someone behind the shed. Nate and Caiden slowed as they walked toward the dog. The fence was shaking, which only meant something was trying to escape.

"Who's there?" Nate yelled. "Come out now!"

Prince was hunched down on all four growling louder than ever.

"What if it's an animal," Caiden whispered.

"Then it won't answer me," Nate replied.

"Good conclusion."

The fence was shaking and the tree above the shed began to move in the windless night. Nate ran behind the small structure with his flashlight in one hand and a pistol in the other, but nothing.

"Damn, whoever it was jumped the fence." Nate flashed the light on the ground to see if anything was left behind. But all looked as it should. Just a few rakes and leftover firewood from the previous winter.

Nate gave Caiden a strange smile shoving his gun back in his holster under his shirt. "Long story," Nate said and Caiden grinned.

Maddie and Tyler were already at the table when the men came back inside with a panting dog.

"Find any bad guys?" Maddie asked.

"Nope," Nate replied.

"Did you really expect to catch one?" Maddie added.

"Nope," Nate answered with a smirk. "Just wanted a little exercise before dinner."

Caiden took a seat next to Tyler and Nate kissed Maddie on the cheek before taking his seat.

"I just love a sarcastic woman at dinner time, how about you,

Caiden?" Nate asked winking at Maddie.

"Oh, well," Caiden started.

"Don't worry about answering that," Maddie added. "That is what I call a trick question. A lose-lose question. Don't answer it."

"Well, this is my Aunt Maddie," Tyler added with a smile.

"Nice to meet you," Caiden said trying to shake her hand from across the table.

"So, you've now been introduced to my weird family. You still have time to run if you hurry," Tyler said laughing.

As they ate, Caiden looked over at Tyler and said, "If all the food is this great all the time, I don't care how weird your family is. I'm staying put."

"Ah, payback," Maddie laughed.

"You catch on fast," Nate winked.

After Tyler left the table to fetch the coffee and dessert, Caiden leaned toward Nate and whispered, "All kidding aside, who are you guys? And are you here to help?"

"Well, if you're in as deep as you claim," Nate whispered, "we shouldn't talk here. So, what kind of help do you need?" Nate asked as loud as he could.

"Oh, well... I'm behind in some of my...um...credit cards?" Caiden replied in a loud voice trying to sound credible.

Nate nodded his head and answered loudly. "I see."

Tyler returned with the cheesecake and gave her uncle and Caiden a weird look.

"Never mind," Maddie said as she took the cake from Tyler. "I'll help you with the coffee."

* * * * * *

"Good morning, Ms. Brighten," the guard said as Tyler swiped her badge through the machine.

Tyler glanced up and grinned. "Morning."

"Hope you had a good weekend."

"Yes, very nice. My family's in town," she added.

"Good, good. Have a great day, Ms. Brighten," the guard added as Tyler headed for the elevators.

"Tyler, wait up."

Caiden's familiar voice was a welcomed sound, especially

this morning. After their covert talks over the weekend, Tyler was now suspicious of everyone at her work... even herself.

"Hey," she said as Caiden handed her a cup of cappuccino. "Thanks."

"You're quite welcome. I stopped by the new coffee shop this morning on the way in."

They were quiet on their ride up. Other people's conversations suddenly seemed more interesting and important than theirs. As the doors pinged and opened for the twelfth floor, they were surprised to see their boss, Ferriday, at the counter.

"Good morning," Ferriday said as they again swiped their badges and looked into the eye scanner.

When the door opened, he followed them inside. Both Tyler and Caiden knew they were in serious trouble before he said a word. Tyler stood next to Caiden with her heart pounding.

"I need to speak with you two," he said.

"Yes?" Caiden replied.

"A new sample was sent over this weekend. We need you to compare it with the other one you've been working on. You've done such a great job we're hoping you'd be just as thorough on this new batch."

Tyler and Caiden gave each other a strange look. Without knowing what else to say or do, they simply nodded their heads.

"Good," he said. "We're on a tight schedule with this one. We'd like it analyzed as soon as possible. Seems it's a little girl and her parents are very anxious to know what's wrong."

With that, Ferriday left with his hands resting in his pockets.

"What was that about?" Tyler asked.

Caiden sighed and shook his head. "I have no idea."

"I want to see that new sample," Tyler said sliding into her lab coat.

Before they started, Caiden called Nate.

"Hi. Could you meet us for lunch today? I'd feel better if you and Maddie knew what we're working on.... great, see you at noon." Caiden hung up and glanced at Tyler. "They'll meet us in the lobby."

"Hey Caiden," Tyler yelled from her computer. "This sample is from the same place as the other one."

Chapter 31

THE GIRLS FOLLOWED Gabe down the dark trail, inhaling the aroma of pine, sassafras and maple. It had been an hour since the sun fell below the large thick trees that surrounded them. It seemed more like midnight than seven in the afternoon.

"Why is the ground so soft?" Lacey asked.

Carrie answered this one for Gabe. "Years of fallen leaves are beneath our feet. Who knows how deep it goes?"

The coolness of the evening and the damp forest floor created a calming effect that could easily have become addictive.

"How much farther, Gabe?" Carrie asked.

"We're almost there," he answered from a few feet ahead of the girls, "it's just through these trees."

"That's all I see are trees." Carrie shouted. "Can you be a little more specific?"

"We're here," Gabe said pointing off to his right.

An old house sat nestled between the tall pines. If it had not been for the light on a telephone pole next to the house, the clearing would have been pitch black. Broken shutters clung to the old structure with what little strength they had. Fallen roof tiles was scattered around the yard. Several of the windows were either cracked or broken. Harsh weather had long stripped the house of its color. The front stairs had been replaced with wooden crates and weeds grew in the flowerbeds. The yard was relatively clean and recently mowed, but grew mostly weeds.

"About time," Skyler stated brushing small insects from her

shoulders and head. "I've probably got ticks all over me!"

"You'll live," Carrie said as she followed Gabe through the small yard. "That dreaded fever you'll get from them only pops up from time to time."

"That's what I'm afraid of," Skyler mused.

"Mom!" Gabe yelled as he got closer to the old run-down house. "Mom, where are you?"

A small woman's silhouette appeared at the screen door. Carrie waved to her and smiled. But the woman took several steps away and disappeared inside.

"Mom!" Gabe yelled again. "My friends… come meet my friends."

Gabe looked at Carrie and shrugged his shoulders. "Follow me."

As she climbed over the boxes to get onto the porch, Carrie was reminded of her youth and living with her father. Her mother had died when she was born and Carrie always blamed her father for her early death. Drunk or sober, the man was a worthless slob and made just enough money to pay the bills. Extras didn't exist in the Clarke house. But of course, booze was considered a necessity. Carrie learned at an early age she was responsible for finding her own way through life. Her clothes came from neighbor's hand-me-downs, lunches were courtesy of the schools, and as for dinners, well, what's a dinner good for anyway except adding on extra unnecessary pounds.

It was the stench that hit her hard. The odor that emanated from inside the house sent Carrie spiraling backward to a time and place she fought so desperately to escape. Fear and revulsion along with some pity stormed through her. Carrie glanced around and wasn't sure if she wanted to run, stay or destroy the small house. Gabe reached out and took Carrie's hand. He helped her up onto the porch then helped the others. Carrie dusted off her pants, took in a deep breath and reminded herself she was on duty for The Agency.

"You okay?" Skyler asked Carrie.

"Yeah, just tired," Carrie answered.

"Mom?" Gabe yelled through the screen. Gabe opened the squeaky door and motioned for the girls. Carrie accepted his invitation and was followed by Skyler and then Lacey. "Have a seat. I'll find my mom. Mom?"

Carrie sat on the couch and the girls found a spot on either side of her. The room was small with only a couch and one recliner. A cast iron stove in the hallway probably heated the house. A kitchen was in the back with a bedroom or two and a small bath. Carrie had lived in just such a house and knew it well. Torn wallpaper hung from the walls and dust lined the shelves of a bookcase. The room was neat and tidy but could use a good deep cleaning.

"Here she is," Gabe said pulling on a small and fragile woman. She wasn't much taller than him, and most definitely weighed a lot less.

"Hi... I'm Carrie Clarke," Carrie said now standing and offering her hand.

The woman stood behind her son grasping firmly to his arm. Dark greasy hair fell past her shoulders. Large brown eyes and thick pink lips created an innocent sensuality. She was wearing a dull floral dress that was about two sizes too big. If Carrie had seen them both in public, she would not have believed she was Gabe's mother, nor a surgical nurse at a hospital. To Carrie, she looked more like his younger sister.

"Mom, say hello," Gabe urged.

The woman smiled but did not speak.

"What is your name? I'm Lacey Harris."

"And I'm Skyler Brighten."

The woman nodded but still did not make a sound.

"Her name's Laflur Jolene Huntington. But she goes by Lafie." Gabe wore a huge smile as he told them her name. It was more than obvious he was proud and loved her very much.

"Please, come sit and talk with us," Carrie urged.

The woman didn't move until Gabe almost shoved her into the chair and ordered her to sit. Carrie wasn't sure, but to her it seemed Lafie was a little slower than most or maybe she was on some type of sedative. As the girls worked on making conversation, Carrie pulled out her small pocket computer to see if she could get a satellite link. Logging onto The Agency's main frame, Carrie punched in the woman's full name. After a few seconds a picture of a much older Lafie and her life history were there for Carrie to review.

It seemed the woman was in her late nineties, although she looked no older than sixteen. Huntington was her maiden name, must of had Gabe with no daddy. She was a registered nurse with the State of West Virginia and did work for the West Virginia State Mental Hospital. That is, until she retired over thirty years ago. *My God...* Immediate family deceased... no brothers or sisters, she has no living relatives listed. What was even more concerning, Gabe wasn't listed.

"Lafie," Carrie said interrupting Skyler in the middle of her sentence. "How old are you?"

Lacey and Skyler didn't say anything. Gabe continued to smile as if not sensing anything was wrong with her question.

"Can you speak?" Carrie asked, her voice rising. "Are you capable of making sounds? You're a nurse... or were until you retired. So I must assume you can talk."

Still the woman said nothing.

"Hello?" Carrie yelled and jumped up to confront the woman. "Are you in there somewhere, lady?"

"Carrie!" Lacey admonished. "That's uncalled for."

"Not really, she's ignoring us. Hey lady, tell me to *eat shit* or something will yah?"

"Please Carrie, Lacey's right," Skyler added. "This is not necessary nor is it proper."

"Fuck proper," Carrie said kneeling in front of Gabe's mother. "I want to know. Can you talk, lady? Because if you don't say something, I'm taking this child into custody and having you locked away. I can do that yah know."

Lacey and Tyler dropped to their knees, but instead of trying to intimidate Gabe's silent mother, they tried to pull Carrie away from her.

"All it'll take is a push of this button and it's all over with," Carrie yelled, shoving the small computer into Lafie's face.

"Please Carrie," Lacey begged. "Stop this."

Gabe remained seated on the couch smiling. Nothing seemed to bother him in any way.

"The town's full of nuts. The train transports zombies to nowhere, and now we're sitting in a fruitcake's house." Carrie's cheeks were red from screaming and her small computer was only inches from the woman's face. "One push, lady. Speak now or it's all over."

Carrie sat back ignoring the pleas from her partners. But it was soon evident her harsh method was working.

The woman looked into Carrie's eyes and said, "That won't be necessary."

Skyler and Tyler sat back, speechless.

"Now can we talk, Lafie? Can we have a real conversation?" Carrie asked.

"What do you want to know?" Lafie asked.

"First off, what in the hell's going on around here?"

"Who are you and what do you want?" Lafie asked. "Did they send you to see just how far you could push me before I talk?"

Carrie pulled out her badge and showed it to Lafie.

"I see, so what do you want from me?" Lafie asked.

"Well, we weren't sent to spy on you if that's what you're getting at. We came to see your hole." With this statement, Carrie could no longer hold it in and began to laugh. Her partners broke out in uncontrolled giggles.

"FBI? How do I know for sure you're with the FBI?" Lafie asked. "How do I know this isn't some kind of a trick?"

"We all have badges," Skyler added, giggling and rolling her eyes.

"Anyone can get a badge made," Lafie added.

"I don't mean to be rude," Carrie said getting to her feet. "But I can't tell you how weird your hometown is. Damn, I mean... here I am sitting in a living room of a woman who's old enough to be my great grandmother but looks young enough to be my little sister, not to mention she has a son half my age. Twilight Zone City if you ask me and I'm not here looking for real estate either. I can tell you that much, and who in the world... wait a minute, what do you know that someone doesn't want told and who are the *theys*?"

The woman was silent again. Carrie studied her knowing there was more going on than she was saying. After a few seconds, Carrie decided it was time to check out the old house. She walked around taking mental notes. Nothing was out of the ordinary other than it was obvious they lived a poor lifestyle. Something was bothering her, but she couldn't quite put her finger on it.

"What are you looking for?" Lafie asked now standing behind her in the hallway.

"Nothing," Carrie answered. She was proud her strange methods got the woman interested in what she was doing.

"This is just a house. Here's Gabe's room and here's mine. We have one bathroom. The kitchen is just off the living room. You're free to look around."

"Not necessary," Carrie said. But something was amiss. Then it dawned on her and she turned to confront Lafie. "Where's your television, phone or computer?"

"We do not have those things in this house," Lafie answered.

"Why not? Everyone does. How can you order your groceries or communicate with others?"

"We do not need them," Lafie said walking back into the living room.

"Something just doesn't add up," Carrie stated when she finished looking around.

"Excuse me?" Lafie replied.

"You heard me," Carrie said, taking a seat on the couch.

Lafie sighed and turned her face away from the agents. She shook her head and rubbed her eyes. "Why are you bothering us? We have done nothing to you or anybody else."

"Because, this whole town is hiding something. Including you," Carrie said. "According to my records you retired before I was born. You're old enough to be my great grandmother yet you look much younger than me... and, if you really did retire all those years ago how is it only recently you were offered a job at another hospital?"

"Are you going to arrest us?" Lafie asked.

"What are you afraid of?" Carrie asked. "And what secrets are you trying to protect?"

* * * * * *

The walk back to their camp was strained and without talk. But once they were all snuggled in their warm sleeping bags, Skyler finally spoke up.

"Carrie, what in the world was that all about?"

"Yeah, I'd like to know too," Lacey added.

"Just trying to get some answers," Carrie replied. "Just answers."

"You're not right," Lacey said. "...and exactly how old is that woman? Ninety, really?"

"That's what I read," Carrie replied as she pulled her sleeping bag higher over her shoulder.

The words stopped floating through Carrie's ears and she was left to dwell in her own private thoughts. Nothing made any sense—nothing. How was it the old woman looked so young... and then there was her son who only goes out after dark and who hates the sunlight. Then the train with the weird people and those men who were not registered as National Geographic photographers. Not to mention the town had no real roads, yet the hotel was constantly booked. No—this place was hiding something and Carrie wanted to know exactly what that something was.

* * * * * *

Gabe sat quietly by his mother not making a sound. His mind raced with wild ideas as his temper rose. No one had come to talk to them except a few people who either drew blood or gave them food.

"Mom?" Gabe whispered.

"Yes," she answered.

"Mom, look at me," Gabe prodded.

"I told you we could not trust anyone," she said.

Gabe slapped his knee. "Mom, look at me."

But she refused.

"Mom," Gabe yelled. "We had no other choice."

Chapter 32

CARRIE JERKED AWAKE so suddenly she almost ripped her sleeping bag into pieces. As her feet hit the cold damp floor, disappointment crashed her thoughts. Her body would not move fast enough to catch up with her mind. It was as if she was in a slow motion movie, moving inch by inch, second by second. Carrie panicked as each of her limbs slowly grabbed the items her mind demanded. With her heart pounding, it took all her strength to break through the imaginary ropes that bound her.

"Shit!" Carrie yelled in frustration. "Shit... shit... shit!"

The faster she tried to get into her clothes, the more entangled she became.

"What are you doing?" Lacey whispered, flashing her light onto the frantic Carrie.

"Shit... shit...shit!" Carrie continued to whisper.

"What is it?" Lacey asked again.

As Skyler slept soundly, Carrie spoke. "I should have seen it, this'll be all my fault."

Lacey climbed reluctantly from her warm bed and into the cold night air.

"Are you still sleeping, Carrie?" she asked.

"No," Carrie stated. "I'm wide awake. Don't you see it? Don't you see what we've done?"

"No, I don't," Lacey replied.

"Wake up Sleeping Beauty. We have to get to them before it's too late," Carrie ordered. "Before they do."

"What are you talking about? Before who does what?"

"What in the world are you two arguing over?" Skyler asked sleepily from her bed.

Carrie sighed as she tied her shoes. "Gabe and his mother. We should not have gone there. They'll come for them."

"Who will?" Lacey asked.

Skyler was now wide awake and dressing as fast as she could.

"You're dawdling, Lacey," Carrie whispered. "Get dressed."

"Will you please tell me what's going on?" Lacey demanded.

"I'll explain on the way," Carrie stated, throwing Lacey her jeans.

The outside air was engulfed in a cold and a misty dampness that hovered just above the ground and muffled any noise. Small animals were no longer rustling beneath the fallen leaves, but sound asleep deep inside their burrows. Insects remained extra quiet in their dry and warm hiding places. All was tranquil, all was way too calm.

"I think we're too late," Carrie whispered.

"Too late for what?" Lacey whispered back.

As they hurried toward Gabe's old yellow house, Carrie explained as best she could. It wasn't easy, for she didn't quite understand it herself. But something told her Gabe and his mother were in danger.

"Whoever destroyed that hospital was trying to cover something up," Carrie said as they hurried. "Gabe's mother said she worked there. Gabe is young. He had to have been born after his mother retired. I'll bet anything he's a by-product of that hospital and whatever they destroyed."

"Are you sure you're not still sleeping?" Skyler asked.

"Look you two." Carrie stopped and glared at the two frightened agents. "That explosion was not an accident. Someone caused it for a reason. No one blows up half a mountain just for fun. Gabe's mother looks young and there's something strange about Gabe. I couldn't put my finger on it until tonight. He's different somehow and that hospital has something to do with it. We went to their house. Whoever blew up that hospital is not stupid. They know we visited Gabe and his mother tonight. We put them in danger."

Carrie marched off and left Skyler and Lacey to their

thoughts. When they finally caught up with her, a bright light danced through the forest ahead.

"Damn," Carrie yelled. "Let's go."

The three ran as fast as they could without tripping over the fallen branches and exposed tree roots. The trail was not easy to find in the misty darkness, but as they got closer to Gabe's house the area became brighter. Dancing orange and yellow light lit the forest and created an ominous orange hue.

"We're too late," Carrie sighed.

As Skyler and Lacey ran ahead, Carrie called The Agency on her cell phone. The girls watched as the flames danced high into the night's sky. The roof was gone, already crashed inside the small wooden structure. The large outside light had melted and the remaining metal was sliding down the burnt pole. Glass crackled as it shattered from the high heat. Carrie wasn't sure if she was angrier at the people who did this or herself. Shrieks from the dark forest filled their ears.

"Carrie," Lacey yelled. "Someone's alive in there."

"No way." Carrie ran toward the house, but the hot flames did not allow her to get very close. "Is anyone in there?"

"Carrie!" a voice yelled from out of the darkness. "Carrie, help, please."

"Over here!" Skyler screamed. "Over here."

On the far side of the yard, a small area once cleared was now overgrown by wild brush of various types. Perhaps it'd been cleared for a small shed or garden that was never built. Crouched in the darkness were two small figures huddled under a blanket.

"Gabe?" Carrie yelled. "Is that you?"

"Hurry," he shouted. "They'll see you."

As the girls knelt down in front of them, a helicopter flew overhead. When it passed, more helicopters followed and a shower of water hit the five people in the small clearing.

"Water?" Gabe asked.

"Help is here," Carrie said with a grin. "You're safe now."

"Who are you?" Lafie asked.

"Nobody," Skyler said. "We're just here to help."

The fire in the house slowly died with the heavy bombardment of water that was laced with special chemicals. Without the burning light, the area was once again consumed by darkness.

"Agent Clarke?" It was a man's voice echoing from the darkness.

"Over here," Carrie yelled flashing her light above her head. "We're over here."

Several men in black uniforms ran toward the huddled and frightened people. Lafie tried to back away, but Lacey took her hand.

"You're safe now," Lacey said with a smile.

Carrie stood and approached the men. They spoke for a few minutes before Carrie allowed them to take the boy and his mother away. As the helicopter rose above the treetops, she glanced over at her two partners. For once in her career, she got there before the bad guys did and it felt good.

"How do you know they're from The Agency?" Skyler asked.

"I just ask them about someone special who used to work there," Carrie whispered. "If they don't know who that person was, then they're impostors."

"Who Lewis?" Lacey asked.

"Nope," Carrie replied. "Maddie… just ask them who Maddie is."

Lacey smiled as she ran toward the waiting chopper. "You amaze me, Carrie."

As the agents hopped aboard, Carrie grinned at Lacey. The night might be over, but their assignment was just getting started.

Their camping gear had already been packed and was waiting for them onboard. Skyler giggled. As the helicopter rose, the morning sun winked at them from behind the mountain ridge. As they flew off toward the west, Carrie sighed. She wondered if Lacey was thinking of another helicopter ride many years before. But instead of flying to a ship just off shore, they were now heading toward Oklahoma City and the safety of The Agency.

Chapter 33

SPANGLEHOLTZ PACED THE boardroom shaking his head. All eyes were focused on him. He was going to blame someone in that room today.

"I cannot tell you how disappointed I was to see this article. I want to know who leaked the story." The doctor glared at everyone.

"Sir." Hope spoke up. Her voice was soft and she constantly cleared her throat. "How would we have known what happened? The child was not born here. We had no idea how the baby looked until she arrived this morning."

"Not quite," he replied.

"What do you mean?" Hope asked.

"This picture in the paper?" Spangleholtz held up the newspaper for everyone to see.

"Yes sir," Hope replied.

"This was the picture I took with my phone in the hospital. I sent it to one person and one person only."

"Oh no," Hope answered.

Hope was a sprite young woman in her mid-thirties, and was Spangleholtz's right-hand person for the last five years. She was not tall since she stood just a few inches over four feet. With her brown hair cut unevenly about her shoulders, she would be considered anything but sexy. Overweight by about thirty pounds, Hope relied on her brains not her beauty to get into the position she held. Self-sufficiency was all Hope strived for in her quiet life. After watching her family and friends endure heartbreaking and financially devastating divorces, Hope decided to remain single. Her work was her family now and it was Spangleholtz she enjoyed spending the days with. As long as she owned her own home and could pay her bills, she could tolerate his daily outbursts of anger and his hot-blooded nature.

"Oh yes!" Spangleholtz turned to gaze at her. "What happened to that picture, Hope?"

"Oh my," Hope said with a sigh.

The hate emanating from his eyes cut jaggedly through her soul. Hope worked there long enough to know unless she could produce a good explanation and quick she would be facing more than just a job termination—it was her life at stake now.

"Is that all you have to say, Ms. Roth?"

Hope glanced around the room at the now-relieved faces. Their fears of retribution were gone since Spangleholtz was focused on her. She felt betrayed by her co-workers and very alone.

"Sir," Hope began. "My phone was stolen the day you left on your trip. I have not seen it since. And that's the truth."

Tears formed in her eyes as she watched the man she had counted on for support over the last few years turn against her. She could see he stepped past the point of hatred and entered the stage of loathing, revulsion and disgust.

"I wouldn't lie to you," Hope pleaded as tears ran down her face.

Spangleholtz stopped staring at her and looked down at the floor. After a few terrifying and long seconds he asked, "Where did you see it last?"

"It was on my desk. I forgot to take it to lunch with me and when I got back it was gone."

* * * * * *

Hope Roth couldn't decide whether she wanted the chocolate cake or the banana cream pie. Both were tempting and looked delicious. As she reached for the cake a voice scolded from behind.

"Perhaps you should stick with just the salad."

"Oh, hi Fannie," Hope replied as she placed the high-calorie dessert on her tray.

Fannie pushed her tray behind Hope's. But her tray held only a simple salad and water. Every once in a while, Hope grabbed something from the counter and added it to hers. When they reached the cashier, Fannie finally made conversation.

"Mind if I sit with you?"

"Why not?" Hope said accepting her change from the cashier.

Once seated, Fannie kept her focus on her food.

As Hope took another bite of her hamburger she looked up at Fannie and asked, "How's your care?"

"Oh?" Fannie replied. "She's fine, just fine."

"Good," Hope said, taking a sip of soda.

"You were smart to report your phone missing as soon as you did."

"I know. I came so close to being canned in more ways than one. Fan, if I hadn't ordered another one right away, I wouldn't have the proof I wasn't the one who leaked that photo."

"Any idea who did?"

"No, but I sure wished I did," Hope said with a frown. "I mean...we must have someone here that doesn't like what we're doing. After all, our work is important. I mean, we're helping the human race to survive right? Why would people be against that? I don't understand."

"Well," Fannie said. "Some people feel we have souls at conception. So any tinkering with those embryonic cells is considered immoral. That's why we have those stupid laws that make it necessary for us to hide our work."

"But Lizzie is so cute and sweet. How can anyone say she's immoral?"

"She is a darling little thing," Fannie said with a smile. "I'm so lucky to be assigned to her. I mean she's growing so fast."

"I know. Every time I see her she seems bigger. How's her mom doing? Do we know what went wrong yet?"

"No, the tests are not back but her mom's great," Fannie said, taking another bite of her salad. "I mean she's on heavy tranquilizers so I guess she has no idea what's going on. But she shares a strong connection with Lizzie. I mean they can almost read each other's minds."

"Really?" Hope asked, enjoying her delicious sweet chocolate cake. "Like what?"

"Not anything conclusive. But the researchers are doing all kinds of tests. So far they can't figure out how or what it is exactly. But it's really cool. Show Lizzie a picture and Mom in the next room can pick it out of several photos. But she doesn't know why the image pops in her head. It'll be cool to see what happens when Lizzie gets older."

"If she gets older," Hope added, lowering her eyes.

Chapter 34

LEE GLANCED AROUND at everyone in the room. She recognized some of the faces but not all. Why she'd been chosen to come to this place was anybody's guess. She recognized a few presidents right away. But those who wore the uniforms didn't ring a bell. Not to mention the men in the business suits. It dawned on Lee she was the only female in the room. *Strange,* she thought to herself.

"May we all be seated?" a voice from the pedestal asked. "Please, take your seats."

Lee looked around for her name tag with a small American flag. Her general emblem was her first clue. As she approached her chair, the name General Longhorn was a warm and comfort-ing sight. Taking her seat she smiled and nodded to the other men around the table. To make it even more intimidating, she was the only military person in her group. Across from her sat five men in suits who ranged in age and to her delight were much older than her. It was an uncomfortable situation, but because of her career choice, Lee was used to uncomfortable situations.

"Please stand for a prayer and our pledge to the New World Order," the man from the podium announced in a loud voice shaking Lee from her thoughts.

Everyone stood and raised their heads and hands to salute the New World Order. Lee listened intently to the quick prayer then the strange chant. The eerie deep voices echoed through her mind and caused her inner alarm to scream warnings. But then at the same time, the chanting was somewhat soothing and trance-like.

"I pledge a vow of secrecy, to live my live devoted… to surpass manhood and gain the carnal understanding, and touch the hand of God… all is good and all is for the conscious awakening whilst we are still in the flesh…it is the realization of our fundamental unity and identity with the ultimate of ultimates… we stand here today to pledge our loyalty to truth, justice and God… we let no other put asunder the true meaning of life… we allow no government to command the abstract… but to carry out the deeper meaning from here to eternity… let death be our new beginning."

What in the hell is that supposed to mean? Lee asked herself as the chant was recited from everyone in the room except her. She glanced around only to see every head raised and all eyes searching the heavens. It was obvious these people where committed to whatever was going to take place here, and she wasn't sure she wanted to know what that was. Once the prayer and chant was finished, they were told to take their seats. As the dinner was served, not one word was spoken. At the same time, Lee had the strangest feeling every eye was on her. Other than the quick glances in her direction from the different people, no one seemed to remove their eyes from their food. The only noise in the room was the sounds of forks hitting the plates and glasses clanking on the tables.

After what seemed like forever, dinner was finally over and they were dismissed for the evening. But not before they were reminded of the meeting the following afternoon at one o'clock. To Lee it seemed she could not get out of that room fast enough. Every step she took someone was in her way.

Once she was in the privacy of her room, Lee pulled out her computer and sent an email back to the States. She had to notify her friend to the weirdness she suddenly found herself in. For some strange reason unbeknownst to her, she needed to make sure someone else knew where she was and what she was doing—just in case tomorrow never came.

Chapter 35

IT WAS ALMOST June and the warm breeze was a welcomed relief from the cold mountain air. Carrie walked through The Agency's newly awakened gardens enjoying the beautiful spring flowers and trees. She often thought of Maddie when she was here and wondered what went through her mind before or after an assignment. The small oak planks creaked under her feet as she stood watching the butterflies. It was so peaceful and serene that Carrie's mind was finally able to rest and wander aimlessly. A small patch of grass between the trees was Carrie's favorite place. She unrolled her blanket and settled down to read her book. As a warm breeze carried the aroma of the flora toward her, she took in a deep breath and let it out slowly.

"Good morning," a man's voice said penetrating her thoughts.

Carrie glanced up and was relieved to see Lewis's warm smile. She smiled back.

"May I join you?"

Carrie waved her right arm as a gesture for him to sit.

"So, how was your last assignment? As usual you were able to make it a success. Finding and befriending the mother and son was an excellent ending."

Carrie continued to smile.

"Well, I've got another assignment, if you're up to it?"

"Like what?" Carrie asked with her interest perked. She knew she had the next thirty days off. It was an agency rule, to be asked to go on another one so soon meant it was important.

"You worked with Skyler these past couple of weeks. How would you like to work with her sister, Tyler?" Lewis leaned toward Carrie and whispered softly, "... and Maddie?"

"Yes sir," she said emphatically. "You don't have to ask me twice."

"Let me tell you a little about the assignment before you get too eager to agree," Lewis added.

"Okay, talk."

"It seems Tyler is concerned her company is up to something. I'd like you to fly to Washington state and do a little snooping around a hospital that's just a few miles away. Many of the samples Tyler examines come from there. I cannot say whether it will be dangerous or not. But if you're interested, I'll set up a briefing."

"Cool." Carrie was definitely interested. Maddie was one of their famous ex-agents, who consulted for The Agency from time to time. Although Maddie was technically labeled as *dead*, Carrie always wanted to work with her. Carrie worked with Maddie's son while employed by the FBI, but never had the opportunity to work directly with the famous *dead* Maddie Edwards.

"I've also assigned Lacey to the case, but I'm sending Skyler to DC on another assignment." Lewis's smile seemed to fade as he mentioned Skyler. "I don't like having relatives working together if I can help it. Causes the brain not to think properly in heated situations, if you know what I mean."

"Oh I know about heated situations. Been there, done that and got the T-shirt in my dresser at home," Carrie sighed.

"I have several of those too I believe."

They continued to enjoy the warm spring day together and talk about the past, present and future. But Carrie's mind was now more on Maddie than Lewis.

Chapter 36

"I'VE GOT THE scoop on your work," Nate beamed at Tyler and Caiden.

"Oh?" Caiden asked with a mouth full of noodles. The Chinese restaurant was the closest place to eat for lunch and they only had an hour.

Tyler looked around the restaurant with a worried face. "Is it safe to talk here?"

"Don't see why not," Maddie added. "People in these restaurants talk all the time."

"Very funny, Aunt Mad," Tyler smirked.

"Well," Nate started. "I'm sorry to report your company seems to be completely on the up and up. Barker Institute is a firm that's been around for about seventy-five years. They're heavy into bio-research, especially DNA coding and de-coding. They're under contract with the US Government for genetic testing as well as owning several large commercial contracts with private firms."

"We know about some of the contracts," Caiden added taking a sip of his tea. "Anything else?"

"They've never been in any trouble from what I've found. They pay their taxes, follow all the laws, nothing's in The Agency's computers to say anything is out of the ordinary."

"But that DNA," Tyler whispered to Caiden. "There's definitely something weird and unnatural with it."

"Could it have been contaminated somehow?" Maddie asked.

"No, it was definitely spliced," Caiden answered.

"What if it was spliced after it was drawn from the person?" Maddie added.

Tyler stopped eating and rested her head on her hands. She was perturbed and bothered because something wasn't right.

"No," Tyler said with a frown, "that sample was taken from a living person. No way could it have been tampered with or contaminated by accident. That sample was definitely from a living human and it definitely had fish DNA integrated within its strands."

"And," Caiden added, "it wasn't even DNA, it was RNA."

"What's RNA?" Maddie asked.

"Go for it," Caiden answered looking over at Tyler.

Tyler took in a deep breath. "Let me try to simplify this. Humans are made up of DNA, double strands that feed off the RNA's single strand." Tyler pulled a pen from her purse and drew a rudimentary strand of DNA for her aunt and uncle. "You see, we have proteins in our DNA and in order for it to bind properly it must first feed through the RNA."

Caiden could tell she wasn't getting through to them so added, "Early life on Earth began with RNA and used the DNA to bind the proteins. There's considerable evidence to prove there was a period of time on Earth where all life grew from RNA. You've heard of genotyping right?"

Maddie nodded her head.

"Life on this world now only exists with DNA strands, the double helix," Tyler added. "But a long time ago, scientists believe earlier life forms were a single naked strand, a collection of RNA. Life forms such as peptides, membranes, mineral surfaces and the like. It's at the heart of the field of molecular biology and chemistry."

Maddie and Nate continued to stare at Tyler like she was speaking a foreign language.

"Let me try," Caiden broke in. "AIDS."

"What, the illness?" Nate asked.

"I'm sure you've heard how the virus binds with our DNA?"

They nodded together.

"Well, viruses use the RNA to bind with the DNA. You've heard of retroviruses? Polio? The flu? Same thing."

"Right," Tyler added. "In order to have a protein bind to the DNA it needs a messenger. DNA uses RNA to talk to the proteins or in the case of AIDS, a virus. That's how we were able to find a cure."

"But the DNA you're studying is not DNA but RNA," Maddie challenged, "and the RNA used the DNA to talk to, or incorporate the protein, which is the exact opposite of life here on Earth?"

"Exactly," Tyler praised. "RNA evolved into DNA—not the other way around."

Tyler showed Maddie her picture of the DNA and RNA strands. "You see, RNA is like a strand of DNA but it's missing one of its sides."

"Like a ladder missing one of the legs?" Maddie asked.

"Exactly," Tyler said.

"And so?" Maddie replied.

Tyler sighed and added, "So..."

Caiden interjected, "RNA is a similar molecule to DNA. There are only two chemical differences. One strand of DNA and one strand of RNA can bind to form a double helix. This made the storage of information in RNA possible in a very similar way to the storage of information in DNA. I'm not going into the names, but DNA uses proteins and RNA uses enzymes. An RNA life form is very unstable. Whereas, a DNA life form is quite stable. Thus you have sustained life on Earth. An RNA life form cannot reproduce... unstable."

"You mean an RNA life form could not have children?"

"Exactly," Caiden answered.

"DNA and RNA are the instructions for life," Tyler added. "They decide whether you have brown eyes or blue. They decide whether you have two legs or four."

"Or can fly or breathe underwater?" Nate asked.

Tyler and Caiden nodded.

"You see Uncle Nate, it's been theorized if you split a gene you can add in the rungs you want in order to force an individual to be either white or black, tall or short, fat or thin..."

"Let me get this straight," Maddie said turning the information around in her head. "The DNA, or RNA you found, was a combination of human and fish?"

"Exactly," Caiden replied sitting back as though they just taught Maddie how to spell her name or something like that. "But had both strands intact."

Nate squinted then asked, "Can you tell which features are which?"

"What do you mean?" Caiden asked.

"Well, um... according to the DNA or RNA, what fish features or human features would the person have—depending on the rungs."

"I see what you're getting at," Tyler said feeling nervous.

By now their lunch was getting cold. Maddie pushed her broccoli and fried rice around on her plate before taking another sip of soda. The others follow suit. The idea or conclusion Nate brought up was frightening and threw everyone into their own terrifying world.

"Now that is an interesting concept," Maddie added. "Can you go back and see where the fish DNA was spliced and determine what changes, if any, would or could occur in that human?"

"I suppose," Tyler replied.

"Yeah, I guess it's doable," Caiden added. "But what would it prove?"

"Don't know," Maddie answered, pushing her plate to one side. "But it would be interesting. I mean, would this person have gills? A fin or two?"

With that last question, Tyler glanced over at Caiden and frowned. Her fear was evident, and so was his. If what Maddie and Nate proposed had any validity, even less than half a percent, then they could all soon be the *walking dead*.

"Wasn't there a law passed about ten or fifteen years ago that made the fusion of human and non-human gene splicing illegal?" Nate asked.

"Yes there was," Tyler answered, "and for good reason."

CHAPTER 37

GABE WALKED AROUND the small room and sighed. It had been days since he or his mother had any visitors. This was not the situation he'd envisioned for them when he agreed to go with Carrie and her friends. Pacing the floor, his patience was wearing thinner and thinner. Unknown to the boy, Doctor Lewis and Greghardt watched on a monitor from another room. Sweat fell from Greghardt's temple.

"I don't like this," Lewis said.

Greghardt wiped his forehead and replied, "And your point is?"

"My point?" Lewis snapped. "Why is it everything has to have a point with you?"

"We have our instructions," Greghardt answered. "Watch and study."

"Instructions from who?" Lewis asked not taking his eyes from the monitor.

"I told you that's classified."

"Classified my ass," Lewis replied shutting off the monitor. "I've had just about enough of this."

As Lewis headed for the door, Greghardt asked, "What's that supposed to mean?"

"Whatever you want it to," Lewis snapped.

"You're not in complete charge here yah know." Greghardt pulled out his cigar from his jacket pocket.

"I'm the head of *The Agency*. If there are others above me, then damn it, introduce me to them. I don't need fucking cowards hiding in the wings."

The elevator doors shut and Greghardt stood alone in the hallway. He smiled and chuckled to himself. "Damn, he was the right pick."

Chapter 38

EARLY WATCHED AS the others entered the room. She had no idea who any of these people were. There were men of different ages, height and weight, each escorting a frightened young woman at his side. Each looked as if she'd been dragged through the roughest time of her young life. Drake held Early's hands as they waited.

"Hang in there, baby," Drake whispered. "They're in the same boat we are."

As each man took a seat by their women, a guard stood protectively behind them. It didn't seem they feared the women would escape, but more as if someone would suddenly spring in and hurt them.

Early's hands shook as she rubbed them against her legs. Visions of her children ran through her mind and her heart ached to be with them again. Although she was told they were dead and shown terrible pictures to prove it, Early knew they were still alive—somewhere.

"Good afternoon," Drake said once everyone was seated. "I know my client wasn't told why she's here, and I'm not sure if all of you have been told either."

Some of the women shook their heads, others nodded.

"I see," Drake answered. "Well then, let's get started."

Several nurses entered carrying silver trays with various sterile instruments. The women's faces changed from curious to concerned and Drake picked up on it.

"We have a visitor for you," Drake announced. "This is Dr. Skyler Brighten from the Oklahoma Medical Research Facility. She'll be taking blood samples from each of you today."

Brighton smiled and nodded her head.

"She'll personally escort them to the laboratory for an analysis."

Brighton tried to stand tall and look as professional as possible. Although she graciously accepted this assignment, she felt ridiculous being an escort service for blood samples. This assignment had to be the most boring Lewis ever sent her on, but it could be the most important of her life.

<h1 style="text-align:center">Chapter 39</h1>

SCHUSTER DIDN'T KNOW if she liked being there nor did she know what was expected of her. She stood near the covered grave and gave a smirk to the other agents examining the ground and nearby trees. Technicians in white shirts took samples of everything they could reach.

This is nuts. But before she could complain to herself again, her cell phone rang.

"Excuse me," she said as she left the group.

"Tabatha?" A familiar voice echoed through her ear.

"Lee? Where are you?" Tabatha asked. "I've been trying to reach you."

"Not real sure," she answered. "Did you get my email? I never heard back from you."

"No. Never did. I'm on assignment this week," Tabatha apologized. "What's going on?"

"I think I'm in trouble."

"Why?" Tabatha asked now worried.

Her friend and lover, Lee, is a United States army general, a five-star, the only woman to ever make it that high. Lee made US history when she was a four-star by keeping her troops safe when all communication died during the war with the Eastern countries. Government and commercial satellites were destroyed as were towers and other communication equipment. All contact with headquarters ended for weeks. Lee's tough interior and her will to survive kept her troops safe. No one died during this sixteen-week nightmare. Lee basically ran the war alone. It was during this time Lee made critical decisions and sent her troops to strategic locations. Other generals argued and fought for their ideas to be heard, but Lee stood her ground. The war was won because of Lee's imagination and knowledge of combat. For her to be so frightened, Tabatha knew something was terribly wrong.

"Where are you?" Tabatha asked again.

"I'm at a conference in a castle in Scotland. What's really weird... I think I'm the only female. Write down what I'm going to tell you," Lee demanded.

As Tabatha wrote, Lee gave her every bit of information she could.

"Okay, I've got yah babe," Tabatha stated as she balanced her phone on her shoulder and scribbled.

"If you don't hear from me in a few days, come find me okay?"

"You've got it, and I love you," Tabatha promised as she clicked off her phone.

She rejoined the other agents with the conversation echoing through her ears. Tabatha texted Lewis and explained everything her friend told her about her situation. She tried to show her concern for her dear friend. A friend since the age of five. Even though Lee was much older, Tabatha grew to love the girl who lived next door and played army every chance she got. Tabatha no less than begged Lewis to check on her and the strange conference she was attending.

There was one special benefit working for The Agency Tabatha cherished. It was the direct communication with the Director and his willingness to help anyone who needed it.

CHAPTER 40

GREGHARDT AND LEWIS stared intensely at each other. Both with their own inner agendas. Both with their own fears and doubts.

"We've worked together for a while now," Lewis said.

"Hmm," Greghardt hummed.

Lewis shook his head. "We've got to work this out Allen. Hitting our heads together isn't getting us anywhere. And we need to figure this out."

"Figure what out?"

"What's going on out there," Lewis sighed. "I've experienced the strangest situations since working here. But our latest cases are most concerning. First, we have bones from a dead person or animal or a combination of both. Then they mysteriously disappear. Wasn't that convenient, which I'm sure was to cover up something. I have no doubts. Then there's that crater in West Virginia, and I just sent two agents to Washington because of the odd DNA results. Not to mention the urgent text I just received from a field agent who's concerned about a friend who just happens to be a high ranking army official who just happens to be listed as missing by the Army. That's WHAT!"

"Lewis?" Greghardt asked in a soft voice.

"What?"

"Perhaps a long rest or something is called for here. If I didn't know better, I'd say you're losing it." Greghardt placed his hand on Lewis' shoulder. "How about a round of golf ol' buddy? We've got a few things to talk about."

"Golf?" Lewis asked. "Are you insane?"

"No, I just think better while swinging my clubs."

CHAPTER 41

"DRAKE HERE," DRAKE said into the phone speaking to his assistant. "Shelby? What's up?"

Early sat listening to her lawyer's voice. She'd given up all hope on her old life and her new focus was to find the truth about her family. Even though she knew she could never fully accept their deaths, Early finally convinced herself she'd never see them again. So she sat and watched as the world revolved around her.

"You found Marty Starling!" Drake declared with his hopes soaring with the good news.

"Well not exactly," Shelby corrected.

"Okay, then you haven't found her," Drake replied as his world crashed down around him.

"Well sort of," she said.

"Shelby, will you quit talking in riddles," Drake demanded. His confusion levels were rising with this strange up and down conversation. "Did you find her or not?"

"It's hard to explain," she answered.

"What do you mean, 'it's hard to explain,'" he shouted into the phone.

"Well, you see... her house exploded when they were supposedly home. A gas leak or some stupid thing like..."

"So they're dead?" Drake added.

"Well, no not really," Shelby said.

Drake sighed.

"The body they found that was supposed to be the mother's... well... this is hard to explain."

"Shelby, slow down and tell me what you know."

"Okay. The body they found, the body that was supposed to be Marty's was too tall, according to Marty's parents. So now the police are not sure if it's really her or not. And the children, well their bodies had been dead for awhile. The time of death would have been weeks before the fire—not after. Now the police are convinced the bodies are not the bodies of the family, but of someone else. Drats, this is hard to explain."

"Would you please repeat that?" Drake asked as the others around the table watched and listened.

Chapter 42

"WELL?" SPANGLEHOLTZ ASKED with an air of smugness emanating from his hungry, dark eyes.

Dr. Crystal Derrier stared with the desire to strangle him running through her veins, but then thought better of it. This was neither the place nor the time for such antics. She glanced around the room ignoring his haughtiness and smiled to herself. After all, what did she have to lose—her job? No, she'd never be that lucky.

"Excuse me, doctor!" he shouted. "Are you deliberately ignoring me?"

"Now why would I do such a thing?" Derrier asked still laughing to herself.

"So, did you meet with Ms. Sutton or not?"

"Yes I did," she replied looking around the dark office.

Spangleholtz's office was huge and dreary. Just the perfect place for the perfect jerk—dark and dungeon-like. Being several miles below ground usually doesn't lend itself to natural lighting, and his office was no exception. Heavy long drapes lined the walls in an attempt to create an illusion of covered windows. But instead of creating warmth, the heavy linen only muffled the sounds and made the room even more wicked and evil. Beautiful ornate carpets were strategically placed throughout the office. But the artificial light just didn't do them any justice. Instead of bringing out their colorful beauty, the darkness suffocated the carpets and gave the room an overall feeling of impurity, of being infected with immorality. Spangleholtz's family pictures hanging on various walls only added to the disturbing mist that hovered inches above the floor. Derrier, not finding anything of interest to look at, decided to take a seat in the huge armchair and embraced the blazing fireplace.

"Why are you not afraid of carbon dioxide poisoning down here?" she asked, staring at the fire. "Perhaps your brain is already so contaminated it doesn't matter. What is it they say about zombies... oh yes, they are the walking dead... or something to that effect."

His temper was rising and Derrier knew it. "Could we please get back to our agenda?"

"Please?" Derrier asked with a smirk. "Where did the sudden rush of politeness come from, Euie? And what were we discussing anyway?"

"The lady you're assigned to, Ms. Early Sutton. Remember that discussion?"

She was getting on his nerves and she knew he loathed her. Derrier felt if he had the authority to fire her he would right then and there. But she also knew this man only fantasized about the power he believed he held.

"And the name's Eugene. Actually I'd prefer doctor..."

"Like I care what you do or do not prefer, Euie baby," she mocked.

"Well perhaps you should."

"Yeah, right, well to answer your question, *yes* I saw her and *no* she doesn't remember a thing. Ms. Sutton is *not* a threat to *you* or your company."

"Is that your official position?" he asked, pulling out his pipe and tobacco.

"For now anyway," she whispered.

Derrier stood and brushed off her pants. "Well, I'm out-a-here, Euie. Let me know if there's anything else I can do for you. After all, you pay me monthly, remember?"

"Don't remind me. What's your next assignment?"

"To snoop on a couple of scientists from Barker Institute. The big building that's just over the next ridge that analyzes your DNA samples. Why?"

"Nothing, just curious."

Derrier sighed and added as she was leaving, "Didn't curiosity kill something once?"

Chapter 43

"GAMMA-AMINOBUTYRIC ACID?" Loomsbury was shocked. The drug was outlawed years ago because of its effects on the kidneys and liver. "Who has this drug in their system?"

"Several young women accused of killing their families," Lewis stated.

"That's impossible!" Loomsbury exclaimed. "There are only a few samples in existence today and they're here in my vault. The rest were destroyed—a worldwide program."

"Don't you think I know that?" Lewis asked, scratching his head.

"I'll get to work right away. When can I have access to the women?"

"Any time you want." Lewis gulped down the rest of his coffee then shrugged, "Ugh I hate cold coffee. Give me some dates and I'll have it arranged."

"Who else have you assigned to the case?" Loomsbury asked scanning his note pad. He was hoping it would be Agent Clarke because she was always so interesting to work with.

"Agent Skyler Brighten... why?"

"Oh, nothing."

Loomsbury turned to leave but stopped when Lewis added, "Gather what you need and be ready to leave as soon as it's arranged. Agent Brighten will pick you up at the airport."

"Yes sir," Loomsbury said as the door shut behind him.

* * * * * *

The plane landed with a bump and Carrie's heart jumped

into her throat. She grabbed onto Lacey's arm and squeezed.

"Ouch," Lacey squeaked. "What's the matter with you?"

"Sorry," Carrie said, "...hate to fly."

"Really? I never would have guessed by the way you've been chewing on those tranquilizers. You'll sleep for a year when we get off this plane."

"Funny," Carrie stated as she rose from her seat, "ha ha."

"Pardon me," a voice said from behind.

Carrie glanced up and recognized the man. She yelled at him a long time ago for being rude on another flight. But instead of being mean, he was actually very polite. Giggling, Carrie grabbed her small bags from overhead and inched her way down the aisle toward the door. *Perhaps my scolding worked after all.* As she exited the plane, her foot snagged on the landing and she lost her balance. As her face aimed for the floor, her heart raced and she panicked. Suddenly and without warning, a strong grip lifted her to her feet.

"Are you okay?" the man's voice asked.

"Thank you," Carrie answered surprised to find the man she had yelled at and embarrassed a long time ago smiling at her.

"I do remember you," he whispered into her ear.

Blushing, Carrie smiled back.

"And I do learn," he said taking custody of her bags from her shoulder. "My name's Adams by the way... Rick Adams."

"Carrie," she responded. "Carrie Clarke."

"Nice to meet you Ms. Clarke. Yah know," he said as they walked down the ramp together. "You really did me a favor when I last... um... saw you."

"I guess I owe you an apology," Carrie added with a grin.

"No not at all. I never realized how irritating I was to people. I mean, we were not going anywhere fast with the aisle full of people and their luggage. I was in such a stupid hurry. I owe you an apology."

"Well, apology accepted then," she said with a half-hardy grin.

Carrie realized she'd completely forgotten about Lacey. As she glanced over her shoulder to check on her partner, Lacey spoke up. "Hey don't worry about me, I'm taggen... I'm a taggen..."

Chapter 44

LEE WOKE WITH a pain attacking her side. She tried to stand, but felt dizzy and sick to her stomach. The phone on the table seemed a mile away. After dialing, Lee fell back onto her pillow wanting to cry.

"Front desk?" the clerk answered.

"This is General Leland Longhorn—Room 21," Lee moaned into the receiver. "I need a doctor."

"Yes ma'am, I'll send one right up."

* * * * * *

Lee's door opened as the manager and a man she didn't recognize entered. But in so much pain, Lee didn't care who it was.

"Madam General, I'm Dr. MacNevin," the stranger said with a strong Scottish accent.

"I'm sorry you are not feeling well, my lady," the manager added. "Is there anything I can get for you?"

Lee felt she would die any moment. Her mouth was dry and her side ached. "Water please," Lee mumbled.

The doctor examined her and decided it was a bad case of food poisoning and gave her several shots—sedative, pain killer and antibiotic. He then promised to see her in the morning. A maid was ordered to sit with her through the night and get whatever she needed. But Lee didn't need any attention that night. Between the sedative and the painkiller, she slept peacefully as her eggs were fertilized in another room.

* * * * * *

Lee woke dazed and confused. It was dark and she had no idea how long she'd slept. Glancing around, Lee was happy to see she was alone. The pain was gone, but she still felt weak and slightly nauseated. Lifting herself to sit up, she realized she was starving. Ringing the front desk awoke a sleepy voice from the other end of the line.

"Yes, what time is it please? I can't seem to find my clock."

"Two in the morning, ma'am. Is there anything I can help you with?" the sleepy voice asked.

"Yes, I'm hungry. Any chance of finding me something to eat?" Lee asked.

"I'll have something brought up immediately," the voice answered, then the phone when dead.

Lee turned on the bedside lamp and found she was in a different room than before. Her laptop was on the desk next to her cell phone, which made her feel a little better. She stood up and almost fell. It took all her strength to get back into bed while clutching her phone.

"Tabatha... It's Lee," she whispered.

"Lee, where in the hell are you?" Tabatha screeched. "We've been looking all over for you."

"I've been right where I told you. I've been sick," Lee answered. "Really sick."

"We sent the police to the castle but the hotel manager said you were never registered," Tabatha replied.

"There's got to be some mistake. Wait, there's a knock on my door. It's probably my food."

Lee dropped her phone onto her bed and yelled for whoever it was to enter. A maid brought in a tray and sat it on her lap.

Lee talked to Tabatha as she ate her meal explaining what she knew, or didn't know. But as she ate, Lee had no idea a new life was growing inside her. A life from her own body, but also a life spliced with a few DNA surprises.

Chapter 45

TYLER AND CAIDEN continued their work late into the evening. They were excited to examine the new DNA. But to their amazement and horror, the new sample was neither DNA nor RNA, but a combination of both.

Caiden sat back and yawned. "Let's call it a night. This crap keeps getting weirder and weirder and I don't like it. I'd feel better knowing you were home with your aunt and uncle."

"Caiden, it's almost like someone is trying to re-design the human body," Tyler said, stretching. "I've studied the results of other DNA at home. With my uncle's suggestions, I found that the fish DNA was spliced in the rung for blood flow. It must have something to do with oxygenation of the blood."

"Had any luck on what type of fish?"

"Sort of," Tyler replied. "In fact I'd say it's along the mammal line, such as whales or dolphins. But I still don't get it. Why would anyone feel the need to try such an experiment?"

"I don't know," Caiden replied.

Caiden followed Tyler's car to her house and waved goodbye as she parked in her driveway. It was late, almost two in the morning, but Tyler was anything but sleepy. Her home office was full of notes and blood results along with various DNA printouts. Instead of bed, Tyler decided to read some of the material again. She was obviously missing something and whatever it was she needed to figure it out. But as she continued to study the material, she heard a bump and loud bang against the side of the house.

* * * * * *

The rental car pulled into the driveway of the small house in the quiet suburb. Lacey was out first but knocked over by a large golden retriever.

"Prince!" Tyler yelled from the front door. "Get over here you stupid dog."

Tyler grabbed Prince by the collar and apologized to Lacey. Nate took control of the dog and pulled him through the gate and into the backyard.

"That should keep him away for awhile," Nate yelled from the fence.

"Are you all right?" Tyler asked.

"Yeah, I'll live," Lacey said with a smile. "By the way, I'm Lacey... nice to meet you... I think."

"I'm so sorry, Lacey, I didn't realize he was out of the yard. I'm Tyler and this is Nate my uncle."

Carrie slammed the trunk and couldn't help but say, "My God you look like Skyler!"

"You must be Carrie," Tyler said from in front of the car. "It's nice to finally meet you. We are twins yah know."

The girls walked to the house after Nate insisted he'd bring in the suitcases. Carrie entered first, anxious to set her eyes on Maddie. But Maddie was nowhere to be found.

"Where's Mad?" Carrie asked.

"Should be around here somewhere," Tyler said following her into the house. "Aunt Maddie? Where are you?"

When there was no answer, Tyler peeked out the back window. But still no Maddie.

"Hope you two brought enough stuff," Nate puffed pulling several bags into the house.

"Where's Aunt Mad?" Tyler asked.

"Oh, she ran to the store, should be back any minute. She invited Caiden to dinner. And by the way, the house is clear, Tyler. Had a technician out today and there's nothing here. No bugs... we're free to talk."

"That is, as long as no one is listening from afar," Carrie added, walking through the house checking out the floor plan.

The one thing Carrie learned during her career at The Agency is nothing is free... and that meant with money and privacy.

"I'm putting you two in the room over the garage. Hope you don't mind," Tyler interjected. "There's twin beds up there and anther full bath. Much more room."

"Hey," Lacey yelled from the kitchen. "Anything is better than a stupid hotel."

"That's for sure," Carrie added walking back from the hall. "Love your house."

"Thanks," Tyler yelled. "I do too."

A honk announced Maddie's return from the store and Nate darted out to help carry in the groceries. Carrie stood in the kitchen leaning against the sink, too excited to move. As soon as Maddie entered she couldn't get her packages down fast enough.

"Carrie!" Maddie yelled as she ran and gave her a hug and kiss. "My goodness it's good to see you again. Tyler, come here and meet Carrie."

"We've met," Tyler added. "She says I look like Skyler."

"Well, she is your twin," Carrie added over Maddie's shoulder. "I feel like I'm staring at Skyler."

"This is really nice having all three of us together," Maddie said, giving another hug to Carrie. "They really do look alike don't they?"

"Yes they do, and it's great to finally be able to work on a case with you. I'm so excited," Carrie told Maddie.

"It is good," Maddie replied. "But I'm concerned over this one. I'll fill you in with what's going on... and you can tell me about your travels to the crater. I heard it might have been a meteor. How exciting."

The others stood aside and watched as Maddie and Carrie walked down the hall toward the back bedroom.

"I just love being left out," Nate interjected grinning over at Tyler and Lacey who only grinned back. "Left out in the cold... left to my..."

Chapter 46

LOOMSBURY REVIEWED THE lab results and scratched his head. There was no way the report could be accurate. Angry and frustrated, Loomsbury grabbed his phone and dialed an extension.

"Lab 4. How may I help you?" a young female voice asked.

"I need to speak with Dr. Hansley. This is Loomsbury."

"Yes sir, one moment please."

Waiting patiently, Loomsbury re-read the report still not believing the carefree attitude the laboratory was giving the samples.

"Hansley," the voice said.

"Hansley what in the world are you people doing down there?" Loomsbury shouted.

"Sir, I am afraid I don't understand."

"I have a report in my hand that states the subject is a combination of human and animal DNA. What kind of..."

"It's no kind of anything sir, the blood samples were obviously contaminated," the young doctor replied.

"I took those samples myself." Loomsbury yelled.

The phone went quiet for several seconds. Neither spoke.

"I need the test re-ran immediately," Loomsbury demanded.

"Yes sir, I'll have a technician take another draw as well. Just to be on the safe side," Hansley replied. "Not sure if the mother and child will be happy but it's the best I can do."

"Whatever it takes," Loomsbury said with an edge to his voice. "But I want accurate results... I hope we understand each other."

"Yes sir, I will run the test myself and will personally report back to you."

Chapter 47

TWO POLICE UNITS pulled up in front of the marble stairs and screeched to a halt. Constable Fahey stepped out of his car and adjusted his pants before heading for the door. He nodded to the other officers. Turning to enter the double doors, Constable Fahey bounced off the butler standing rigidly to assist him.

"May we help you sir?" the butler asked.

"We wish to see the manager right away." Fahey regained his balance and walked around the butler straight into the large structure. He wasn't waiting for an invitation. The butler followed the officers into Stonefield Castle anxious to deter him from entering any of the other rooms.

"Sir, I beg you," the butler requested, "please allow me..."

"I'll take it from here, Douglas," the manager stated from his office door. "What can we do for you, Constable?"

"We have a warrant to search the premises," Fahey stated with an air of authority.

"And may I ask what it is we're looking for?" the manager asked calmly.

"General Longhorn from the United States. We believe she may be in room twenty-one." Fahey announced boldly.

"Let me check the records for you, sir." The manager motioned for the officers to follow him to the front desk. He punched a few numbers into the computer and shook his head. "I'm sorry but we have no record of a General Longhorn ever being registered here. Weren't several of your men looking for her a couple of days ago?"

"Yes, but if you don't mind, I'll have a look for myself," Fahey demanded.

"Certainly," the manager motioned for the butler. "Douglas, would you please escort these two officers so they do not get lost."

Douglas nodded.

"Thank you for your cooperation," Constable Fahey added as the three walked away.

"Everything has been taken care of I presume?" a man in a suit and tie asked with his pipe smoldering in his left hand.

"Yes sir, everything," the manager replied.

CHAPTER 48

MARTY STOOD NEXT to her daughter who was sleeping peacefully in her crib. She hugged her eldest, Macie. They watched as little Lizzie's chest rose up and down.

"Mommy, she looks just like any other baby except she has fuzzy hair all over her. When did you say they were going to remove her tail?"

"I'm not sure yet," Marty replied. "They want to make sure it won't damage anything if they do. It wouldn't be good if they crippled her now would it?"

"But Mommy, she can't go around with a tail. I mean, how could she wear her pants?"

"We may have to cross that bridge when we come to it." Marty tried to reassure her daughter. "But until then, we are here and we are safe. So let's just enjoy our new baby and don't worry about it."

"I love her, Mommy," Macie said, smiling down at her baby sister.

"I love her too," Marty replied.

"What are you doing?" little Eliza asked, entering the room.

"Hi sweetheart," Marty said giving her a kiss on the cheek. "We are watching Lizzie sleep."

"Why?" Eliza asked.

"Because we love her," Macie replied.

"Oh," Eliza said satisfied with the answer.

Macie, who's six, and Eliza, who's four, have light reddish-blonde hair and dark green eyes. Not once since arriving in Washington have they asked about their father, nor has Eliza asked anything about her new strange sister. Only Macie noticed something was a little different. But both girls loved holding and playing with her. Marty was happy and content with her small family. Never once did she question how or why her life changed so suddenly. Nor did she question why she couldn't see her parents or friends. Only little Lizzie knew something wasn't right about being whisked away in the middle of the night and hidden deep in the forest. Only Lizzie was asking questions no one could hear. Only Lizzie was paying attention to what was going on, and Lizzie was only a few weeks old.

Chapter 49

"I AM NOT going to stand here and try to justify my position on this matter any longer. Our conversation is finished." The coffee spilled over the side of the cup and burnt his hand. He shook his head and sighed shaking the hot liquid from his skin. "I don't even know *why* we are having this conversation in the first place."

Director Vernon Geeshmore's glasses slid down his oily nose as he vigorously paced the floor. He adjusted them, too afraid to look into the eyes of the angry man. The situation was way out of control, and Geeshmore didn't like the path they were headed on. The carpet muffled his forceful steps as he carefully contemplated his next move.

"As I said," Nestle stated. "Our conversation is done. You may leave now."

Geeshmore paused, stretched out his neck by rolling his head around, and took a deep breath. After twenty-five years in the military and obtaining the rank of agency head of the National Institute of Health, he was surprised his courage was failing him at this crucial point in time. He turned to confront the man who was about to ruin a society created to protect the truth centuries before they were born. Decisions about life and death were ever present in his life, but today of all days, Geeshmore felt alone and unable to find the strength and courage he so desperately needed.

Slowly and methodically, Geeshmore spoke as his hands shook uncontrollably in his pants pockets. "The ancient and accepted rite of our society is, above all else, to seek out the truth. We do not teach men about the truth, instead we guide them toward a truth that can be accepted by every member—every chosen man on Earth. We all must find the truth for ourselves, we cannot, nor do we try to find it for anyone. Our journey is self-discovery and self-growth. We seek a common ground to philosophical and religious ideas in order to align our standards of right and wrong. We protect the reality of God. We are *not* gods, in and of ourselves. Nor do we pretend to be. I came here to state my objections not so much as to what we are trying to accomplish, but how we're going about it."

Dr. Nestle didn't move; he didn't speak, either. He stared into a dark corner of the room as though in deep thought.

Geeshmore breathed a short sigh of relief. *So far so good,* he said to himself. "Roland, my friend, my brother... you must hear me. We are destroying families in our efforts of human refinement, not to mention the lives of the individuals, all at the *whim* of our discretion. Have you *honestly* thought this through? Do you *honestly* believe what we're doing is what our founders had in mind?"

Silence was the Director's answer. Dr. Nestle didn't say a word. Geeshmore felt it was safe to continue his small, memorized lecture.

"I understand the university will benefit financially from our research, but at what price? How do we put a price on a two-year-old, or a three-year-old? Or for that matter on any living soul. We are tampering in areas where we have no business. We are treading on God's soil. I see everything exploding in on our society and there will be no way of stopping it. We have enough to worry about with the conspiracy theorists nipping at our heels. New members are joining every day, yes, but what legacy are we leaving them and those who follow?"

Nestle started to laugh. He laughed uncontrollably.

"What's so funny?" Geeshmore asked.

"You," Nestle yelled. "You."

"I have stated my concerns and objections. I am not in agreement with what's going on. I've had my say." Geeshmore closed the door behind him as he left.

The room became silent except for the remaining chuckles escaping the old doctor's lips.

CHAPTER 50

THE SMELL OF bacon was more than Carrie could resist and the empty bed next to hers was a clear sign she was probably the last one to wake up—again. After grabbing her bathrobe and slippers, she headed for the kitchen.

"Hey sleepy head," Maddie said handing Carrie a cup of coffee. "You must have needed the rest."

"Tell me about it," Carrie answered. She sniffed at the bacon sizzling on the stove then sat down at the kitchen table. "Where is everyone?"

"Well, Lacey went to check out the city; Tyler's at work, and Nate is running some errands. So it's just you and me. How do you like your eggs?"

Carrie took a sip of coffee. "Scrambled's fine. So tell me, how'd you get mixed up in all this?"

"Well I'm not really sure what *all this* is yet," Maddie answered as she plopped a couple of eggs into the bacon grease. "But I don't like what I've heard so far."

"Don't keep me in suspense, spill the beans." Carrie sipped her coffee and watched the birds eat at the feeder through the kitchen window. The small home was cozy and comfortable and just as she'd expected.

Thinking back, Carrie felt sorry for Maddie, but it didn't take long for her to realize Maddie didn't need anyone's pity or sorrow. Maddie was a strong woman and knew what she needed and how to get it. Never during her life did Maddie ever give up or throw in the towel. Never had she regretted anything she said or did. Every word, every action had a reason Maddie could defend. She fought for everything that was good in life and hoped to make a difference in this crazy world. If Carrie could accomplish only half of what Maddie did, Carrie could feel she too had succeeded in life.

Chapter 51

"CHARLOTTE!" THE YOUNG maid screamed. "Charlotte, don't move. Stand still."

Charlotte was perched at the edge of the roof five stories above the gardens. From her position, Charlotte could see over the trees and across the valley. It felt wonderful and she longed to be free. As her wings spread out in the sunshine, her blood warmed and the feeling was energizing, giving her a sense of strength she never felt before. It took an enormous amount of effort for her to flex her wings, her back muscles were still weak. Charlotte was never allowed to open her wings in the castle. She had to keep them bound to her back. But now standing on the high rooftop with the sun warming her blood, Charlotte knew she could do anything, anything she wanted. The sensation and essence of just being high above the Earth gave her a comfort and a deep longing for more. Something Charlotte could not resist.

"Charlotte. Don't move, " Bart coached trying to push his large body through the small window, "we're coming to get you."

The little girl turned and smiled proudly at the man who wore an anxious and worried look. Then, in just a split second, she turned her back and glanced over the edge. Charlotte spread her wings as far as she could to allow her body to feel the rush of air that was just beyond the edge.

"No! Charlotte, don't do it! Your wings are not strong enough... Charlotte, NO!"

But it was too late. Charlotte had already leaned far enough over the edge to allow the wind to catch her wide and colorful wings. Her back ached as the air pushed against her outstretched membranes. Her body and legs were pulled toward the Earth as her wings tugged high into the blue sky. It was as if her body would be torn into pieces at any moment, but it felt exhilarating.

No fear flowed through Charlotte, only a wonderful sense of freedom. As she glided toward the concrete below, Charlotte used all her strength to flap her wings. Never before had anything felt as wonderful. Her breathing rapidly increased in both strength and frequency. It didn't take long for her to realize that using her shoulder muscles eased the strain on her back. She soared over the tree tops toward the large lake. As she reached the water's edge, Charlotte allowed her left wing to drop, which raised her higher on the right side. If she shifted her body, she glided in a half circle toward the left. A few flaps of her wings and a small upward tilting of her head sent her body soaring higher.

The air was cool up here, but the hot sun warmed and thinned her blood as it rapidly flowed through her veins. The higher she soared the less restricted she felt. Her boundaries were limitless. For the first time in her life Charlotte was free.

Bart and the young maid ran outside followed by Stewart. He stood in awe watching the little girl conquer her fears and dominate the elements. The scientists concluded the human body would never be able to withstand the strain of the air current and the gravity, the wings would detach from the body and the person would die a painful death. But Charlotte was proving them wrong. She was flying, just like the birds flew freely in the sky. Charlotte was flying.

Unlike her sister whose fragile bones broke even as she slept, Charlotte's were light but strong. When her sister was born, Stewart named her Angel. For the little girl looked just like one. But Angel only lived a few years, and each year was filled with pain. It was both a blessing and a curse when she passed. Stewart cried for weeks after Angel's passing.

When they decided another child would take Angel's place, they knew the bones had to be stronger. They also surmised the stronger bones would be heavier thus not allowing the child to fly. But there she was, soaring above the trees and proving them all wrong. Stewart watched as Charlotte glided toward the ground, but before her feet touched, she fluttered her wings to slow her descent. She touched down so delicately, it was as if Charlotte had stepped off a cloud.

The maid and Bart ran to her and began scolding. Charlotte ignored them stretching out her wings even further, taunting them. It felt wonderful to finally release the muscles she had to keep constrained all the time. Then as if she were a bird, Charlotte flapped them a few more times before folding them against her back. Her eyes met the doctor's and they smiled together. Stewart winked at her with a twinkle in his eye.

<h1 style="text-align:center">CHAPTER 52</h1>

"GOOD AFTERNOON, MS. BRIGHTEN and Mr. Harding," Crystal said introducing herself as she sat across the table from Tyler and Caiden. "I'm investigating the mysterious deaths of the family murdered by the wife and mother—Early Sutton."

Caiden and Tyler glanced at each other surprised they would be questioned about something they knew nothing about.

"You look confused," Crystal said responding to their reaction to her statement. "I understand you are the DNA experts. Is that correct?"

Caiden shrugged his shoulders and replied, "I wouldn't necessarily say that, would you, Tyler?"

"Not really," Tyler replied. "What is this all about anyway and who do you work for again? I don't believe I caught that part."

"I didn't say," Crystal answered, pulling out a badge and flashing it briefly, she added, "the FBI. Now as I was saying..."

"Can I see your badge again?" Tyler asked.

"That isn't necessary," Crystal added. "Now back to where I was... oh yes, I believe you tested the DNA samples of the baby girl born at Mercy Medical Center?"

"I'm sorry," Tyler spoke up. "First off, we have no idea as to what samples you're referring to. Second, I didn't get a good look at your badge. And third, our projects are classified and only our clients are privy to the results. So if you'll excuse us, we have work to do."

Caiden and Tyler stood and gave the woman another glare before leaving the room. Crystal laughed to herself as she gathered her papers from the table. *At least someone is using their heads,* she said to herself. *Thank God for small favors.*

* * * * * *

Crystal drove down the winding road away from the large complex all the while laughing at the whole situation. Lewis answered her call on the third ring and after briefing him, she called Spangleholtz, the man she loathed. When there was no answer, she was awarded with his voice mail.

"Euie baby! It's Crystal. I'm sorry I missed you darling," she lied. "I've spoken to the two scientists and all's clear, they know nothing, absolutely nothing. That trail, I'm afraid, is a dead end. I'll see if I can find out exactly where those blood samples were sent. It's obvious they didn't go to Barker Institute. Maybe one day you can tell me what's so special about these samples... maybe? Anyway, later Euie baby... later."

Crystal clicked off her phone and continued to laugh as she headed for the expressway that would ultimately take her to California. It would be good to finally sleep in her own bed.

Chapter 53

"HELLO?"

"Ms. Clarke... how are you and how is your friend?"

"Jeff? What a nice surprise," Carrie replied. "We're both fine."

Carrie glanced up at Maddie who smiled. As Carrie listened and Lewis spoke, Maddie finished the breakfast dishes and straightened up the kitchen. Carrie was still on the phone when Maddie shoved a load of dirty clothes into the washer. Maddie was folding bath towels in the living room when Carrie finally clicked off her cell phone to join her.

"Hmmm, seems there's more going on than what meets the eye," Carrie mused.

"What do you mean?" Maddie asked while folding a dark green bath towel.

"Well, Jeff sent us out here to investigate a hospital, right? But he just called and changed our plans. It seems one of *our* agents interviewed Tyler and Caiden today. She wasn't there for The Agency, but on assignment from a classified research facility that also doubles as a mental institution. Lewis gave her the assignment years ago to get in tight with the facility's Director just to keep a tab on him. I guess he never gave it much thought. But, she'd done her job rather well. After all this time, she still works for the facility as an investigator. He wants Lacey and me to go there and do some snooping. We'll be posing as hikers... campers who just happen to stumble into their backyard."

"Really?" Maddie added, now separating the freshly dried and folded towels by their color and size.

"Funny how this stuff works, isn't it?" Carrie asked.

"What do you mean?"

"Well, Tyler calls you because she's concerned about where she works and she doesn't feel safe. Then Jeff sends us out here to investigate a hospital. And our agent secretly working for a place that's connected with it… that research facility, and then that same agent visits Tyler and Caiden asking about blood samples. It just seems weird, that's all."

Maddie looked at Carrie and frowned. "What blood samples?"

"Don't know. But I do know Skyler's escorting samples from those women who killed their families to headquarters. Jeff's notifying her to watch out for anything unusual. But why?"

"I don't like this. The last time our government decided they could do whatever they wanted many children were murdered. Just ask Lacey about it, she'll tell you. This is not a good sign," Maddie surmised staring into Carrie's eyes.

"She's a pretty tough girl, that Lacey," Carrie added. "Whatever happened to her as a kid doesn't seem to affect her now."

"Don't be so fast to jump to conclusions. We can hide our feelings for years before they surface," Maddie added before grabbing the towels and leaving the room.

Carrie's phone rang and she was pleased to hear her boyfriend's voice. Carrie and Devon talked for only a few minutes before he had to run. She stared at her now quiet phone and wondered if she still loved him as much as she used to. They hardly ever saw each other anymore, and they were never home at the same time. Over the last couple of years, Carrie's work at The Agency changed her, made her more independent. But there was still a little something inside her that needed Devon. Every time she heard his voice, she felt secure and safe. Not to mention it was still wonderful to hear his voice even if it was for only a few minutes.

Chapter 54

EARLY LAY ON her cot as memories of her family flooded through her mind, shifting her soul from calmness to torment. Tears rolled down her cheeks as she remembered her precious daughters, Nevada and Dakota, and how hard they worked to make a snowman in their front yard. They were so cute with their thin hair pulled into ponytails and little knitted scarves wrapped around their necks. No matter how hard they worked, the dingy little snowman never seemed to get any higher than a couple of feet.

Their bedroom was always neat and tidy. Dolls of different kinds lined the shelves fully dressed, as if ready to go out for the day. If one hair was out of place, the girls immediately attended to their little people's need. Green floral curtains and matching spreads decorated their bright yellow room. Twin beds were never slept in, the girls preferred to cuddle on the floor under tons of blankets and pillows.

Dakota was the first to walk and talk. She was a little bigger than Nevada but to look at them now, it was impossible to tell them apart. Their love filled a room with warmth and their smiles calmed even the most hostile of emotions. At only three years of age, they spoke in clear and concise sentences. They were toilet trained before two, and wanted nothing to do with being dirty.

Her son Daren, on the other hand, was all boy. At seven, dirt clung to him like iron to a magnet. His favorite place was high in the trees, where he could hide in the branches and watch the world go by. Daren's room was always a mess with his cars and trucks scattered about the floor. Daren's hugs and kisses were worth waiting for every afternoon as he bounced off the school bus. Early and the girls waited anxiously on the corner every day, Monday through Friday, for the bus to climb the hill and stop two houses away by a big oak tree. Daren was always the first off.

"Mom," Daren yelled. "I got an 'A' in science." Or math, or whatever it would be.

Early always lagged behind as Daren and the girls strolled to the house. She'd wave to the bus driver as he headed down the road to drop off other children.

But now, instead of tucking her babies into bed, Early laid alone on a cot in a jail cell. She did not know where her children or husband were, or whether something really happened to them. As the minutes turned into hours and hours into days, Early reminisced about her life and family. Evenings and nights were especially hard, because Early only had her memories to comfort her.

Sometimes she'd think back to when she first met Alex and relive those precious moments. In college, she majored in music therapy, which meant her days were filled with dance and song. Aside from the psychology classes, modern dance was her favorite. She practiced her turns on the empty dance floor for hours, twirling in place or gliding across the room. The soft music was soothing and gave her a feeling of warmth and serenity.

One afternoon, as she came out of a perfect turn, a shadow appeared by the double French doors. With her arms still above her head, she tilted back and saw a handsome young man. Her body was lean and slender, and she always allowed her hair to flow freely down her back with long wavy curls.

"Hello," Alex spoke from the door.

At first Early wasn't sure what to do. It was as if time had suddenly stopped and she was frozen between breaths.

"I'm Alex. I didn't mean to frighten you, please keep dancing." Alex walked toward her as she relaxed her arms and righted herself. "I've watched you before, I hope you don't mind. I mean, dancers are for watching. Correct?"

"I guess so." Early was not sure how to accept his advances.

"Well, please… by all means… then dance," he urged.

With nothing else to do, Early swayed to the flowing tune of the music as Alex watched. It was an erotic sensation knowing he followed her every move as she glided across the smooth wooden floor. Early danced since the age of three. Her toeshoes were worn and tattered, but she loved them and refused to throw them away.

From that day on, Alex watched Early glide across the room every other afternoon. Her heart grew for this handsome young man who never asked for anything other than the simple pleasure of watching her dance.

It was during her senior year he finally asked her out. That was when Early learned he was a medical student. They dated throughout his senior year, and the summer after his graduation he proposed. It all happened so fast. She was dancing and practicing for her thesis and he proposed in the middle of the dance floor. It meant so much to know he understood music was everything to her. So much so, he used her platform to ask for her hand in marriage.

The remainder of the night moved slowly. Early's pillow was soaked from the tears that continuously ran down her face. She wondered if she would ever see her love again. He had been her whole life, her mate, her lover. But today and tomorrow and for many more dreaded hours she would be alone.

Chapter 55

LOOMSBURY RAN OVER the results of the blood samples scattered across his hotel desk. It was impossible what he was seeing, but they ran the tests several times. Gamma-Aminobutyric Acid was detected in each woman's blood sample. So much that traces remained to this very day.

He stood back and stared at the results. His mind raced faster than his thoughts could keep up. Rubbing his eyes, Loomsbury stretched and glanced over at the clock on the bed side table. It was four in the morning and he still wasn't tired. *Perhaps if he ordered another test just to be sure.* But no, he'd already done that several times and each time the results were the same.

The outcome of the tests explained why the women retained no memory of the killings or for several months after. But how did so much of the drug get into their systems without killing them? The remaining amount was not high enough to continue the memory loss, but it was enough to be detected by The Agency's sophisticated equipment.

At the levels the women were given, nothing they experienced would pass into their long term memory. Although they functioned and seemed normal to any person who observed them, everything they saw, spoke or experienced would be as if it never happened. But why and for what purpose?

Loomsbury was only twenty-five. As a boy genius, he received three PhDs by the age of fifteen. When The Agency recruited him at sixteen, he was given his own laboratory to do whatever was asked of him. But for the first time in many years, Looms-bury was stumped. Each woman had the same exact amount of Gamma-Aminobutyric Acid in their system, which only meant they were still receiving the drug—somehow. But that was impossible—or was it? Suddenly it hit him. It hit him harder than anything ever before.

"An implant!" he cried.

An implant would explain everything. It would explain the heavy enough dose to cause the memory loss, and the lesser amount showing up in his results. Loomsbury called Lewis to explain his theory. It was important each woman undergo an MRI or X-ray as soon as possible to determine if any foreign bodies were hidden beneath their skin. It would be the only way such a large amount of the drug could continuously be administered without detection.

When he hung up the phone, he felt tired and decided he earned his time for sleep. It felt great he figured it all out. He wouldn't need to see the MRI results, Loomsbury already knew the answer. He was sure that the women had been implanted with an Automatic Medical Drug Administrator device, better known as an AMDA. The device was used to administer drugs to people with diabetes or other life-threatening illnesses which required constant medication. It was the only logical explanation and he knew he was right, for if given the assignment on how to do it, that would be the course he would take.

It wouldn't be hard to implant the devices. If they were inserted just above the uterus there would be no scar, no outside appearance anything was done. No one would know and the secret would go to their graves with them. Unless someone knew exactly where to look, they would go undetected even during a sonogram or pregnancy.

Loomsbury flipped off the lights and pulled the blankets over his shoulder. He was now tired and could easily fall asleep. Trying to clear his mind, Loomsbury thought of the women and how they must have felt waking up in a courtroom with no memory or idea how or why they were there.

"Amazing," he said to no one. "Brilliant ... but amazing."

Chapter 56

AS THE SUN rose over the mountain range, Carrie and Lacey hiked higher up the trail that wound precariously through the pine and maple trees. At times the path was so rugged Lacey had a difficult time keeping up.

"Need a break?" Carrie asked stopping a few feet ahead of Lacey.

"No. Just keep going."

It took two hours to reach the summit, and when they stopped to admire the view they were both in complete awe. The horizon was nothing aside from amazing. From this vantage point, the girls could see for miles in every direction. Ridge upon ridge of heavily forested mountains, tumbling rivers and flower-dotted meadows were visible as far as they could see. Off in the distance the snowy top of Mount Rainier was a soul-inspiring sight.

"Oh my!" Lacey exclaimed. "This is beautiful."

Carrie pulled out her digital camera and started clicking. "Here," Carrie said handing the camera to Lacey. "We need a few pictures of each other so we're more credible as hikers."

They rested under a tall hemlock tree to relax and eat their lunch. Aroma from the various foliage was a wonderful sensation. It was cool and faint sounds from the rustling of small animals echoed through the mountain. The only other sound was from the wind as it filtered through the trees.

"I could live here," Lacey surmised. "This place is like a nature's wonderland... a postcard... wish you were here."

Carrie laughed. "Hey, we're deep in the woods. You think we'll run into Bigfoot?"

"Ha ha, very funny." Lacey joked back.

Carrie pulled out her GPS and double checked the map. "We're right on target."

"How do you know where to go?"

"Lewis gave me the coordinates he wants us to check out. That's all we can do for now. If we find something, great, if not, we'll just have to wait and see what he tells us to do next."

They gathered their packs and headed toward the side of another large mountain range. The peaks and valleys seemed to continue forever. They soon found a clearing and decided to pitch their tent and call it a night. Lacey gathered what dried wood she could find for a fire as Carrie went shopping for dinner.

Slightly before dark, Carrie returned with the remains of a rabbit attached to a small branch. As the meat roasted over the open flames, Lacey prepared a salad from eatable foliage, which was mostly herbs and mushrooms. Carrie even ran across a small patch of wild potatoes. Their meal was delicious and they ate until they couldn't eat any more.

"How do you know how to do all this stuff?" Lacey asked as they nibbled on the freshly cooked wild apples Carrie found right after lunch.

"It's not hard. Devon Arvol, my boyfriend, is half Native American. He was taught how to live off the land. He was raised on the reservation by his mother and grandparents. His dad was a white-man who never came to see him much. We used to go camping a lot... traveled to different national parks and all." Carrie lowered her head wishing she were camping with Devon right now. "Anyway, he's the one who taught me *less is better*. The less you carry in the less you carry out. I didn't believe him at first, but I learned how to tell the difference between eatable and poisonous plants and where to find them. He also taught me how to catch small animals like rabbits and to fish without a fishing pole. Comes in handy at times."

"Oh? So that's why we're carrying staples instead of pre-packaged food?" Lacey asked.

"Yep, I can do a lot with just a little sugar and flour and salt.

We'll have fresh berries and biscuits in the morning, and of course, coffee."

The girls laughed as they turned in for the night. They were past exhausted and just wanted to crash. Once the fire died down, they rolled over and fell peacefully asleep listening to the natural sounds of the wild.

Chapter 57

LEWIS READ THE report twice while glancing at Greghardt only once. He knew he could trust Loomsbury's conclusions completely, and was amazed and shocked at what he was reading. Instead of giving answers, the report only filled his head with more questions.

Strickland waited patiently from the couch sipping on her Scotch and water for her turn to read the report. Not knowing was always the worst. As Lewis read to himself, she watched as Dr. Greghardt puffed a few times on his cigar while tapping his fingers on the coffee table.

"My grandfather used to smoke a pipe," Strickland interjected between sips. At last her nerves seemed to be calming and her hands finally stopped sweating. "I love the smell of good pipe tobacco."

"Cuban." Greghardt winked at her.

Lewis handed the report to Greghardt who passed it to Strickland.

"Already seen it," he said as she looked at him with surprise.

"Well I haven't," Strickland said taking the paper. As she read the report the expression on her face turned from calm to alarm. "This can't be. This drug was banned years ago. If I remember correctly, the last of it was destroyed under the strict supervision of The Agency."

"Well, apparently not," Greghardt replied taking another puff.

"Or, it was re-created," Lewis suggested.

"Impossible," Strickland said.

"Why?" Lewis asked.

"Because," Strickland answered as she rubbed her now sweating hands against her pants. "It takes too long to make it."

"How would you know?" Lewis asked.

"I worked for the FDA prior to becoming vice president... remember?"

Greghardt smiled at her and added, "That's right, Jeff, she was one of the leading scientists if my memory serves me right."

Lewis nodded while giving Strickland a stunned glance.

"I'm not trying to be a smart-ass or anything, but that drug takes years to make. That is if you don't want to kill someone. It's not something you wake up one day and say 'Hey I think I'll make some Gamma-Aminobutyric Acid today.' It just doesn't work that way, and for that matter, if someone knew they would need it this year, they would have had to start on it at least four or five years ago. It simply doesn't make any sense."

"And your point?" Lewis asked.

Greghardt let out another breath of heavy tobacco smoke and shook his head. "What she is trying to tell you is the drug must not have been destroyed. That isn't hard to believe is it? If I'm not mistaken, I think we have some of it in Loomsbury's secret stash...his outdated, outlawed and banned substances."

"But *we're* The Agency," Lewis declared taking a large gulp of whiskey he just poured over ice. "It's different where we're concerned."

Greghardt chuckled. "Please, Jeff, as though The Agency is the only agency on the planet that has access to illegal substances. Honestly, maybe the drug is being secured by Peter Pan or the Easter Bunny."

Lewis gulped down the rest of his whiskey. It was time for another drink. Heading for the small kitchenette, he also grabbed Strickland's glass and filled them both to the rim. He didn't speak a word until he'd finished drinking the whole drink. Then with another in his hand, he took a seat next to Greghardt and stared at Strickland.

"I do not believe we live in a fantasy world, and I've been

around long enough to know what goes on out there. But we were in charge of destroying that stuff and I'm pissed we failed to find it all." Lewis stood and yelled for Connie who came running into the room.

"Yes sir?" Connie asked with pad and pen ready to write down any orders no matter how strange or how frightening. Connie worked at The Agency for years and was always ready for anything.

"Pull the files on the destruction of the drug Gamma-Aminobutyric Acid. Then tell Loomsbury to be ready to brief us on the subject in an hour."

"Yes sir," Connie replied writing down her instructions. "Sir? How do you spell Am..in...o?"

Lewis grabbed the pad from Connie and printed the words on the paper.

"Thank you sir," Connie grinned. "Before I go, Agent Schuster and her crew have returned, and she's asked to have a private moment with you. She said it's important. It's about the..." Connie's voice changed to a whisper, "General."

Lewis took in a deep breath and gave a heavy sigh. "Now what? Fine... give us about ten minutes then send her in." Lewis gave Strickland and Greghardt a long sorrowful glance then returned to his desk. It'd been a long day and a long night, and he knew it was about to get even longer.

Chapter 58

"MOM?" MACIE SAID trying to wake her mother. "Mom? I think Lizzie's sick. Mom?"

Marty rolled over and blinked her eyes. She'd been so tired and sleepy it took a couple of seconds for her to realize what her daughter was talking about. "What? Lizzie?"

"Yeah, Mom. I think she's sick. She's hot and crying."

Marty jumped out of bed and ran down the hall to the nursery. The lamp next to the crib was on and Lizzie was whimpering.

"What is it, baby?" Marty asked picking up her little girl. "Oh my God, you're burning up."

"Mom? She needs a doctor," Macie demanded.

"I know, baby, but we're miles from the nearest hospital," Marty sighed.

Not knowing what to do, Marty began to panic. She knew she had to get the fever down fast. Carrying the baby close to her chest, Marty ran into the bathroom.

"Mom? She doesn't need a bath!" Macie screamed. "She needs a doctor."

"Honey, we must get her temperature down and this is the only way I know. Now help mommy okay sweetie?"

"What do I do?" Macie asked with tears in her eyes.

"Get some clean towels," Marty said turning on the bath water.

As she undressed Lizzie, Marty began to cry. She couldn't lose her special little girl; little Lizzie was all she had that kept her going. Marty's tears fell as she watched Lizzie go limp in her arms. Her breathing labored and her eyes rolled back in her head.

"No baby no... be okay..." Marty cried out, "please be okay."

"Here's the towels, Mom," Macie said laying them down next to the tub. "Now what?"

"Get her a bottle of water, put an ice cube in it, and grab the baby aspirin. It's best for a fever. You're not supposed to use it, but I need her temperature to go down fast and aspirin works the best...now hurry."

"Mom? Can she take aspirin? I mean, is she like us?" Macie cried. "I don't want anything to happen to her."

"She's fine, baby, now get me those things." Marty gently laid her little Lizzie into the cool bath water. She rested her left hand under the baby's head and used her right to spread the water over the child. The water was cool and Lizzie responded right away. *Good,* Marty said to herself. *Good.*

Macie returned with the medicine and baby bottle and tear-streaked cheeks. "Here mom," Macie cried.

Marty took the aspirin and crunched it between her fingers and rubbed the medicine under little Lizzie's tongue. She knew this was one of the most sensitive parts of the body and would absorb the medicine fast. Then she offered little Lizzie some water. Lizzie sucked down the precious liquid which cooled her tummy. The blood flowing in her veins began to chill and her temperature slowly fell.

Lizzie opened her eyes and drank the cool liquid. Marty exhaled a huge sigh of relief. "Thank God. It's working."

"Lizzie's going to be okay?" Macie asked.

"Yes sweetie, she'll be fine. You did a great job helping mommy."

With Lizzie wrapped in a towel and drinking the water, Marty grabbed the phone and dialed the help number. The voice came through the intercom.

"Do you need assistance?"

"Yes, I need help. Lizzie has a fever," Marty yelled. "Where have you guys been? When I don't need you you're always bugging me. Now I need you and you're nowhere to be found."

"What is her temperature?" the voice asked.

"I DON'T KNOW!" Marty screamed. "I just know it's high. Now get someone out here."

"We're on our way," the voice stated.

Marty dressed both girls and put a diaper on Lizzie. She didn't want her to get hot again so didn't dress her. She laid her on a blanket to leave her open to the cool air. The doctors arrived within minutes and took all three to the clinic. As the doctors escorted them in, Spangleholtz greeted her. He took custody of Lizzie in his arms as Marty and her two daughters were escorted to a private waiting room.

* * * * * *

"What's ailing her?" Spangleholtz asked the doctors staring at little Lizzie.

"Not sure yet," one doctor replied.

"Some kind of an infection," the other added.

"Wait," the first doctor exclaimed, reviewing the blood analysis reports. "We need to change the antibiotics."

The doctor's eyes widen, "Why?"

"She has a streptococcus equi infection," the other doctor replied.

"A what?" Spangleholtz asked. "Can it be treated?"

"Most definitely," the doctor answered. "But what's interesting is our little lady's a little more horse than human. Even though she has more human characteristics on the outside, she is more horse on the inside. Or at least where her blood is concerned."

"What exactly are you telling me?" Spangleholtz demanded.

"She needs a veterinarian more than a physician," he chuckled. "I'm calling Dr. Stalkswarts. He's our equine specialist."

"I'm beginning to hate my job," Spangleholtz stated under his breath.

Chapter 59

SPANGLEHOLTZ WAITED FOR the call, which arrived at exactly eight in the morning. It was the conversation he'd been dreading for days. Usually he was a strong man, but today at this moment, Spangleholtz was a coward. How one phone call could change a man was beyond his comprehension. Waiting for the phone to ring was the worst. But he didn't have long to wait. Within seconds the ring echoed through his office and jolted him. His heart pounded and his hands shook. He was afraid to pick up the phone, but knew he had no other choice.

"Yes sir," Spangleholtz answered, a crackle of fear emanating from his lips.

"Dr. Spangleholtz?" a young female voice asked. "I have Director Geeshmore for you sir from the National Institutes of Health."

"Put him through," Spangleholtz replied. He hesitated for only a moment to regain his composure and courage and falsely exclaimed, "Vernon. How wonderful to hear from you. It's early in DC isn't it... about seven I believe?"

"I didn't call to compare time zones, Gene," Geeshmore said. "We have pressing problems and you know how I do not like problems. Now, tell me, what do people know?"

Spangleholtz hesitated for a moment. He wasn't sure how he was going to answer the question. It wasn't a question that could be answered with just any reply. What he said now would determine how and where he would spend the rest of his life.

"Yes, well..." Spangleholtz stumbled. "My investigator still contests no one knows a thing. That the reports in the papers had been fabricated. I can guarantee you nothing slipped out of this office." Spangleholtz wasn't sure if his answer would appease the listener or not, but it was the truth as far as he was concerned.

"I understand there was a meeting of the mothers with their lawyers recently," Geeshmore said. "Why would they have met if no one knows a thing? Doesn't it seem odd they would find each other?"

"Not really, sir. I would expect a good lawyer to eventually listen to the news and pull them together."

"Gene," Geeshmore yelled. "I did not call to listen to your stories and you trying to weasel yourself out of this; I've had just about enough. You have exactly twenty-four hours to fix the problem. Understand?"

Spangleholtz stood holding the now quiet phone in his hand. The other party hung up. He knew what he had to do and wasn't happy about it. Since accepting this position he had to make decisions on who lived and who died. But he knew what he had to do to save his own life.

Chapter 60

"DRAKE ANDERSON, IT'S Ash Kranton." The voice pounded into Drake's ear. "Did you get your report yet?"

"Yes," Drake said. "Good work by the way."

"Well I've ordered an MRI for Lark. I want to know if there's an implant in her. If there is..."

"Look... Ash," Drake stuttered. "I don't think that's such a good idea. I mean we don't know who put those things in them, we don't know what can happen."

"It's an MRI for Christ's sake. I'll call when I get the results. You should do the same for your client."

Drake thought for only a few moments then called Dr. Barnes. He needed to know if Early had an implant but also wanted to make sure it was safe first.

* * * * * *

Early screamed as they wheeled her into emergency surgery. The pain was severe and she knew she was going to die. Drake rushed out of the office as soon as he received the call.

A breathing mask was placed over Early's mouth and nose. From her view, she could see the worried faces of people she didn't know. Fear rose from within and she wanted nothing more than to go home.

"Breathe in deeply sweetheart," the doctor coached from above her head. "You'll be just fine, just fine."

Early glanced around and saw several doctors and nurses

running about preparing her for emergency surgery. But what she didn't see was Dr. Loomsbury standing in the corner tapping his foot. He was upset over the phone call he just received.

"Loomsbury."

"Sir, Dr. Hensley here."

"You have the results?"

"Yes sir, but I do not believe you'll be happy."

"Why?" Loomsbury asked.

"Because the results are the same."

"What?"

* * * * * *

"I am sorry Dr. Loomsbury could not be here this morning," a young lady announced from the podium. "My name is Dr. Leonora Priddleton. I'm Dr. Loomsbury's assistant."

Priddleton was young, only a few months past her twelfth birthday. But her actions were more of a forty-year-old woman. Dark black hair pulled into braided ponytails gave her an even younger look. An almond colored face accented with dark-rimmed plastic glasses enlarged her dark eyes. Standing at just a little over four feet, her lab coat all but draped the floor. As she stood composed, light yellow tennis shoes with pink shoestrings poked out from under her long white coat.

Greghardt chuckled and leaned over to Dr. Lewis and whispered, "They get younger every year don't they?"

"Hey, I wouldn't want to get in that little lady's path. There's more brains in that skull than in both of ours combined."

"After careful review of the material left for me by my colleague Dr. Loomsbury, I've concluded the drug was destroyed. There's no evidence that any remained. The records are clear and concise. There were four agents who worked the disposal process, checks and balances... cross checks... checks and rechecks."

"Excuse me, Dr. Priddleton," Greghardt interjected.

"Yes sir... you have a question?"

"Why couldn't several doses have been confiscated and kept hidden?"

"Simple answer," Priddleton said clicking on the large monitor covering one wall. "Special precautions were taken to ensure all of the drug was gathered from around the world. Each specimen was hand carried by two of our agents. The laboratories would have lost their licenses if the samples presented were not real. It took two agents to open the sealed case. Even then, only The Agency had the third key. It was The Agency who ensured each vial was genuine and destroyed. The paperwork is complete and accurate."

"So we can conclude this drug was specifically created for these women?" Strickland asked from her seat.

"We believe so, yes," Priddleton replied. "It takes exactly fifty-eight months to create the drug at the intensity required to keep someone under the influence and not kill them."

Priddleton waited for more questions.

"Jesus, exactly who are we up against?" Lewis asked no one in particular.

"We do not know the answer at this juncture," Priddleton replied. "But we hope to gain more insight from the instrument Loomsbury brings back. We expect his return within the day."

Lewis sat back in his chair and allowed his mind to wander. Whoever or whatever had the capability and money to re-create that drug—the drug The Agency took such precautions to destroy—must be powerful and dangerous. But it was the purpose behind the whole situation that worried him the most. Why? Why kill all those innocent people... and their families? What are... or were they trying to hide? And who are included in the *they*?

"Dr. Priddleton?" Lewis asked after a moment of thought. "Have you examined the bone fragments Agent Miranda and his crew are assigned to?"

"Yes, but we're still waiting for the test results. I would not like to make conclusions or statements until all the results are in sir."

"Yes of course." Lewis turned and stared at Agent Miranda before he continued. "Would you debrief us now please?"

"This should be quick," Miranda said standing. "We found nothing. We examined every square inch of the burial plot, but it'd already been sanitized. We also spoke to several people of interest and again... nothing."

"Damn," Lewis shouted. "Can't one damn thing go right around here?"

Chapter 61

AS LARK LAY nervously inside the cramped hollow tube, the machine clicked and barked several times. Never having experienced an MRI before, she was frightened. Even with the earplugs, she could still hear the attendant announce they would soon begin. Lark took in a deep breath hoping the fresh air would relax her, but it didn't seem to help. Her heart pounded hard against her chest. It'd been months since her family was murdered and she wanted her husband more than ever. People were directing her life, pushing her to go here and there. Now she was being examined for something implanted inside her. The machine clicked a few times and once again the attendant's voice came over the small speakers next to Lark's head.

"Are you ready, Mrs. Winters?"

"Ready," Lark hollered. *Might as well get this over with.*

As the machine sprang to life the miniature device implanted just above Lark's uterus also sprang to life. The invisible waves of magnetism energized the multi-dimensional particle cells deep inside the small implant and collided with the magnetized plasma. Lark didn't feel a thing. She had no idea what was about to happen.

The explosion first blew apart the light plastic casing and then ripped through the surrounding tissue deep inside Lark's abdomen. Her heart was next, it was liquefied by the intense heat. Her large blood vessels shredded and the fluid bubbled from Lark's body. The only sensation Lark felt was the urge to sleep, and sleep was what Lark did... forever.

The explosion from deep inside resembled a mini cosmic gamma-ray burst. After destroying Lark's body, the intense blast rippled through what little remained of Lark and continued outward into the MRI machine. The heat melted the plastic and metal pieces before the force from the blast had a chance to catch up with it. The room filled with dark smoke and flames shot out in all directions. The attendant barely reacted before the severe heat melted the protective glass. As the waves hit the attendant, his flesh melted from his body. Strong energy tore through his remains and he died instantly.

The ground vibrated beneath the explosion and rocked the entire building. The rooms adjacent to the MRI laboratory vaporized as was anyone unlucky enough to be near. As the blast continued outward, what it gained in momentum it lost in intensity. Eventually the blast became a small mushroom cloud that hovered precariously above the medical center as if a vulture circling its prey.

Lark was now at peace with herself and with her life. She was with her maker who knew and understood she was indeed an innocent victim. Lark became the guardian angel to watch over her family but at a distance.

* * * * * *

"Get over here," the fireman yelled. "Now!"

Nurses, doctors, orderlies, patients and visitors ran through the smoke-filled corridors anxious for a small breath of fresh air. Screams bounced off walls before hovering over the firemen's heads.

"My God!" shrieked a fireman. "What in the hell happened here?"

It was a free-for-all frenzy. Flames danced to the rhythm of the unlucky victims' heartbeats and grew wilder with each passing minute. More and more water sprayed out from the hoses. Many, who were too ill to move on their own, were trapped inside rooms coughing and wheezing from the deadly fumes. Many were burnt beyond recognition, but thank God, had long since left this world for a much better place. They were the ones who were blessed. Those who remained were suffering—they were the cursed.

Darkness adhered cautiously to the walls as the flames continued to grow and spread. A reddish-orange light emanated from the exit signs creating an evilness far more sinister and threatening than the firefighters had ever seen. Light fixtures and other objects melted before their eyes. The water droplets were no match for the sizzling blaze that consumed anything and everything.

"Get out of here!" the Fire Captain cried. "Hurry... everyone... get out of here, the building's going to collapse."

But before anyone could move, the ceiling caved inward as though embracing the clinic one last time. Billowing plumes of smoke rose hauntingly over the small facility that was once a rather nice building. Flames leaped joyously toward the stars as though dancing wickedly and rejoicing in their victory.

Bystanders stood in terror and disbelief. The cars across the street peeled and bubbled from the heat. People ran screaming from the now demolished building that was once a place of hope. Those trapped inside were lost forever—the only logical thing for the rescuers to do now was to save their own lives. One by one, people ran as far away from the evilness as possible.

Chapter 62

THE SMALL TABLE set romantically for two was lit by one candle in the middle of the white linen tablecloth. Some of the tables were draped in either gold or black to create a mixture of intimacy and sensuality. Sounds from the vibrating guitar strings echoed through her mind as the man sang only a few feet away. Tyler glanced into Caiden's eyes and smiled. Her heart pounded harder than ever. It was a wonderful sensation being with Caiden away from their daily work. Today he was hers and she was his. It felt wonderful and sinful to take a day off just to be together. But they needed the short break.

"Madam?" the waiter asked pulling out the chair for her to sit.

Tyler felt like a million dollars as she took her seat. The waiter placed a golden cloth napkin with black embroidered letters over her lap. Today was magical and it could only get better.

The song *Don't Worry* played softly in the background, but the only sounds Tyler heard came directly from Caiden.

"Tyler?" Caiden asked. "Hello, anybody home?"

She smiled waving his hand across her face. Tyler blinked then blushed.

"Oh... I'm sorry, and you were saying... um what?"

"Yes ma'am," the waiter said again. "I was asking about drinks?"

"Um, yes... I'll have whatever he's having," she replied.

"Tyler," Caiden whispered across the table. "I didn't order

anything yet."

Tyler felt not only stupid but out of control. All she wanted was to crawl into Caiden's embrace and melt into a warm nothingness.

"We'll each have a Vodka Blush please," Caiden said to the waiter.

"Certainly," the waiter replied.

"Having a good time?"

"Yes," Tyler answered not able to remove her eyes from Caiden's gaze.

He chuckled. "What? What is it?"

"Nothing. I'm just having a good time."

"Good," Caiden said glancing down at the menu. "Know what you want?"

"You," Tyler replied before she realized what she said.

Caiden glanced over the top of his menu and raised an eyebrow. Tyler was still staring at him.

"I guess I'll order for us," he added with a slight chuckle in his voice. "Our tickets are for the early showing, so we'll be fine. It's only two o'clock. We have plenty of time."

Tyler smiled not hearing a word he was saying. She was engulfed by the love that was swelling within her heart.

Chapter 63

A COOL BREEZE drifted through the tall trees that lined the mountain ridge and invigorated the girls. Carrie was several steps in front of Lacey as they climbed the overgrown mountain path. The aroma of various trees and flowering brush warmed their hearts and soothed their souls. The day was hot but also cool, sweet but also sour. Every few steps Carrie checked on Lacey's progress.

"Need to stop?" Carrie asked.

"Nope," Lacey yelled as she lost her footing.

The ground beneath her gave way and she slid down the side of the tall mountain slope.

"Carrie!" Lacey screamed as her body dragged leaves and other debris with it.

"Damn," Carrie screeched. "Grab onto something."

Dropping everything right where she stood, Carrie sighed. Cautiously she ran after Lacey only to get caught in the flowing avalanche of packed leaves. Small branches and twigs bore into Carrie's palms and legs as she tried to brace her speeding decent.

"Carrie, help!" Lacey screamed.

From up ahead, Carrie could only see the top of Lacey's head and her hair flailing wildly. Then suddenly she was gone. Only the trees in the distance were there—no Lacey.

"Lacey!" Carrie screamed as she realized they were both dead. Obviously Lacey flung over the side of a mountain cliff.

Carrie tried to dig her heels into the soil to stop her wild and crazy ride. But instead of dirt or rock, Carrie felt years of packed dead leaves under her feet. The more she tried to stop, the faster she slid. Until suddenly, she was falling into darkness, into her death. Then there was nothing but a soft landing on years of buildup leaves accompanied by an eerie silence.

"Nice of you to drop in," Lacey said with her face hovering just above Carrie's face. "Are you hurt?"

Carrie lifted herself up onto her elbows and tried to regain her senses. "I don't think so, are you?"

"No, I'm okay. I think we're in some kind of a room."

"A room?" Carrie asked trying to stand up.

"No I'm lying," Lacey mused. "Honestly, I think we're in a cave or something."

Lacey held her flashlight in one hand while reaching down to help Carrie up with the other. The space was dark except for the small ray of light emanating from Lacey's hand.

"So now what, oh Great Explorer?" Lacey moaned. "The opening's about fifteen feet above our heads; there's no way we're going to get out the same way we came in."

Carrie looked up at the small hole that was way above her reach. Dead leaves fell around her as she stared into the dusty sunlight. The sounds of small animals didn't give her any warm or fuzzy feelings, either.

"Okay, now what do we do?" Lacey asked again her voice echoing through the chamber.

"Well?" Carrie moaned. "Do you have another flashlight on you?"

"Where's yours?"

Carrie lifted her gaze longingly into the heavens. "Up there."

"Real smart," Lacey added. "At least I brought *my stuff* with me."

Carrie took the flashlight from Lacey and scanned the small cave. The floor was smooth, too smooth, and the area was massive. Carrie could almost make out a...

"Wait a minute," Carrie whispered. "This is no cave."

"What else can it be up here in the middle of nowhere?" Lacey asked.

"Look, over there, a table with glass bottles on it." Carrie pointed across the room with the light. Lacey squinted trying to adjust her eyes to the darkness.

"Hold on," Lacey stated as she dug through her backpack.

"What are you doing?" Carrie asked, flashing the light directly onto Lacey.

"This," Lacey declared, pulling out a larger flashlight.

"I thought you said…" Carrie began but finished, "…oh never mind."

The room was huge with many large stainless-steel tables. It was a sprawling maze beckoning them to try it out.

"Wow, where are we?" Lacey asked walking through the room.

"Not sure."

"You think anyone's still here?"

"Doubt it," Carrie stated as she continued to examine the mysterious place they just landed in.

Shelves lined the walls with large glass jars containing a liquid with what appeared to be skinned animal parts.

"Yuck," Lacey stated. "What *is* this stuff?"

"It reminds me of a laboratory of some kind," Carrie surmised trying to get a closer look. "Oh my God!"

"What is it?" Lacey hollered.

"Ah shit."

"What?" Lacey screamed.

"These are not animal parts," Carrie whispered turning away.

"Then what are they?"

"Human," Carrie exclaimed shivering.

Carrie glanced around the dark room and tried to absorb everything. It was hard since the only light came from her flashlight. The room was huge and the walls were lined with row after row of shelves filled with what could only be explained as body parts. The more she studied the large and small jars, the more Carrie felt she just entered a side show exhibit on the weird and unnatural world of human evolution.

"What is all this crap?" Lacey asked.

"I'm not sure," Carrie answered.

The middle of the room was filled with stainless steel tables bolted to the floor. Some tables were pulled from their studs and shoved to one side. Probably by animals trapped after falling in as they had. Each table housed a large sink, flushed and drained by a hose hanging above it. The room was draped with these strange contraptions which gave it a more sinister feel.

"I feel like we just entered a house of horrors or something," Lacey whispered.

"I think we did. I mean look at this... it looks like a human fetus but look at the feet!"

"Wow, they almost look webbed or something," Lacey surmised.

"And look at the eyes, they don't look at all human," Carrie added.

"No they don't, they look really weird, they're round like an animal's." Lacey glanced around the room. "Do you get the feeling we shouldn't be here?"

"Yes, I do, and what really bothers me is why? There's a reason this place was abandoned. It's almost as though people left in the middle of something. That desk over there has papers on it. It's like everyone left in a real hurry."

"There's got to be a door around here somewhere," Lacey said, glancing over her shoulder. "I'm going to look for it."

The thing in the jar stared at Carrie with saddened eyes. It was only a couple of feet long. No hair, no legs and no arms. The ears were deformed and so was the nose. The skin was rough looking, not smooth like a normal baby. Carrie was sure she was staring at a newborn human of some kind. Everywhere she looked, jars contained strange creatures floating in a yellow liquid. As she walked through the room, she noticed most of the jars contained body parts instead of a whole baby. Deformed hands and feet, floating within their eternal liquid of existence— eyes, ears, noses, mouths. It was a shopping mall of discarded human body parts and it made her sick.

Heads were next, hundreds of deformed human heads preserved in this disgusting room to be examined and studied. Several skulls were deformed, with cleft lip and pallet, they ranged from mild to severe. Carrie wondered if these babies were killed for just this purpose—to show the progression of the ailment to others.

"Sick," Carrie said to no one in particular.

"Over here!" Lacey yelled. "I found something... hurry."

"What is what?" Carrie asked.

"I'm not sure. What is this thing?" Lacey asked wiping the dust from the wall.

"What is what?" Carrie asked kneeling down to get a better look. "Let me see... it looks like some kind of a.... wall mount... or plaque of some kind."

As she flashed her light upon the emblem she shrieked.

"What now?" Lacey asked.

"Do you know what this is?"

"A picture of a skull, I mean it matches the weirdness of this room," Lacey surmised.

"Duh... am I the only person with brains?" Carrie scolded.

"Excuse me?"

"Lacey... look at this thing," Carrie said pointing to the skull that was sitting on top of two crossed bones. "This emblem is a signature."

"Signature of who?"

"This is not good. We shouldn't be here." As Carrie talked she couldn't remove her eyes or her hand from the plaque embedded in the stone. "It's the signature of The Order of the Skull and Bones."

"The what?" Lacey asked.

"Honestly, don't you read? They were known as The Brotherhood of Death... a secret society from Yale University. This secret society housed some pretty famous and powerful people."

The more Carrie explained the more she felt she was being watched. She didn't like this place and wanted out.

"The members are called *Bonesmen*," Carrie explained.

"Are?" Lacey's eyes widen. "You mean they still exist?"

"Yes. I'm telling you this isn't good."

"Okay, so what do they have to do with this God forsaken place," Lacey asked.

"I don't know. Maybe they abandoned it a long time ago? But we shouldn't be here. I don't think anyone wanted this place found."

"A little late for that now. We're here and we're not going anywhere. We definitely cannot get out the same way we came in. I do hope this place was really abandoned as you say."

"Let's keep looking. We need to find a way out," Carrie said shinning her light around the room.

In one corner of the massive, dark room a large cabinet had fallen against the wall. Lacey peered under one corner and was surprised to find a door.

"Hey, over here Carrie... look what I found."

"Thank goodness," Carrie replied heading in her direction. But before Carrie reached her she stopped to study what appeared to be a body of a two- or three-year-old child. The glass jar was the largest so far and Carrie was surprised she hadn't noticed it before.

"Carrie... help me!" Lacey screamed as she tried to move the cabinet frozen in place.

But Carrie didn't move. She was mesmerized by the beauty of the little girl floating inches from her face. She was tiny but perfectly formed in every way, except for her...

"Carrie?" Lacey asked, now standing behind her. "Egads, what is that? Are those... wings?"

"I believe they are," Carrie surmised. "Isn't she beautiful?"

"Yeah, right. Can we go now?"

"Look at this thing... help me turn the jar," Carrie coached as she reached out to touch the dusty glass.

"Don't touch it!" Lacey screamed, pulling her away. "You don't know if it can hurt you."

"It's dead," Carrie answered placing her hands on both sides of the glass.

Lacey sighed as she helped Carrie cautiously turn the container. "I'm going to regret this, I can tell already."

Chapter 64

GEESHMORE PACED THE floor of his office located deep inside the National Institute of Health's central annex building. He was anxiously awaiting any word of the situation that was now out of control. It was his fault—it had to be. He should have handled everything himself. It would have been the smart thing to do.

"I can't trust a damn soul," he screeched. "I'll have to clean this shit up myself."

As Director of the Center of Excellence for the nation's health, Vernon Geeshmore was the pit of disappointment for his family. It was he who was supposed to make sure every citizen had adequate health coverage and every man, woman and child received only tried and tested drug therapies. But to his wife, he was a failure and to his parents an embarrassment. At a little past forty and a little over six feet, Geeshmore's life had finally come full circle. Time was no longer on his side. With ten years of dedicated serviced to the institute, it would be only natural he concerned himself with his future and not the millions of others who *didn't give a shit* and complained daily about the poor health care they were or were not receiving.

There was a time when Geeshmore listened and changed laws to help those in need. But the more laws he changed and put into action, the lazier people became. The more he gave, the more they took and the less they did for themselves. It was a vicious circle and now he was back where he started with nothing to show except an empty bank account, an ungrateful family and graying temples.

"Director," a voice said through the phone's speaker. "I have Dr. Spangleholtz on line two."

"Thank you, Lellie. Patch him through." As he waited, Geeshmore's temper rose.

"Vernon?" Spangleholtz beamed. "What can I do for you today?"

"Destroy all those damn units," Geeshmore screamed. "NOW!"

CHAPTER 65

EARLY WOKE TO a stabbing pain deep inside her abdomen. Tears rolled down her cheeks as her hands aimed for her stomach.

"Ms. Sutton. Are you in pain?" a woman's voice asked.

"Yes," Early cried.

"I will increase the dose," the friendly voice responded. "Take some deep breaths for me Ms. Sutton. Very deep."

The deeper the breath, the more pain Early felt. She wanted to die, just die and be anywhere but here.

"How is your pain now, Ms. Sutton?" the nurse asked. "Between one and ten?"

"Ten," Early cried.

"I will give you more," she said. "Please take in another deep breath for me."

Early didn't understand. The more she breathed the more it hurt. Why did this woman keep telling her to breathe? But the sharpness was dulling and Early's body was starting to relax.

"Ms. Sutton, what is the pain now... between one and ten?"

"A six," Early said in a slurred voice.

"I'll give you a little more," the nurse said as she checked the instruments and tubes attached to Early's body.

Early continued to breathe as deeply as she could. The pain was definitely easing and she was slipping into a wonderful darkness.

"Ms. Sutton, your pain..."

"A two," Early whispered as she fell into a peaceful slumber.

* * * * * *

Loomsbury was stumped. With the latest odd cases assigned to him, he didn't know if he was coming or going. He studied the DNA results from the young boy. It matched his mother's, but then again it did not. Although human, a few strands were most definitely from the *Surnia Ulula* species, or better known as the Northern Hawk Owl. A bird native to Washington, which is where Carrie and Lacey are currently assigned. The odd DNA strands were added where the boy's eyesight would be affected. He read the report again. He thought about Carrie and Lacey, and then the boy. He tumbled them around his mind contemplating the results. As the minutes ticked, Loomsbury had a large pain in the pit of his stomach.

"I've got to examine that boy!" he yelled.

* * * * * *

Drake jumped out of his chair in the waiting room.

"How'd she do?"

"She did good, very, very good..." the surgeon answered. "We got it and she's fine. It was much deeper than we expected. Much deeper."

"How long had it been in her?" Drake asked.

"For some time, years probably. Her tissue had already fused with it. The infection caused her initial pain. If I had to guess I would say it's been in her somewhere in the neighborhood of five or six years."

"My God!" Drake exclaimed. "Where's the damn thing now?"

"The lab has it for analysis," the doctor answered. "They'll let you see her soon. She's in recovery and will be for a few more hours. Why not get something to eat? You could use the break."

"Come on, babe," Vickie urged. "We can do nothing for her now, we'll come back."

Drake glanced at his wife and frowned. It hurt him deeply to think of what Early had just gone through. It angered him. Why was it there in the first place and for what purpose? As they left the hospital for the nearest restaurant, Drake's phone rang. He listened to the hysterical Shelby scream and cry about Lark and could only stare at his wife in horror.

* * * * * *

"Hi sweetheart," Drake said as Early opened her eyes a couple of hours later. He had a strong but loving grip on her hand. Vickie's eyes were tearing as she watched her husband soothe a woman she felt she knew better than herself. At first Vickie just knew Early was guilty. But after meeting her and reading over the case file, it was clear Early did not hurt her family. Witnessing an innocent person go through hell to prove their story, scared Vickie to death. What if something like this happened to her someday? Who would take care of her and fight to find the truth? Vickie loved her husband and was proud of him. She was about to say something when a man entered the room.

"How is she?" Dr. Barnes asked.

"Not sure," Drake replied not taking his eyes off Early. "She hasn't spoken a word."

"They had to go deep, went through layers of muscle. Moved her organs around... I'm sure she was in pain when she came to. She's on some strong meds that'll make her sleepy for awhile."

"Yes," Drake whispered. "They're taking good care of her."

"Did you hear?" Barnes asked.

"Hear what?" Drake added glancing at the doctor.

"Four of the accused women were blown apart, that's what. It was the same device implanted inside your girl. I highly recommend you and the other lawyers pretend *your* clients were also blown to pieces... unless... you want them dead too. They'll be safe if people think they're six feet under."

"I heard about them. Thank God we got Early's out in time. And just how do you suggest we fake their deaths?" Drake asked sarcastically.

"I'm sure it's not hard. But I know where they *would* be safe," Barnes added. "But I'll need to make a few calls first."

* * * * * *

Gabe stood protectively in front of his mother as Loomsbury entered their room. "My name is Gabe, and this is my mom. Her name's Laflur Jolene Huntington. But she goes by Lafie." Gabe smiled at the man, but Lafie continued to stare into her hands.

Loomsbury took a seat near Gabe and his mother.

"Hi Gabe, nice to meet you," Loomsbury said, "but it's your mother I need to talk to."

"What answers do you need?" Gabe asked.

"Mrs. Huntington... Lafie. We know Gabe is a hybrid. But we don't understand how or why."

Lafie raised her head and said softly, "He's not a hybrid."

"But the DNA..."

"His genes were spliced... upgraded. He has a human mother and a human father."

"How... why?" Loomsbury asked.

"Are you going to kill us?" she asked.

Loomsbury sat back. With her question came a pounding in his chest.

"No," Loomsbury stated. "Absolutely not."

"Who are you?" she asked.

"I am Dr. Loomsbury, the head scientist here."

"And where is *here*?"

"Has no one talked with you?"

"No, no one."

"I see," Loomsbury was surprised; this was completely against The Agency's protocol. "Well, perhaps we need to."

"Perhaps," she replied.

Chapter 66

THE AFTERNOON SHOWERS created a newness that was mesmerizing and soothing. Greghardt stood in the middle of the Oval Office and stared down at his brown leather shoes. His pants flowed flawlessly around the curve of each loafer. Lewis studied Greghardt's movements while shaking his head. He knew his friend was getting old, but now he wondered if perhaps his mind was also out of date.

"They're called shoes, Allen," Lewis mused.

"Really?" Allen answered not taking his eyes off the floor. "I did not know that."

"Funny," Lewis added turning to glance out the window, "it stopped raining... for now. Strange how a nice shower can make everything seem so clean and fresh."

"Yes it is," Greghardt replied not taking his eyes off his shoes.

Lewis watched Greghardt staring at his feet.

"Okay, I give up," Lewis said walking toward Greghardt. "What's wrong? Did you accidently wear two different types or something?"

Greghardt looked up and snickered. "Please, I'm not that bad off... not yet anyway."

"Honestly, what's wrong?"

"I just realized where I'm standing," Greghardt said then added, "and I'm bothered by the realization."

"Explain please?" Lewis asked sitting on one of the sofas. "We've been here many times before, this is nothing out of the ordinary."

Greghardt inhaled a deep breath and let it out slowly before he spoke. "This room has been here for how many years? A hundred or so? Since, ah... Taft if I remember correctly... in 1909 I believe it was... yes, in 1909 William Howard Taft walked this very room. Way over a hundred years ago. This very office."

Now Lewis knew Greghardt had lost his mind. "Okay, and your point is?"

"This office has seen a lot of action, has it not," before Lewis could answer he added, "and it has seen many faces both new and old. But only somewhere in between does the answer lie."

Lewis sighed and clasped his hands together. Not only had his dear friend Allen Greghardt lost it, but now he wondered if he ever had it to begin with.

"Thus," Greghardt continued, "we must examine what little we have to conclude we're right back where we started."

"Which is?" Lewis asked getting up to stand next to his friend and co-worker.

"Here," Greghardt pointed to the floor. "We started here and we'll finish here. They made this room round for a reason, and that reason was to show how everything comes back to its origin at some point."

In a strange and scary way, what Greghardt was saying actually made some sense to him. Now he wondered if he too was losing his mind. Lewis stared down at his feet. "Full circle, huh?"

"Full circle," Greghardt repeated.

"What are you two looking at? Did you put on different shoes or something?" Strickland entered the room only to witness two grown men staring down at their feet. "Or did you lose something? Need help finding it?"

"No and no," Greghardt answered.

"What's going on then?" Strickland asked as she laid her papers on her desk.

"Come see," Greghardt said.

Strickland stood between the two men and stared down at the floor, then up at their eyes. They did not blink.

"Full circle," Greghardt whispered.

Strickland raised her eyes as she said, "Huh?"

"Allen here has it all figured out, Madam President," Lewis

said smiling. "It has to do with walking in circles."

"Oh, I figured there was a simple explanation to everything," Strickland stated with a bewildered look on her face. "Okay, start talking."

"Well let's look at what we have." Greghardt said. "It all began with the women who woke up in court remembering nothing. Not one, mind you, but several. Then we're told they were drugged with the help of an implant. Next we have a company in Washington that's analyzing tampered DNA. We've assigned two agents to investigate a hospital in the same region and odd bones were stolen from a lab. Not to mention the female Army general who's missing, or for that matter, those poor women blown to bits from the implants."

Greghardt stopped talking and glanced up at Strickland. His face was red and flushed. She'd never seen him so angry before. He frowned adding, "I'll bet our government is involved... somehow."

Strickland didn't respond. Memories of years past and how she was used by her predecessor became vivid in her mind. The idea of another person using his or her government position to gain personal wealth angered her. Would this crazy world ever be a safe and wonderful place? Why couldn't people accept the only way to get ahead in life was to work hard and be honest?

"It would have to be someone in either the CDC or Department of Health, that's the first place I'd look," Strickland said staring at Greghardt. "Why always on my watch?"

"It's not you sweetheart." Greghardt said patting her arm. "Let us check it out."

Strickland nodded.

"Safer that way," Lewis added.

"Safer for who?" she asked.

Chapter 67

CHARLOTTE SAT ON the armchair next to the smoldering fireplace. Although she was in deep trouble, she felt better about herself and more in control than ever. The feeling of empowerment overwhelmed her. Before entering the room, Charlotte decided she'd fly away and be free of them forever if they punished her. The large room was cold and the warm fire was inviting.

She always loved this room with the huge marble and brick walls and large squared floor. Her patent-leather shoes echoed as she walked. If she had to flee for her safety, she would miss this room more than any of the others. The large sculptured lion heads seemed to be smiling at her. She wasn't sure if they were mocking or if they were proud of her for being independent.

"Now what's keeping them?" Charlotte whispered. Sitting on her knees, she glanced around the chair to see if anyone was coming down the stairs or through the wooden front doors.

Charlotte sighed and slid onto the floor. Her bare feet touched without making a sound. She stood in the middle of the large room with her hands on her hips. Her anger was rising. They scolded her over and over and sent her to her room. It's been days and now she was waiting to be punished, but no one was showing up.

"Pssst!" a voice echoed into the room.

"Who's there?" she asked glancing around. She was sure it was one of those stupid kids playing a joke on her again.

"Pssst... over here quick!" the voice said a little louder.

Again Charlotte scanned the room only to find no one. "Who's there?"

"Over here!" the voice yelled. "Here!"

Squinting toward the sound, she made out the dark figure of a boy trying to get her attention. He was partly hidden behind a statue in the far corner where the sunlight didn't reach. After glancing around to make sure she was alone, Charlotte half ran, half walked into the dark.

"Who are you?" she asked.

"You must follow me." His voice was full of urgency and his eyes showed a fear Charlotte had never known.

"Why?" Now she was curious how this boy was able to get into the house with no one seeing him. "How did you get in here anyway?"

"Look, we have no time for talk. Follow me."

His sternness scared her and she backed away.

"I'm not going to hurt you, but they will. They'll cut off your wings now that you've used them. You should never have let them see you. Do you want that to happen?"

"Well of course not," Charlotte answered but then added, "How would you know what they'd do to me?"

"Are you going to follow me or not? I'm not going to get caught because of you. Now stay here if you want. But I'm out of here. Are you coming?"

Charlotte thought for a few seconds then decided it would be more of an adventure to follow this boy. Besides, she could always come back if anything wasn't right and if the kids were playing another joke, she'd tell.

"Okay, let's go," she said.

"This way, and hold on to this rope. It's dark down here. Hang on okay?"

"Okay." She giggled.

The boy pushed a wooden plank. It moved slightly. Then he pushed on an emblem engraved in the floor. He turned it right, then left, then right two times. A small shaft opened a few feet away and they darted inside. They walked only a few feet before the shaft closed behind them.

"Don't talk until I say so," he whispered. "And be as quiet as you can."

Charlotte nodded as she grabbed tightly to the rope. Every so often she reached out and touched the brick wall. The floor was smooth and level which made it easy for her to follow this strange kid. They descended a round staircase, one step at a time. In the dark it was hard for her to keep her balance. When they finally reached the bottom, the boy flicked on a flashlight and handed one to her.

"We can talk now, no one can hear us down here."

"Who are you?" she asked.

"I'm your brother. My name's Charlie, we have the same parents. We've watched you grow over the years and how you've changed. But when I saw you fly, I knew they would have to do something. What they're doing here is bad and no one can know."

"No one? What's that supposed to mean and *what's a parent*?" she asked. "And, you said you're my brother?"

"Okay, slow down," he said as they walked side by side through the long tunnel. "Listen up. Each person has a mother and a father... okay? But a mother and a father can have lots of kids. You're a kid, a girl like you is called a daughter." As they walked, Charlie explained to Charlotte how she came to be and how they're related.

Her eyes brightened as she realized she was a part of someone else, and she shared the same blood with another living person. Perhaps she was not alone after all.

"Are our parents still alive?" she asked.

"No, they killed them a long time ago. But our grandparents are. That's where I've been living and where I'm taking you."

"But I don't understand," she added. "How old are you?"

"I'm fourteen," he said. "We lost a couple of sisters before you were born. Their bones were too soft."

"I still don't get it," Charlotte added.

"You will," he replied. "Now follow me, we're almost to the trees."

* * * * * *

Lee woke feeling much better. The pain was gone and so was the fever. The attendant smiled as she adjusted her covers.

"We must be feeling better today," she said.

"Yes," Lee answered. "I am. I would like to get up."

"Let me find the doctor first," the attendant replied. "Just to make sure it's okay."

The attendant left the room and Lee reached for her cell phone. It took a couple of seconds for the call to go through but soon her friend was on the other side.

"Are you all right?" Tabatha yelled. "I've been worried sick about you. Where have you been, I must have left a million messages."

"How long has it been?" Lee asked.

The phone was silent for a few seconds before there was an answer. "Long since what?"

"Since we last talked."

"At least a week," Tabatha groaned. "I'm worried, Lee."

"A week?" Lee screamed. "No way has it been a week."

"Yes way," Tabatha yelled. "And I'll feel much better when you're home. When do you come back?"

"I don't know. Look if I don't call in a couple of hours, come and find me, okay?"

"Right," Tabatha sighed. "I'll just jump on the next plane and fly right over... to where ever *over* is."

Chapter 68

A KNOCK AT the door announced Tina's presence.

"I'm sorry to interrupt Madam President, but Dr. Lewis has an important call on the secure line."

"Thank you, Tina," Strickland said as she waved Lewis to the phone.

Lewis clicked the speaker button. He knew whatever Martha had to say affected everyone. "Lewis here."

"Dr. Lewis, I'm sorry to intrude sir, but I have a few messages for you," Martha announced. Martha's one of Lewis's personal assistants and is extremely formal and accurate. If Martha was calling, then it was important.

"That's fine, Martha," Lewis urged. "What are they?"

"First, we'll have a new visitor soon, a Ms. Early Sutton. She's to be transferred in a few days," Martha said with a pause.

"That's great, Martha. Thank you. I hope that's all that's going on right now."

"No sir."

Lewis cleared his throat before speaking. "You called me *sir* which can only mean it isn't good."

"I'm afraid not. We've lost contact with Carrie and Lacey."

"What do you mean *lost contact?*"

"We cannot reach them by cell or radio, nor do they show up on the scope. It's as though they fell through a hole in the Earth or something."

"Martha," Lewis scolded. "People do not fall into a hole and disappear. I want to know as soon as anyone finds anything. Understand?"

"Jeff," Greghardt said.

"Don't Jeff me," Lewis argued. "I know it's not my fault. But damn it. I sent them on this mission and I didn't think it through first."

"Jeff!" Strickland shouted. "I think you should hear this."

The three stared at the television as the news caster discussed the latest developments.

"... the seventh woman this year to suddenly wake up and find herself in a courtroom with no idea as to how she got there or why, Meredith Creeten, collapsed shortly after screaming out in shock. Her lawyer, Justin Monish, moved for a continuance in lieu of the recent developments. The judge has asked for a psychological examination before the case continues and ..."

"My God, it's happening again," Lewis exclaimed.

"How can this be?" Strickland asked. "What's going on?"

"We need to get a full scale investigation going right away," Greghardt added.

"I thought I already did that," Lewis said.

"I canceled it," Greghardt replied.

"You what?" Strickland and Lewis yelled at the same time.

"... I'm Jackie Peters coming to you live from..."

* * * * * *

Constable Fahey stood in front of the castle wondering what would be the best course of action. He knew Dr. Nestle was not someone a person played with or challenged. Nestle was a dangerous man with a long list of powerful associates. But the longer he waited, the more Fahey knew something terrible would happen. He took in a deep breath before climbing the stairs and opening the door.

He entered the lobby of the Stonefield Castle Hotel only to be greeted by men he did not recognize. Each nodded his head as Fahey walked past. Fahey calculated there were about sixty. Some wore military uniforms and others plain suits. Fahey noticed the bar out of the corner of his eye and decided a stiff drink would be good about now.

With glass in hand, he turned to study each person. No one

spoke, each seemed to be engulfed in his own private world.

Damn strange. Then he saw him. Dr. Nestle stood only a few feet away staring at him with his dark and intent eyes. As the doctor walked toward him, Fahey gulped down the rest of his drink.

"Good day to you, Doc," Fahey said.

"What may we help you with, Constable?"

"Nothing," Fahey responded turning to the bartender. "I just came for a drink."

"Long way to come for a short glass of ice and liquor, Constable."

"Perhaps," Fahey replied taking a sip. "But I like the drinks here. They're better than anywhere else."

The men stared at each other for a few minutes before Fahey added, "Another Bones affair I suppose, obvious as to the way no one mingles with anyone else."

"What do you want, Constable?" Nestle asked. "This is our annual conference. We have one every year, as you well know. So what do you want?"

"As I said, a drink."

Nestle glanced around. He loosened his tie and adjusted his slacks. "I see. Very well then."

Fahey watched as Nestle became lost in the crowd. Then as if they were never there, the men disappeared, one by one, through various hallways and doors. When Fahey finished his drink, the lobby was empty of everyone except him and the bartender.

* * * * * *

Nestle paced the floor pounding his fist into his hand. The situation was out of control and if things didn't calm down soon, the organization would be in jeopardy. What wasn't adding up was the general. She concerned him. Why would a volunteer act so standoffish and confused? Then there was the Constable who would not stop snooping around. What was he searching for, it couldn't be the general. She agreed to be here. Pacing the floor, his temper rose and his heart pounded. His head ached. The decision of what to do about Geeshmore kept nagging at him and he would have to make a decision soon. A knock at the door woke Nestle from his thoughts.

"Yes?"

"Sir, it's me," a voice echoed back.

"Enter," Nestle replied.

A young man entered wearing a concerned expression. They stood and stared each other before either spoke.

"Sir, I've been asked to speak with you about some of the problems plaguing us recently. Perhaps you would like to join us downstairs so we can talk as a group."

Nestle nodded. "Let's get Spangleholtz and Geeshmore on a conference call, they'll have a few words to add."

The young boy bowed slightly then left. Nestle walked to the window and peered out. His emotions were running wild. He watched as a flock of birds flew past. The waters were calm and the air clear. It was a beautiful day outside, but inside it was storming.

"I'll be damned," he whispered, "if I will allow anyone to break down this society. We have not been around for as long as we have for nothing."

Chapter 69

"EARLY!" DRAKE YELLED running into her hospital room. "I found them."

"Found who," she asked sitting up in bed.

"Feeling better?"

"Found who? And yes I am, thank you," Early replied.

"I found the doctors who handled your daughters' eggs."

"Really? I could have told you who they were."

"No no, you don't understand," Drake interrupted. "The building was destroyed in a fire. But we've track the doctors down."

"A fire? Where? When?"

"A few days after you were arrested," Drake continued but was interrupted again.

"What are you talking about?"

"The clinic, it was destroyed in a fire," Drake declared.

"And what does that have to do with helping me?"

"Oh Early, sweetie, we have to bring you up to speed," Drake said.

"Okay, explain."

"The clinic where you were impregnated wasn't a real clinic. In fact, there's no record of a clinic ever being there."

"But..."

"Just listen. I figured someone had to have rented it so we searched and found the owner. The owner didn't want to talk at first. But the more we pushed and paid, the more he did. We found them sweetheart, we found them."

"And?"

"Listen to this. We tracked the doctors to a hospital in Washington, and not just any hospital either. It's a research facility." Drake glanced down the page he held in his hands. "Ummm, here it is... Barker Institute. It's located in the mountains, not easily accessible either."

"And that means?"

"It means you were set up," Drake surmised, "somehow."

"How in the world do you connect *me* to that facility?"

"Don't you get it?" Drake asked. "Why would a research facility in Washington set up an invetro-fertilization facility in New York? Now all I have to do is connect your husband to this facility, no wait, that other lady... darn what was her name, Sterling... Stalling... Starling..."

"Marty Starling?" Early asked.

Drake stopped reading his paper and stared into Early's eyes. "I've got to go. If I can somehow connect Ms. Starling and your husband to that clinic."

Early watched Drake dash out of her room. She rolled her eyes and laid her head on her pillow. What was left of her life was becoming more and more complicated every day.

* * * * * *

"You may see your daughter now," the nurse whispered to Marty who'd fallen asleep. "I'll stay here and watch your girls if you'd like."

"May I take them with me?" Marty asked, not wanting to be away from them.

"Yes, of course."

Marty towed her little ones behind her as she entered her sick daughter's room. Tubes and wires were hooked into Lizzie on just about every place of her little body.

"Oh my," Marty exclaimed.

"It isn't as bad as it looks," Spangleholtz said from a corner in Lizzie's room. "She's going to be fine."

"What's wrong with her?" Marty almost cried.

"She has a streptococcus germ, that's all."

"Is she contagious?" Marty asked concerned for the welfare of her other girls. "I mean, I don't want..."

"No, she isn't contagious," he answered. "But when she's well, we need to talk. It's time you fully understand everything about your daughter."

Marty stared at the man with a quizzical look. She already knew everything she needed to know about her daughter. Whatever could this man be talking about?

Chapter 70

THE DOOR WAS not easy to open. It was sealed tight by the corrosion of time. Carrie needed some things from her backpack, but unfortunately it was way above her head and out of her reach. It'd been a long week and she was ready for it to be over—although she did thrive on adventures, this was getting ridiculous.

"Now what?" Lacey asked.

"Need to find the key," Carrie surmised.

"Excuse me? A key, you want to find a key? Are you insane?"

"I've been told I am," Carrie replied searching the massive room.

Lacey rubbed her face with the back of her hands and sighed. It didn't take long before Carrie returned with various bottles along with some other strange objects.

"Like I said, I needed to find the key. Now, help me please."

"What are we doing?"

Carrie handed Lacey a bottle. "We have to unlock this door. I found some acid and other things to use. If we drip this stuff around the frame it'll eat through the corrosion. Then I can freeze the lock with this dry ice stuff. The metal should shatter. Like I said, a key."

The girls worked carefully dripping the acid around the door frame. Carrie's feet were planted firmly on a solid metal chair placed near the door. Large rubber gloves protected her hands and lower arms, and a long metal tongue held the glass container housing the acid. Lacey stood on another chair wearing the same type of gloves and dripping the same type of acid. As they talked, they worked, which helped to make the time pass faster.

Not once did they discuss their situation or what would happen if they couldn't find a way out. They shared stories about their lives and their past experiences. Lacey finally told Carrie about her time in South America and what she could remember. Although her memory was vague and spotty, the feelings of what she experienced were still very vivid in her mind. Through their hours of work, Carrie admired Lacey for talking about herself, the things that made Lacey, Lacey. Not often did people speak so freely around her. It never occurred to Carrie that perhaps she wasn't the only person who had a sad beginning in life. Carrie told Lacey about her drunken father. She explained how her mother died giving birth to her and her father never forgave Carrie for killing his wife. Living with a drunk left a bruise on Carrie's soul she knew would never completely heal.

Those few hours together brought Carrie and Lacey to a closeness that frightened and enlightened them. Both girls grew not only in spirit but in a knowledge about life that day.

* * * * * *

Lacey giggled as the old metal door creaked open. It took all their strength along with a metal rod, but the door slowly gave way. The area beyond was dark and damp, and held a musty odor.

"Okay, are you ready?" Carrie asked.

Lacey nodded.

"Don't touch the door," Carrie cautioned. "There's still acid on it."

Together they cautiously entered the dark hallway.

"Do you have a gun?" Lacey asked.

"Yes," Carrie answered. "And you?"

"Yes."

As they walked, they scanned the hallway the best they could with the dim flashlights.

"Wait," Carrie said squatting to the floor.

"What?"

"I play video games and unless you make a map of where

you are and where you've been, you can get lost real fast." Carrie pulled out a pencil and paper from her shirt pocket and scribble out a rough map.

"Where'd those come from?" Lacey asked.

"Found them in an old desk."

Carrie drew a round circle to indicate the room they just left, she then added the hallway where they now stood. "I don't know which way is north, but I believe we're headed deeper into the mountain. So I must conclude we're walking west. Anytime we make a turn or go up or down, we must remember to add it to this map. Okay?"

"Okay," Lacey replied. "Perhaps I should make one too?"

"No, too confusing," Carrie said shoving the paper into her shirt. "Let's go."

They walked down the hall encased in a strange smooth surface. It reflected their lights and reminded Carrie of a metallic substance. But she couldn't tell for sure what it was made of. They reached the end of the hall, and had to decide to go either right or left.

"Now what?" Lacey asked.

"You pick," Carrie replied.

"Umm, left," Lacey answered.

"Okay, left it is."

But left only took them to a dead-end with small rooms on both sides. One room was a closet for brooms and mops. The other was a restroom for both men and women.

"Yah gotta go?" Carrie asked.

"Actually, *yes*," Lacey answered. "I wonder if it works."

Carrie pushed on the handle and the toilet flushed. "Well, there's water."

"Okay, you keep watch for me and I'll keep watch for you."

"If I wasn't so hungry," Carrie began, "I'd recommend we just sleep here tonight. But we need to find something to eat."

"Food would be good about now," Lacey said as she shut the door behind her.

* * * * * *

The corridor seemed endless as the two walked down the metallic hall. Echoes from their footsteps muffled as they came to the end. A large door blocked their way to either freedom into the fresh mountain air, or their death... a dead end.

"Now what?" Lacey asked.

"We try the door."

"Oh like it's just going to open?" Lacey asked.

But as Carrie turned the knob and pushed, the door opened and fresh cool air swirled passed. Beams from their flashlights danced into the room as they scanned the area for hidden dangers.

"So far so good," Carrie whispered.

"Where are we?" Lacey asked.

"Not real sure."

The door shut behind them when they walked in. The sound echoed loudly for a few seconds and made both girls cringe. Frozen in place, they waited for someone, or something to jump out of the darkness and attack. But only silence greeted them.

"Something's off," Carrie whispered.

"I know," Lacey said. "I feel like we're being watched."

The room was big, but not as large as the laboratory. Instead of a tile floor, this room was carpeted. From the dim light, Carrie could tell the place was clean and tidy. Several couches lined the walls and small tables with chairs sat in the middle. At the far end, which was only about twenty feet away, Carrie could make out what appeared to be a kitchenette.

"Some kind of a conference room?" Carrie whispered.

"Maybe," Lacey answered.

Standing side to side, the girls examined the room. Several doors on both sides led to places unknown. They stood and listened for whatever would attack them.

"Did you hear that?" Lacey whispered.

"Yes," Carrie replied. "Sounds like heavy breathing."

"I don't think we're alone," Lacey whispered through her tears.

Chapter 71

CHARLOTTE STOOD IN awe in front of the man and woman smiling down at her. The small-framed house was not what she was used to. The modest living room would only sit about six and was miniature in comparison to the large room with the two carved lion heads. The house was a single story, and Charlotte was used to many floors.

"Charlotte," the woman said. "What a pretty name. I'm your grandmother."

"Hello."

"Charlie told us all about you and I've so wanted to meet you." The woman spoke with such a smooth and wonderful voice it gave Charlotte a warm and secure feeling.

"I don't understand," Charlotte said with a frown.

Charlie handed a picture to Charlotte and explained who everyone was and how she was related to them.

"So my mother was your daughter?" Charlotte asked.

"Yes that's correct," the woman replied.

"And she's dead?"

"Yes, I'm afraid so," the woman added.

"How?"

"Well," the woman said, holding out her arms, but Charlotte didn't want to go to her. "You see, not all people are good. Your mother and father volunteered to have their children in a special way. They wanted the perfect child, the smartest and the prettiest. I wasn't for it, but I couldn't talk them out of it. Their minds were set. Their doctors were bad people. I never saw my daughter again once she checked herself into *that* clinic. We moved here fourteen years ago to be close to her. We just couldn't say goodbye. Then one day Charlie found us. He'd sneak out of the compound from time to time to explore. After a while we became friends. One night he broke into a file room and stole his records. That was when we discovered he was our grandson. He was five at the time. Later we learned of you and your sisters. Charlie ran away from that place and has lived here ever since. I asked Charlie to leave you alone, unless you needed us. But when he told us about your ability to fly we knew you'd no longer be safe. So, here you are."

"But," Charlotte started then stopped.

"But what sweetie?"

"But why don't you have wings like me?" Charlotte asked.

"I don't know," the woman answered. "I can only assume it's because of the altering of your genetics. How you have wings, we have no idea. But you *are* our granddaughter. You belong here with us. If you'll have us?"

Charlotte glanced around the small but comfortable room. She was frightened and curious at the same time. She thought of her room back at the castle and wanted to be there right now.

"Where would I sleep?" Charlotte asked.

"We have a room for you," Charlie replied. "Come, I'll show you."

Charlotte followed Charlie down the short hallway. The thick carpet under her feet felt warm and soft. A small kitchen off the living room was neat and tidy. She counted four bedrooms. One small bathroom with pretty yellow walls was across from her room. She smiled when she saw a window framed with pink and yellow fluffy curtains. Her eyes widened when she saw the single canopy-bed with matching drapes. Dolls and books filled the shelves of a built-in bookcase. The rug beneath her feet was even more soft and warm than in the hallway.

"Well?" Charlie asked.

"Is this my room?"

"Yep, if you want it."

Charlotte glanced around her new room and smiled at Charlie. Her heart pounded and her head was spinning. The room was nice and warm and the people seemed so friendly, but something was bothering her... something just wasn't right.

* * * * * *

Constable Fahey paced his office. Nestle being in town could only mean one thing—trouble. And why were they hiding the woman general the US government was looking for? People just don't disappear off the face of the Earth, or for that matter from inside a castle. Something was going on and he was going to get to the bottom of it. Reaching for a cigarette, a thought flashed through his mind. He had to get back inside the castle.

"Henley, get in here."

"Yes sir," a young man replied running into Fahey's office.

"I'm tired of being afraid," Fahey said. "You hear me, tired."

"Yes sir, tired sir," the man repeated.

"Well I am," Fahey said gathering his thoughts, "tired."

* * * * * *

Constable Fahey stared into the dark eyes. His heart pounded and sweat dripped down his face. With his hands tied behind his back, he had no other choice but to endure the salty sting.

"Tell me, Constable," Roland Nestle said pulling a small chair under him. "Why do you always do this to yourself... to me?"

"What do you mean?"

"You just can't help yourself can you?"

"I said, I like the drinks here," the Constable replied with a half smile.

"Well you can have as much as you want, after you tell us why you have the need to continuously spy on us."

"I'm not spying," the Constable defended.

"Then what else explains why you're hiding in our bushes all the time?" Nestle asked. "People don't hide in bushes unless there's a reason. Especially if they only want a drink. They come inside. Do they not, Constable?"

The Constable nodded his head. He knew he was in trouble, and there was nothing he could do about it. As Nestle asked the questions, an older man with long graying hair entered the room with a syringe filled with a greenish liquid.

"My night cap I suppose," Fahey whispered.

"I always said you were a smart man," Nestle replied.

"Were?" Fahey asked as Nestle shot the warm green liquid into Fahey's arm.

"Yes," Nestle stated holding the empty syringe in front of Fahey's eyes, "*were*."

"Well, good night then," Fahey mumbled falling into an empty darkness.

"You mean goodbye," Nestle added.

Chapter 72

DRAKE STOOD IN front of the research facility in Washington. The building was huge with large tinted windows. It looked out of place in the heavily forested mountain terrain. Over ten stories of glass and concrete greeted him with a cold and starch facade. Just standing in front of the huge structure gave Drake an eerie and foreboding feeling of doom.

"Lost?" a young lady asked from behind.

"Oh my." Drake exhaled. "You scared the shit out of me!"

"I'm sorry." Tyler giggled. "I'm Dr. Brighten, people call me Tyler."

"Nice to meet you, Doctor," Drake said shaking her hand.

"Again, lost?"

"Well, perhaps you can help me," he said.

"Oh?"

"I'm here to see a doctor and maybe you can direct me," he said hoping for a break.

"Well I'll help in any way I can."

"Tyler?"

Tyler turned and grinned as Caiden hurried toward them.

"This is my partner Dr. Harding," Tyler said. "This is... I'm sorry I didn't get your name."

"Sorry, Drake Anderson."

"What's going on?" Caiden asked.

"Not sure," Tyler added.

"I'm here on business," Drake answered.

"I see, and what business is that?" Caiden asked.

Not sure how others would respond to him bringing up the recent murders, he tilted his head and sighed. But he couldn't just stand there looking crazy. With nothing to lose, Drake said, "Have you heard about the women who woke up in court with no memory of murdering their families? Well... I'm the lawyer for the first one, Early Sutton. She's innocent and I'm going to prove it." Drake lowered his head and waited for a response.

"And you need a doctor because?" Tyler asked.

"I don't believe we can help you, Mr. Anderson," Caiden said.

Tyler rolled her eyes and continued where she left off. "How can we possibly help?"

"My client was impregnated by invetro fertilization. I've traced the doctors who did the procedure to this place. This is my last hope," Drake said not raising his head.

"We can't help you," Caiden added.

Drake looked up at Caiden and frowned. His last lead was going nowhere. "I see. But if you should change your mind... think of anything, I'm staying at the Wayside Inn on the main highway." He handed Tyler his card.

"No one here can help you, and if you know what's best you'll be on the next flight out of town," Caiden replied.

Caiden grabbed Tyler's arm and pulled her into the building. As they entered, Tyler glanced back and watched as Drake walked toward the parking lot. He looked lost and alone.

* * * * * *

Tyler re-read the reports for the fifth time. The words blared out at her. After wiping her eyes, she re-read the words again not believing what she was seeing. Tyler tossed the papers aside and rubbed her face. She yelled, but no words came out, just a high-pitched screech. She rubbed her face again.

"What in the world is the problem?" Caiden asked, turning to get a better look. "Are you okay?"

"No I'm not!" she yelled. "I'm not fucking okay."

"Wow, such language," he scolded. "Let me see what you're looking at."

With shaking hands and sweat running down her temples, Tyler handed Caiden the report. He read over the words and numbers and shook his head.

"This cannot be."

"But it is," she replied.

They stared into each other's eyes, neither wanting to give in to the other's beliefs. Tyler blinked and Caiden froze.

"This cannot be," he whispered.

"But it is. RNA strands are continually made, broken down and reused. No one could possibly survive, much less flourish. Any unknown RNA or DNA entering the body would be destroyed, and the UV rays, my God the implications," Tyler whispered scratching her head.

"So we're back to whispering, are we?" he asked with a wink.

Ignoring his comment, Tyler continued, "This is a blood sample from a young girl. About six, I believe."

"She must be very ill," Caiden added.

"I don't know, but how can a human be alive with RNA strands instead of DNA? That's impossible isn't it?"

"Obviously not," he answered. "What were you supposed to test on this sample?"

"Deoxyribose and ribose sugar levels," she replied.

"But you ran tests on everything else. Why?"

"Because only ribose sugar was detected," she said with a frown.

"Then this person can't be alive," Caiden replied. "You must be testing samples from a dead person."

"Nope, this child's alive. Here's her chart." Tyler handed Caiden the file who scanned the words.

"You know what, Caiden, this crap scares the shit out of me."

"That's not what concerns me," he answered. "How this person came to be... now that does."

Chapter 73

LOOMSBURY SAT SILENTLY as Gabe's mother was briefed by an internal agent. He watched as she listened with confusion written all over her face. He waited a few minutes before he decided it was time to step in and help out.

"Excuse me," Loomsbury said standing behind the agent. "I believe you've confused them enough. Allow me to take it from here."

The agent nodded and left the room. With not much else to do, Loomsbury smiled at the two very frightened people.

"We're here to help. I'm sure this is puzzling, but please believe me when I say we're here to ensure your safety. It's obvious someone wants you out of the picture, whatever that picture may be."

"Maybe I can help," Lafie said. "Perhaps if I..."

"You really don't have to say anything."

"You're a doctor, you'll figure it out anyway," Lafie said with a strange smile.

"I'm listening," Loomsbury replied anxious to hear her story.

"I'm ninety-three. My son is twelve, he'll be thirteen in about six weeks. I worked for the Warrington Mental Hospital until a few weeks ago when it..."

"Exploded?" Loomsbury added.

"Yes, until it was destroyed," she said with a frown. "My son's an invetro baby. Mine and the head scientist at the facility. We fell in love and decided to give it a go. However, Gabe's

DNA strand was upgraded a little."

"You mean with owl DNA?"

"Yes, but only for his eyes. It worked, the downfall is Gabe has a hard time seeing in daylight. His vision is much better at night. We didn't realize it would destroy his day vision. Otherwise, he's normal in every way."

"Interesting," Loomsbury said.

"The doctors and scientists were experimenting with other DNA splicing besides Gabe's. Such as to lengthen lifespan, regrow limbs, along with other things. At times I felt they were trying to play God."

"But who wanted to shut everything down?" Loomsbury asked.

"Those who funded the facility. The more the scientists and doctors pushed the DNA, the stranger the babies. Some had terrible deformities, living only a few hours after being born. Some of the pregnancies had to be terminated. The whole experiment was going wrong. It seemed as though nature was trying to stop them. As the babies aged something had to be done because the abnormalities started to show, and on a few, it was bad... really bad. Many were uncontrollable, bad tempers, wild even; they had to be caged, or put to sleep. They aged faster than regular children. Gabe's twelve? Not really, he's only four."

Loomsbury gasped and sat back in his chair. Lafie nodded her head. Her grin was evil.

"Within a few years they reached adulthood. The facility was becoming over-crowded. It was decided the hospital and all the subjects had to be destroyed, for the betterment of mankind—if you can believe that story. Gabe's father and I didn't want anything to happen to him. We never told anyone about his special eyesight. Everyone thought he was a normal child. But since I knew what they were doing, I was a risk. My genes had been upgraded with a virus. My aging process was reversed—well, slowed because I've not aged a day since my last treatment. That was about ten years ago."

Loomsbury rubbed his eyes and forehead. Shaking his head and sighing, he asked, "So they killed everyone in the facility?"

"Not the scientists or doctors. They transferred them. I didn't wish to go. I was over it, tired of the whole thing. When they killed those poor people, we hid and prayed they'd leave us alone."

"But they didn't," Loomsbury added.

"No they did not," Lafie said with a tear in her eye.

"The people who funded the facility, do you have any information on them?"

"Not really, only that their research goes way back... for centuries from what I understand. But I *do* know they're a very powerful and rich group."

"They'd have to be in order to keep all of this a secret." Loomsbury said.

* * * * * *

Gabe had never spoken to so many people before—this was something exciting and entertaining. With a large grin, he studied each person with a profound purpose that showed in his eyes. After a long silence, he spoke. "So are you going to ask me some questions, take my blood, or just sit there and gawk at me?"

"Excuse me?" It was a young woman.

"We've been here for almost an hour and you're not saying anything."

A young woman in the front spoke up. "But neither are you."

"You invited *me* remember?" Gabe stated.

The scientists smiled as they watched Gabe.

"Are you really part owl?" a young man finally asked.

"Uh, no," Gabe replied.

"But you can see in the dark," another woman stated. "And we can't."

"So? I can stand and pee and you can't," Gabe replied.

Several of the scientists laughed.

"Who told you I was part owl?" Gabe asked.

"It's in your DNA," a man answered. "Didn't you know?"

Gabe studied the people with an unsteady stare. It was obvious they just told him something he didn't know. But his expression soon changed to enlightenment.

"Well, that explains a lot doesn't it?" Gabe asked. "Everything makes a lot more sense now."

"What does?" a man asked.

"My life," Gabe replied with a grin. "And how I can lay real eggs."

"You can lay an egg?" a male voice asked from the back of the room.

Gabe laughed. "Of course I can't and since when does a male bird lay eggs anyway? Are you *sure* you people know what you're doing? Are you *really* scientists?"

Dr. Leonora Priddleton giggled. Gabe hadn't noticed her standing near the door.

"All right, enough of the jokes," she said. "Let's get down to business?"

Gabe stared at the young girl who approached wearing a long white lab coat and holding a clipboard.

"What exactly can you do?" Priddleton asked with a smile.

"Nothing impressive," Gabe replied squinting his eyes.

Chapter 74

THE GROUP OF men stared blankly at the speakerphone. Only the large oak table and chairs decorated the large granite-lined room. Nestle's nerves were about to explode. He counted in his head to ensure his composure remained calm and under control.

"I have Dr. Spangleholtz and Dr. Geeshmore on the line sir," the voice announced through the speakers.

"Vernon? Eugene? So glad you could join," Nestle stated.

"Yes sir," Geeshmore announced.

"Thank you," Spangleholtz added.

"How's the newest little one? I do hope she's getting along fine. I heard she had an illness?" Nestle asked.

"Yes," Spangleholtz replied. "A little infection but she's fine now."

"Good, good," Nestle said. "We have a slight problem and I was hoping you two could help."

The incoming line became quiet.

"There's been a lot of information on the news lately. Perhaps, Vernon, your idea of how to handle the mothers wasn't such a good idea after all."

The incoming line remained quiet.

"My statement was meant for you, Vernon," Nestle added.

"Sir, it was the only way," Geeshmore said in his defense. "If I remember correctly it was agreed by *everyone* that the children would be better off if raised in a facility. Unless we planned on indoctrinating each mother."

"But now we have the courts involved and the local law and worse, the press. What are you going to do about it?"

The incoming line became silent again.

"That was a question for both of you. Eugene, I didn't like the article in the *New York Times* a few weeks back. To me, that leak is proof of a reckless disregard of protocols."

Again, no sound came through the speaker.

"I see," Dr. Nestle said with anger rising in his voice. "Gentlemen, we have some problems and they need to be corrected immediately. Our society was created to advance the medical and scientific field in regards to enhancing the human race—to evolve it to a higher physical level. We've been around since the days before Jesus Christ. I will not stand by and watch our organization falter. I'm demanding some action, here and now. I'm looking at all of you who sit around this table as well as you two on the phone for answers. I do not wish to have to say this again. Fix the goddamn problems!"

Chapter 75

IT FELT GOOD to be home with her daughters. But at the same time, Marty felt sick and disgusted with herself. She reached for her purse and pulled out her wallet. She flipped through the pictures until she found one of David. Tears filled her eyes as the realization of his death hit her.

"Why?" she cried. "Why?"

Everything flooded through her mind at once—the birth, his death, the sudden move to this place. But through it all, not one ounce of remorse or loss did she feel. It wasn't right. Her husband of twelve years died and not one tear did she shed for him... until now.

Marty thought of her mother and sister. She thought of David's parents and realized they must have gone through hell after her disappearance. Not to mention her daughters hadn't seen their grandparents in months. Why did she go along with everything so easily?

Lizzie lay on the blanket smiling as her sisters talked to her and handed her toys. Marty loved her girls but missed her husband. It was time for her to go home and take her babies with her. Marty knew they were no longer safe here. How dare these people tamper with her child without her knowledge... how dare they.

* * * * * *

Marty took only the necessary items she could carry—one

change of clothing for each, two blankets and other small items. The girls used their school backpacks and Marty grabbed her exercise duffle bag. She did, however, take as much powdered formula and water as she could carry. The evening was cool so they wore light jackets. Since she never left the compound, Marty wasn't sure what she would find. But it was something she would have to risk to save what was left of her family.

It felt wonderful to be in the cool night air without someone hovering over her. She'd forgotten what it felt like to be alone. She still didn't understand why it took so long for the remorse to hit her. Why didn't any of them think of David? It just didn't make any sense.

She locked up her house and they left through the back yard. Owls hooted as they strolled down the path through the tall pines. A full moon was out so their way was well lit. Little Lizzie slept peacefully in her harness strapped to her mother's chest. The girls didn't ask where they were going or why. They simply followed their mother's instructions.

The small family walked for what seemed like miles before Marty realized they never came to a fence of any kind. She could hear running water in the distance but other than that, complete silence. Why wasn't anyone coming after her? It was a strange sensation, but felt wonderful to be free and have her children close to her. Marty felt she was in control of her family for the first time in months.

Marty and her girls hiked up the mountain path until their legs could go no further.

"Mommy," Eliza asked as she dropped her small backpack onto the damp forest floor. "I'm tired."

"Me too," Macie stated, pulling little Lizzie from her mother's carrier.

"All right, girls," Marty said. "We rest here. We don't have a tent, but I brought a couple blankets. " Marty smiled at her girls and dropped her pack onto the ground. "Macie... are you okay with Lizzie while I make a fire?"

"I'm fine," Macie said, sitting on a small blanket she laid out for them.

Lizzie reached for her sister. Macie hugged her and kissed her cheek.

"She's growing so fast," Eliza said brushing the curls from Lizzie's face.

"I know," Macie added smiling at her little sister.

Lizzie cooed and drooled as her two sisters laughed. Lizzie was happy.

Chapter 76

LACEY WAS THE first to see it coming and screamed. Carrie turned just in time to see the large wooly hands reaching out from the darkness and grabbing Lacey around the face. As she reached for her gun, Carrie felt a strong grip pull on her arms.

"Carrie!" Lacey screamed.

Carrie couldn't move. She was on her stomach with someone or some *thing* sitting on her back. Lacey's screams were muffled, and Carrie could tell she was panicking. Struggling seemed useless and a waste of energy so Carrie relaxed her muscles and rested her head on the carpet. The more she relaxed, the less her attacker tried to restrain her. The room was a pitched black except for the wobbling light from the fallen flashlights.

"Who are you and what do you want?" a strange-sounding voice asked from somewhere in the room. It was female from what Carrie could tell, but something was wrong with it.

"We fell through a rotted ceiling and have no way to get out. We were searching for a way to leave," Carrie said as calmly as she could. "We mean you no harm and we don't want anything."

The room brightened by several desk lamps. Carrie still could not see who or what was restraining her, nor could she see who had talked.

"What are you names?" the voice asked.

"I'm Carrie Clarke and that's Lacey Brighten," Carrie said. "We're hikers."

"Hikers?" the voice asked.

"Yes hikers," Carrie answered.

"Hikers?" the voice asked again.

"Yes... hikers," Carrie repeated.

"I know no hikers," the voice replied.

"If you'll get off me," Carrie said, "perhaps we could introduce ourselves properly."

The person restraining Carrie hesitated for a few moments before releasing his or her grip and backed away. Carrie waited a second before sitting up. But what greeted her eyes terrified and amazed her. Lacey ran to Carrie's side as soon as she was released and snuggled as close to her as she could. Horror griped them as they stared into the faces of creatures they never knew existed.

"You Carrie?" the female voice asked. "I'm Learl."

A beautiful but strange woman's face smiled at Carrie. She wasn't young, but she wasn't old either. She was only about four feet in height and was hairless with round pink eyes and a flat dark nose. Black lips framed her large smile. Sharp teeth protruded from her lips where flat teeth should have been. Her hands were small and her fingers were half the size of a normal human's. Pinkish-brown and wrinkled skin framed her small body.

"Hi Learl," Carrie said smiling.

Carrie and Lacey stood up at the same time. Lacey maintained a firm grip on Carrie's arm. Other strange creatures emerged from the dark corners of the room. Their faces resembled humans but with oddities that skewed their features in one way or another.

"Do you live here?" Carrie asked.

Learl gave Carrie an odd stare then nodded.

"How many of you live here?"

Again, Learl looked as if she didn't understand.

"We live here," Learl replied. "This is our home."

Carrie glanced around at the frightened faces. Her arm ached from Lacey's strong grip.

"Lacey, loosen up will yah?" Carrie whined. "Can't you see they're more afraid of us than we are of them?"

"I don't understand," Lacey cried. "What... who are these people? How did they get here?"

"We have always been here," Learl answered.

"Who takes care of you? Who brings you food?" Carrie asked.

"What do you mean?" Learl replied. "You hungry? You need food?"

Carrie glanced over at Lacey and then nodded. "Yes, we could use some food about now."

Chapter 77

EARLY PACED HER cell. She was anxious to hear back from Drake. He left several days ago to research the invetro fertilization doctors in Washington—by himself. If anything happened to him, who would there be to help her? If anything happened to him, everyone would probably blame her. Early was tired of being blamed for something she had nothing to do with. The more she thought about everything that happened over the last several months, the more everything bothered her and the more she wanted less to do with anyone, including herself.

"Ms. Sutton?" a guard shouted. "Please come with me."

Early stared blankly at the guard and said, "Where's my lawyer?"

"Please come with me," the guard demanded again.

Early didn't recall ever seeing this guard before. Fear was growing inside her. As she followed the man down the hall, there were no other guards in sight. Even the other inmates' cells were empty. Something was going on and Early didn't like it.

* * * * * *

Drake stood by the window of his hotel room enjoying the view of the colorful mountain terrain. If nothing else, at least the beautiful landscape was worth the trip. As he watched the birds soar among the trees, there was a knock. Not having any reason to feel his life was in danger, Drake opened his door with a smile.

"Drake Anderson?" It was a man just a little over six feet and in his late fifties or early sixties.

"Yes, and you are?"

"The name's Edwards, Nathaniel Edwards." Nate held out his hand and Drake shook it. "Most call me Nate."

Drake nodded but didn't speak.

"I understand you've been inquiring about the doctors at Barker Institute." Nate said in a calm tone.

"Yes, is there a problem with that?" Drake asked. He was annoyed the doctors were so protected and guarded.

"Not really," Nate replied. "May I come in? We should talk."

Drake normally would be reluctant to invite a stranger into his room; however, since his recent case was anything but usual, he decided to take the chance.

"Mr. Anderson, why is one of the lawyers from the amnesia murders here in Washington to speak to one of our doctors?"

"Is that what they're calling it these days?" Drake asked with a slight chuckle. "The *amnesia murders*? Sounds like a title of a good mystery novel doesn't it?"

"Perhaps, but that's what the press named them," Nate replied choosing a seat by the window.

"Who wants to know why I'm here?" Drake asked.

"Let's just say we have a mutual friend, a Dr. Barnes."

"I see," Drake replied feeling betrayed.

Nate explained The Agency and Barnes's relationship. For over twenty minutes, Drake tumbled into a world centered on undercover agents fighting corrupt government officials. He realized to his horror these people practiced the art of exploiting justifiable homicide. It was a world Drake knew nothing about when he first met Early Sutton, but one that scared him to death.

"So as you see, I don't quite understand how you believe Barker Institute is involved," Nate added.

"My client, Early Sutton, had invetro fertilization at a clinic that wasn't actually a clinic. I traced the tests results back to this company. I'm hoping to find the doctors who worked at her clinic."

"I see," Nate said with a frown. "But I'm afraid the people you seek are not at the Barker Institute. It's simply a biological research facility that does intensive tests on DNA samples. We have checked out the company and they're on the up and up. Not to mention my niece is one of their top scientists. By the way, that is how I found you. She gave me your card."

"Oh?" Drake replied. "So that nice young woman I met out front, that's your niece?"

"Yes," Nate answered.

"Mr. Edwards," Drake said.

"Please call me Nate."

"Nate," Drake repeated. "It's important I find the doctors from the fake clinic. It's the only way I can help my client."

"We have been asked to protect your client as well as the others who are still alive. The Agency agreed because we believe there is more going on than what we know."

"And do you know what's going on?" Drake asked.

"Honestly," Nate replied. "We have no idea."

Chapter 78

THE FOOD WAS eatable but stale. Army rations stacked in cartons reached the ceiling and ran wall to wall. Carrie surmised there was enough food to feed a hundred people for years. Carrie and Lacey were so hungry they couldn't stuff their mouths fast enough. The fuller their stomachs got, the more they wanted to know about these subterranean strangers.

"I'm sorry we frightened you," Carrie said as she gulped her water.

"And we're sorry we frightened you," Learl replied.

Carrie walked out of the food room patting her stomach. It felt good to not be hungry. From where she stood, the room could only be described as a make-shift common area. Several odd-looking individuals sat in awe with questioning eyes. Carrie glanced around and realized there were three other doors she had not noticed before.

"Do you mind if I take a look around Learl?" Carrie asked.

"Look around?" Learl replied.

Carrie realized the woman had no idea what she was talking about. Although her English was good, her comprehension was not.

"Those doors," Carrie asked, "where do they go?"

"Sleeping," Learl answered. "And office, but we don't go in there."

"Office?" Lacey repeated.

"I show," Learl replied.

The office was actually a file room. There were no desks or tables, only several filing cabinets. Carrie pulled out a drawer and grabbed a folder at random. It was a case history of a person. There was an eight-by-ten color portrait of the individual along with their genetic code and an ancestral chart. Also in the documents were a medical overview and date of death. She pulled out several other files and they were all in the same format.

"Only deceased people in this cabinet," Carrie said closing the drawer.

"I've hit pay dirt," Lacey exclaimed. "Well, I mean I found Learl's file."

"Oh?" Carrie replied grabbing the papers from Lacey's hand.

A quick scan of the pages gave Carrie a view into Learl's family lineage. A picture of her mother and father were glued to the inside front cover. They were human and, from all appearances, perfectly normal. The file did contain an explanation to the strange appearance of the woman.

"We are not allowed in here," Learl explained. "We must leave now."

Carrie reached out and touched Learl on the shoulder. "I think we're okay for now."

"But..."

"It's okay," Carrie said trying to reassure her.

As she read, Carrie discovered Learl's DNA was spliced with pig DNA. She had been altered, which explained the dark strange skin and the thick lips and nose. It dawned on Carrie as to what may be taking place with these people. She gave the file back to Lacey who replaced it and closed the drawer. Carrie pulled Lacey from the room.

"What?" Lacey asked. "You're always pushing me around, what's up with you anyway?"

"Shhh," Carrie whispered. "Watch and learn."

* * * * * *

"Where are all the doctors and workers?" Carrie asked.

"They'll come back," Learl answered.

"No they do not come back." A man covered with light yellow fur yelled from across the room.

"Seith!" Learl screamed. "They will come back. They promised."

"No," Seith yelled. "Too long."

"How long has it been?" Carrie asked Learl.

Learl paused for a few seconds before she answered, "Long time."

"Months," a woman with long red and black hair answered from the other side of the room. Her arms and legs were long and skinny with sparse little white hair. She had the blackest skin Carrie ever saw on a person. There was not an ounce of fat on her body anywhere. Her eyes were red with streaks of black, and she wobbled as she tried to walk. Her balance was off.

"There's been no contact at all?" Lacey asked.

"None," Seith cried. "They leave us to die."

"Is there a way out of here?" Carrie asked.

"Just the trains," Seith answered.

"We go there we die!" Learl screamed.

Seith and Learl started to argue. Others joined in and before Carrie could stop it, everyone was screaming and yelling at each other.

"Stop it!" Carrie shouted. "Shut up!"

The room became quiet. All eyes were now focused on Carrie.

"Just stop it okay?" Carrie said in a calmer voice. "Let me think for a minute."

"We need to review those records again," Lacey urged.

"Don't you think I know that? Go and look through those files. I'm going to talk with Learl and Seith. Will you be okay in there by yourself?"

"I guess so," Lacey answered glancing around at the strange creatures who were just sitting and staring at the new strangers who invaded their private world. "But whatever happened to watch and learn? I'm watching, but I'm definitely *not* learning."

* * * * * *

The small office was secretly harboring a door to the outside world. As several of the inhabitants moved the cabinets from the wall, Learl took a chain from around her neck.

"I was told never to allow anyone to leave this place," Learl warned.

"Traps," Seith added.

"Traps?" Carrie asked. Her voice quivering.

Seith nodded.

"Maybe Seith go with you," Learl suggested. "He spends nights exploring beyond this door."

"Oh?" Lacey asked.

"Yes," Learl answered. "We look for them to return."

"But they never come back," the strange looking skinny black woman said.

Carrie nodded. The door creaked as Learl pulled it opened. Expecting darkness, Carrie was surprised the tunnel beyond was well lit.

"If I don't return in..." Carrie started to say.

"Don't even go there," Lacey grunted with a grimaced face.

Chapter 79

"MADAM PRESIDENT," TINA announced through the speaker. "Dr. Trabolinie from the USGS is here to see you."

"USGS?"

"United States Geological Survey," Tina replied. "It's one of your Agencies ma'am."

"Do I have him on my calendar?"

"No, he just dropped by. But he says it's important," Tina whispered as loud as she could.

"Would you please come in here first."

Tina entered and shut the door behind her.

"Ma'am," Tina said as she approached Strickland, "he came running down the hall saying it's of the utmost importance he sees you right away."

"Is he for real?"

"The guards let him in. So I guess so."

"Never heard of the USGS," Strickland said.

"They are on the list, ma'am."

"Show him in," Strickland replied, reluctantly.

"Madam President!" Dr. Trabolinie shouted entering the oval office. "We have to evacuate Washington immediately."

"DC?" Strickland asked.

"No, not DC," Trabolinie yelled. "State... Washington state, it's going to blow."

Strickland sat at her desk and rested her head in her hands. *Now what?* She looked up at the man and frowned. "And how in the hell do you suggest I do that?" She slapped the button on her phone. "Tina, call Dr. Greghardt. He *has* to hear this one."

* * * * * *

"I'm sorry Madam President," Greghardt said sitting in the chair that gave him the best view. "Would you please repeat what you just said?"

"I said, I've just been told to evacuate most of Washington state. That's what. I've never heard of such crap in my whole life. How in the world am I..."

Strickland ranted and raved into the phone as Greghardt glanced over at Lewis.

"What?" Lewis asked sipping on his morning coffee.

"You are not going to believe this one," Greghardt whispered. "Vivian, calm down. We'll fly out at once. We'll get to the bottom of this... together."

* * * * * *

"... I'm Jackie Peters coming to you live from Marblemount, Washington. We're about twenty miles from Diablo Peak, a small but beautiful mountain just north east of Seattle. As you can see from our satellite imagery, there is already smoke coming from the mountaintop.

According to the United States Geological Survey Agency, this is an active volcano and they expect an eruption within the next few days, if not hours!

The USGS serves our nation by providing reliable scientific information to help us understand our Earth. Their mission is to minimize loss of life and property from natural disasters, such as this.

From what we've been told, the USGS was also involved in the investigation of the West Virginia explosion that occurred several weeks ago. It was a relief to hear it was a meteor and not volcanic and it was an isolated incident.

But now, we are being told this mountain is about to blow and the blast could be much larger than Mount Saint Helens..."

"This is nuts." Maddie yelled at the television. "Oh my God!"

Maddie ran to the phone and dialed.

"Dr. Lewis." A familiar and soothing voice echoed into her

ear.

"Are you asleep on the job or what?"

Lewis cleared his throat. He was concerned hearing from her.

"Don't worry," Maddie said in a calmer voice. "It's safe for me to call, no one cares about me anymore. Now are you asleep or what?"

"What are you talking about?" Lewis asked.

"Do you know what is on the news right now?"

"Sort of," Lewis stated honestly.

"A volcano in Washington that's what, don't you get it? Something's going on up here and whatever it is... well, I think they're about to blow it up, just like what happened in West Virginia. We have to get Carrie and Tyler out of there and now."

Lewis was silent. Maddie impatiently tapped her foot.

"Jeff, is what I'm saying getting through to you?"

Lewis sighed then added, "Mad, we can't make contact with the girls."

Maddie turned her attention back to the television as she thought of what she should do.

Chapter 80

THE OLD TRAIN tunnel smelled of rotten damp rags. Carrie could tell Seith wasn't comfortable walking with her. Although the tracks were well lit, the tunnels felt eerie and ominous... almost alive.

"Thanks for coming with me Seith," Carrie said, wanting to start a conversation. The only sound was the echo of their grinding footsteps on the gravel and it made her nervous.

"You are welcome. But I can only go a little more."

"Why?" Carrie asked.

"I must stay here," he said as they walked down the darkening tunnel.

Eerie shadows bounced wickedly from the tunnel walls and ceilings. Although they were alone, Carrie couldn't shed the feeling of being watched. The tunnel was large enough for two tracks, but only one was in the middle. It made her think of a carnival ride through the mouth of horror. Whatever came in on these tracks had long since left. Rusty spots along the rails showed they hadn't been used for some time. Whoever paid to have this place built used some big money.

"Do you know your doctors' names?" Carrie asked.

"Doctor?" Seith replied. "What is a doctor?"

"Weird," Carrie said as they walked.

Seith suddenly stopped. Carrie turned expecting an explanation, but Seith simply shrugged his shoulders and said, "I go no further."

Carrie smiled and replied, "No problem. I'll go just a little more and then come back. You wait for me?"

Seith nodded as Carrie continued on alone. The dampness was making her shiver and she wished she had brought her jacket. But she was not about to turn back now. Carrie was determined to find out just how far the tunnel went before opening into the forest. She continued to walk for about another twenty minutes when her eyes focused on what could only be described as body parts.

"Oh no..." Carrie almost screamed before she caught herself.

Parts of human and animal remains were all along the tunnel's ceiling and walls. At first her heart raced up to her throat, and her instincts begged her to turn around and run. But she knew better. Nothing here was going to hurt her. It was already dead. She studied the rotting and dried carnage and realized what she was looking at.

"Ah shit," she whispered.

A breeze of fresh air hit her and when Carrie glanced up, she could see the end of the tunnel. It was about two hundred yards ahead. This was a way out, but not for everyone. After a long sigh, Carrie turned and headed back toward Seith.

How could anybody be so evil to create such a terrible place?

The more she thought about it the more it bothered her. This place was not only Seith's home, but also his prison and cemetery. She now understood why they could never leave... their bodies would be blown apart.

* * * * * *

"Well?" Lacey asked as Carrie and Seith entered the small office space.

"I'm not sure," Carrie answered.

"What do you mean you're not sure," Lacey whispered. "You've been gone for hours and you don't know what you found?"

"We need to talk," Carrie replied as she grabbed Lacey by the arm. "Alone."

Lacey smiled at Seith who was busy looking at some papers and rolled her eyes.

"Okay," Lacey said. "I'll play the game... where? Where exactly are *we* going to be alone?"

"Good question," Carrie added glancing around. "Um Seith, could you get me something to drink? I'm really thirsty."

"Of course," he answered and walked out of the room.

"Not much on words?" Lacey teased but Carrie ignored her.

Once the office door was close, Carrie turned and frowned at Lacey.

"What?" Lacey whispered. "What did you find?"

"I know why no one can leave," Carrie whispered. "I'll bet they're all implanted with some type of an explosive device."

"A what?"

"Listen," Carrie demanded through clenched teeth. "Just before the opening of the tunnel there's body parts splattered everywhere. The smell is awful. The only thing that could cause such a mess is an explosion... and since I was there and didn't blow up... it has to be inside of them. We can't take them with us. At least not now."

Before Lacey could say another word, Seith returned carrying a glass of what could only be lemonade.

"Thanks Seith," Carrie said before gulping down the cool liquid, "I was so thirsty."

Seith nodded then said, "Did you tell her?"

"Tell her what?" Carrie asked.

"Tell her what you found," he replied.

"What do you mean?" Carrie asked.

"The dead," he said, "did you tell her about the dead?"

Carrie was shocked. It never dawned on her he might know what was at the end of the tunnel. "You know about that? How far have you gone?"

Seith lowered his head. "I've almost gone as far as you. But before I got there..." Tears formed in his eyes and he looked away as he explained. "Yaggart was ahead of me... then he was gone. Just like that he was gone."

Carrie put her arm around Seith and gave him a reassuring hug. "It's okay... I understand what it's like to lose someone you care about."

"I was afraid, I ran back as fast as I could," he cried. "I told everyone Yaggart got away. I lied."

"Shhhh," Carrie wanted to console the man, but didn't know how. "I understand, it's okay."

As hard as she tried, she couldn't get past the way his arms felt so muscular. Not soft like a human's but firm like an animal. His fur was rough to the touch. She wanted to scream and run from the revulsion that was building up inside her. But she knew it wasn't his fault. Seith was a living breathing person with feelings and wants and desires, and who deserved to be treated with respect and compassion.

All it took was for her to look into his golden eyes and her heart melted. Carrie cuddled him and reminded herself she would judge Seith by his actions and not his looks.

"Seith, no one ever has a great life anymore... no one. Every person on this stupid planet has a story to tell and almost all of them have very sad endings. Some children are treated bad by their parents, or teachers or others."

"You... you were sad as a little girl?"

"Yes, Seith, even me," Carrie said with tears in her eyes. "I try not to talk about it 'cause it still hurts. My grandmother told me my mother died giving me life. As hard as the doctors tried to save her, she was just too weak. The worst part was her death destroyed my father. He always blamed me. He was an alcoholic and when he looked at me..." Carrie couldn't hold back the tears and began to cry on Seith's shoulder, "there was such hate in his eyes for me. I couldn't leave the house fast enough when I turned eighteen."

"I don't know who my parents are," Seith whispered. "I don't know what would be worse, the knowing or the not knowing."

"The knowing," Carrie cried.

Chapter 81

"WHAT?" DRAKE YELLED into the phone. "What do you mean she's missing? How in the hell does a prisoner come up missing?"

"What is it?" Nate asked.

"Early's not in her cell," he answered trying to hear what Shelby was saying. "They don't know who took her or how they got her out. She's just missing."

"Missing?" Nate repeated grabbing his cell phone.

"Yes, missing... hold on a second Shelby," Drake said while turning to Nate. "And the DNA results are back. Those bodies that were supposed to be Early's family, well they're not. No DNA match. Not even close... now who are *you* calling?"

"Dr. Lewis," Nate said with his shaking hands. "They're on the move."

"Who's on the move?" Drake asked holding his cell away from his face and looking confused.

* * * * * *

Early was in a dark small room. She was cold and frightened. The guard brought her to this place and left her alone. Where was her lawyer and why was she here? There were no windows, only a single door. There were no pictures, just a lone chair placed along one of the walls.

As she walked around, Early knew this would be the end of her life. Being labeled a baby killer meant everyone had it in for her. There was nothing she could do but wait for whoever it was to come in and kill her. She just hoped it would be quick and painless.

Memories of the other prisoners yelling *kill the baby killer* and other terrible things echoed through her mind. She was a sitting duck. Her whole life turned upside down, torn away without an explanation. Before, her life was full of love, but now it was filled with pain. Nothing would ever be the same, not even her dreams.

Before she could think any more wild and depressing thoughts, the door opened and her eyes planted firmly in the middle of Alex's face. The husband whose murder she was accused of committing.

He looked both wonderful and terrifying to Early. The man she loved and devoted her life to was standing only a few feet away, and he was smiling. Thoughts ran so fast through her mind she felt dizzy and sick. Where had he been? Where are their children? Why did he leave her alone in such a terrible place?

"Early," Alex said softly, "Early sweetheart, I'm so sorry." Alex held out his arms for Early to run into, but she didn't move.

Her eyes showed her disgust for the man she once loved. Early didn't know what to do or what to say to this stranger who stood before her. She wasn't sure if she loved or hated him. With her mind confused and her heart broken, Early didn't know if she should laugh or cry. She felt dead inside—numb.

"Early, I can explain," he pleaded.

But Early wasn't going to fall for anything anymore. Unless she knew for sure something was real and not just an illusion, she wasn't going to simply accept it. Her marriage was an illusion, she realized that now. The murder of her family was a deception, she knew that now too. But what she didn't know was why? Why would her husband betray her after all the promises they'd made to each other?

"Talk to me, Early," Alex pleaded. "Please understand, they made me do this. I had no idea it would turn out like it has. Think of our children, Early. None of this was any of my doing. They're stronger than we are. I had to protect the kids. Early? Please."

But his words were falling on deaf ears, and he was pleading to a wiser but hardened heart. Early was exhausted and emotionally drained. Not a nerve in her body seemed to be working. All she wanted was some food and much-needed sleep. But with her dead husband standing directly in front of her, sleep would be the last thing she'd expect.

"Early, would you at least talk to me?" Alex pleaded.

Early couldn't take it any longer and exploded on the man. "Just who in the hell do you think you're talking to? Your wife? You could have fooled me, which is exactly what you did."

"Early please," he pleaded with tears in his eyes.

"'Please' my ass!" she screamed. "For months I was told you and the kids were dead and I did it... I did it. My name's in the news. I'm a killer of my family while you're living it up as Daddy. I'm the sick Mommy. And... where are MY children anyway?"

Alex remained silent.

"Oh so now you're quiet. I just can't believe after all this time you come waltzing in here and for what?" Early quieted for a few seconds before saying in a softer voice, "Why are you here, Alex?"

"To take you home," he whispered.

"Home where?"

"I can't say," he replied.

"Where are my kids?" she demanded.

"They're safe and you'll be with them soon." He lowered his head. "You probably won't want to be married to me any longer and I can't say I blame you. But I wish you'd hear me out before you decide on anything."

A knock at the door startled them.

"It's time to go, Early," Alex said lowering his eyes. "You'll have to come with us. You don't have a choice."

"I haven't had a choice in anything lately," she replied. "Why should now be any different?"

Chapter 82

THE LARGE GATHERING of brothers quieted as Dr. Nestle took the stage. He was proud of the way they handled the problems. Everything was starting to come together and he was sure all issues would soon die down.

"I want to thank each and every one of you here today and to say I'm impressed with your accomplishments, and with just a little more effort, we *will* be successful with our plans."

The large gathering cheered and clapped. Nestle raised his hands and the room fell silent again.

"This is not to say we allow our guard to drop, in fact the opposite is true. We all must be on the alert for anything. We must follow our instincts and search the shadows, listen to conversations, and keep our eyes on everyone. *We will be victorious!*" Nestle yelled and the men cheered.

Spangleholtz stood proudly at the back of the room soaking it all in. It was a wonderful sensation being a part of the New World Order that would soon revitalize the world. Birth defects and inherited illnesses would soon be a part of the past. As he wallowed in his arrogance and false illusions of magnificence, his cell phone vibrated from inside his jacket pocket.

"Spangleholtz," he whispered leaving the auditorium for a more private spot.

It was Hope, his assistant in Washington. She was hysterical and shouting. At first he wasn't sure what was going on for it sounded like she was saying Marty had run away, and he knew that was impossible. But the longer he listened the more he understood that's exactly what she was trying to tell him.

Spangleholtz's heart raced realizing the Order's future depended on finding Marty. In the room behind him, Nestle was speaking of a future success, but the longer Hope screamed the weaker that success became. Thoughts raced through his mind trying to think of what to do. Should he tell Nestle or just handle the situation on his own? After all, this was his problem and not something that should be brought to the attention of the whole Order. No, he would take care of his own problems.

"Hope," Spangleholtz said. "Assign a search party. I'm on my way back. I'll be there by morning."

Chapter 83

GREGHARDT, LEWIS AND Strickland sat in the middle of the Oval Office. The room was on the cool side so each suffered a chill that ran up and down their spines. Each sighed, not knowing what to say or do.

"Allen…" Strickland started, but was cut off by Greghardt.

"I know what you're going to say, Viv, but I'm afraid we're helpless until we get more information. Our key witness has disappeared, or been kidnapped, and by whom we have no idea. Almost the whole state of Washington is about to go up in smoke and we don't know why. Until we hear back from our agents in the field, I'm afraid we're stuck."

"Someone has to know something," Strickland yelled before catching herself. "Someone is hiding something, and we must find out what that something is before it's too late."

"And where do you suggest we begin?" Lewis asked, feeling vulnerable for the first time in years.

"With that research facility being evacuated, all signs point in that direction. We should start there," she said.

"That will be hard to do once it's blown up," Greghardt added.

"Then we'll get there before it does," Strickland said.

"Madam President," Tina yelled as she rushed into the room. "Sorry to disturb you but you need to see this."

Tina hit the *on* button on the television. They gasped as they watched a huge fireball roar above the treetops.

"Where is this?" Strickland asked.

"Washington, ma'am," Tina replied.

"But this can't be from the volcano?"

"No, it can't," Greghardt added. "It's too small."

Lewis was already on his phone ordering a team to investigate the small explosion. They had to know what was going on.

"Madam President," Lewis said. "You just may be correct in your assumptions of where to focus our attention."

"God, I hope I'm right," she replied, rubbing her hands vigorously against the side of her skirt. "Something is really bothering me," Strickland mumbled to no one in particular.

But Lewis heard her loud and clear. "What's bothering you?"

"Hold that thought," Strickland said as she opened the door to the Oval Office. "Tina, can I see you for a moment, please?"

Tina entered with her pad and pen.

"Tina, I want to know where all my directors and congressmen are. Can you track them down … without anyone knowing? I also need to know where they've been over the last ninety days."

"Certainly, Madam President," Tina said in a warm but professional manner. She then left the room.

"What's that all about?" Lewis asked.

"I have a hunch some of mine are involved in all this. I've just got this feeling. And I'm afraid I'm the one that hired them."

"I have a feeling you may be on to something," Greghardt added. "And I think we can help."

Greghardt got on the phone and called The Agency to help track down all the cabinet members, congressmen and directors of several US agencies.

Chapter 84

CARRIE DIDN'T WANT to leave them behind but she knew she had no choice. She'd come to know the small group as friends.

"We'll be back," Lacey said hugging them one by one.

"We will return," Carrie promised wrapping her arms around Seith. "I will come to get all of you."

Seith's eyes filled with tears as the two girls walked through the door in the small office. Learl and Seith pushed the cabinets back into place and sighed when finished.

"They'll be back," Learl said trying to reassure Seith.

"I hope they be safe," Seith answered.

"Me too," Learl said leaving Seith alone in the small office.

* * * * * *

Carrie and Lacey walked for what seemed like hours down the long vacated track. Lacey was amazed at the size of the tunnel, it was all she talked about.

"I can't believe this tunnel never collapsed," Lacey said.

"I'm sure it was built to last."

They walked until Lacey stopped and yelled, "My God! What is that awful smell?"

"Death," Carrie whispered.

Lacey fell to her knees gasping for air.

"Lacey, are you all right?" Carrie remembered Lacey's past and knew what was happening to her young partner. She had to get Lacey out of that tunnel. Carrie grabbed Lacey by the arm and dragged her through the carnage, not slowing down until they reached the outside.

"Lacey, grab a hold of yourself," Carrie ordered.

"I'm trying," Lacey cried out gasping. "I haven't felt like this in a long time... I'd forgotten."

"I know."

"I'm sorry," Lacey said taking in another breath of fresh air. "It won't happen again."

"You can't help it," Carrie replied. "It's just the way it is. Certain things trigger feelings and memories from our past and we begin to re-live them. It's just what is."

"I know but," Lacey started to say then squinted her eyes. "Hey, there's people over there."

"What?" Carrie asked turning around to see what Lacey was staring at.

One adult and two children were walking through the trees.

"How did they get way out here?" Lacey asked.

"Not sure, but we're about to find out," Carrie replied dashing toward the hikers.

"Hey, wait for me," Lacey yelled running after Carrie.

"Hello?" Carrie screamed and the small group of hikers stopped.

It was a woman and two girls. The woman looked terrified and the girls looked exhausted.

"Are you okay?" Carrie yelled still running toward the small group.

After everything she'd just been through, Carrie refused to dismiss anything at this point. And to find a mother and her children walking through the wilderness only meant one thing— trouble.

The mother started to run, and Carrie had to think fast. "Please stop, I can't run after you. I'm too tired, please stop."

"We're not here to hurt you," Lacey yelled. "We can help, honest."

That seemed to work. The woman sat down on the ground and huddled the children close as they approached. Carrie noticed they were wearing tennis shoes and carrying small packs. Not one of them was prepared to be hiking in these woods.

"Hi, I'm Carrie and this is Lacey," Carrie panted as she spoke. "We were hiking and fell into a cave. We just found our way out. Why are *you* way out here?"

"Yeah, did you fall into a hole too?" Lacey asked. "Like stupid us?"

The little girls laughed at Lacey's statement but the woman only shook her head. The girls sat on their packs and stared at their mother. Carrie and Lacey sat down on the damp earth next to them. It felt good to rest their legs after the long trek out of the damp cave.

"Why are you way out here?" Lacey asked. "In fact, how did you get way out here?"

Marty began to cry. The girls wrapped their arms around their mother. Carrie's mind raced for answers. But Lacey knew what was wrong. She had been there before as a child and knew what they were feeling and thinking.

"You're running for your lives aren't you?" Lacey said.

"How did you know?" Marty asked between sobs.

"She just does," Carrie answered winking at Lacey. "Believe me, she knows."

"I have the T-Shirt at home," Lacey mused. "You're safe now, really."

"I need to find my backpack." Carrie giggled and Lacey laughed.

They laughed so hard their sides were burning. The girls laughed along with them even though they had no idea what was so funny. Then Marty began to giggle. All of them were soon laughing as hard as they could in the middle of a wild and vast wilderness.

"What are we laughing at?" Marty asked.

"Life," Carrie replied and they all laughed until they cried.

* * * * * *

Carrie ran down the slope yelping.

"I guess she found her pack," Lacey mused.

Marty smiled and nodded. "They'll be coming for us soon. We have to go now."

"Who'll be coming?" Lacey asked.

"I have to find a place to hide and where the kids can rest. I can't tell you everything now," Marty answered.

Panting, Carrie plopped down next to Lacey with a huge smile. "I think I know where we are… sort of."

"Marty needs to make camp," Lacey added. "She needs to hide."

Carrie stared at the children. "Have you eaten?"

Marty shook her head.

"We have to feed the kids." As she spoke, Carrie noticed Marty's jacket was moving. She glanced over at Lacey and nudged her with her elbow. When Lacey gave Carrie a glaring look of non-approval, Carrie tried to use her eyes to get Lacey to see the moving jacket. But Lacey wasn't following her.

"What?" Lacey asked.

Carrie rolled her eyes and again pointed her head and turned in the direction of the moving jacket. Lacey shook her head as her eyes widened. She still wasn't following Carrie's clues. Carrie took in a gasp of air before leaning over until her head and body were between Lacey and Marty. Again Carrie jerked her head toward Marty and blinked her eyes several times.

"You have something in your eyes?" Lacey asked. "I hate it when I get stuff in my eyes."

"I give up. Hello? Anybody home in there?" Carrie knocked on Lacey's forehead with her knuckles.

"Owe… that hurt," Lacey complained, rubbing her head. "What's the matter with you anyway?"

"Nothing," Carrie sighed. "I think I saw a good place to camp a little way up the slope. We can stay there for the night."

"Will they see us?" Marty asked.

"No. It's pretty secluded." Carrie stood and brushed the leaves off her pants.

"Thank you," Marty said as she followed them.

As the small group hiked up the mountain slope, Lacey leaned over to Carrie and asked, "What was all that about back there?"

"Nothing, Ms. Dense," Carrie smirked as she hurried her stride.

* * * * * *

Carrie stood at the cave entrance with her mind reeling.

How in the world was she going to get the girls and the mother past the walls of the decaying human flesh? She glanced over at Lacey who looked green. Carrie knew this was probably not the smartest idea she'd ever had. But it was the best place to hide this family until she could figure out what to do.

"Look," she said to the group. "Through this cave is a warm and dry place where you can hide. There's bathrooms and beds and a kitchen with food. But to get there I have to take you through this tunnel."

"And it stinks," Lacey said almost crying.

Carrie gave Lacey the evil eye and ignored her statement.

"I'm really sorry about this," Carrie said, "but I'm going to have to put my jacket over Macie's head and Lacey will have to put hers over Eliza's. We'll guide you. It's going to smell and I apologize. But it'll be okay… I promise."

Marty stared at the girls and hugged her jacket. Carrie knew she was hiding something, but that didn't matter right now. She just had to get them to safety. They guided the girls through the stench and Marty gagged all the way, but eventually, they made it to the door. The filing cabinets had been pushed back into place, but with Carrie and Lacey pushing together, they moved them out of the way.

"Seith… Learl!" Carrie yelled. "Hello? We're back."

Lacey pushed the cabinets back into place and followed everyone into the common area.

"We were not excepting you so soon," Learl said giving Carrie a hug. "Who's this?"

"We met some new friends outside," Lacey said.

"This is Marty," Carrie said pulling her to the front. "And this is Macie and this is Eliza."

"You look funny," Eliza said staring at Learl.

"So do you," Learl replied sticking out her tongue.

"Okay," Carrie interrupted. "Everybody looks funny. So can we feed these guys please?"

"You want food?" Learl asked.

Chapter 85

AFTER DINNER, CHARLOTTE and Charlie decided to take a walk. She listened to his words but kept a cautious eye on the whole family. Nothing was making any sense. Why would he suddenly show up now? If they were her grandparents, why wasn't she always in their lives?

"I'm sure you're confused, Charlotte, but once you're here for a while you'll see. Having a family is the greatest." Charlie picked up a rock and tossed it through the trees.

"Why don't you have wings?" she asked.

Charlie studied her for a few seconds then replied, "I don't know."

"What makes you different?" Charlotte added.

"Different?"

"I know I'm different than everyone else. I know everyone doesn't have wings. I'm not stupid. So if we're really related, then why can't you fly?"

"I don't know. Maybe you should ask our grandparents. Maybe they'll know."

Charlotte watched as Charlie threw a few more rocks before they headed home. But Charlie walked slowly, almost as if he was feeling guilty about something.

* * * * * *

The sound of the explosion ricocheted so violently through the small home the house was almost knocked off its foundation.

"Grandpa?" Charlie screamed from his bedroom. "Grandpa... Grandma, is it an earthquake?

Charlie ran into his grandparents' room but it was empty. When he got to the living room, the front door was wide open and he could see his grandparents and Charlotte watching what looked like a fireball high over the treetops.

"What is it?" Charlie asked running out to join them.

"We think the home was demolished," his grandmother replied stroking Charlotte's head.

"I want to see!" Charlotte's bravery shocked everyone.

"No, you can't," Charlie yelled. But it was too late.

Charlotte ran into the wind. When the current caught her wings, she soared effortlessly into the sky. Exercises her grandfather taught her were making her stronger. Taking off from the ground was almost painless now. With a sense of pride, Charlotte flew around the house to gain height. As soon as she cleared the treetops, she could see the fireball in the distance. Being cautious, Charlotte didn't get too close. All she needed was someone to see her.

Charlie was running, yelling for her to come back. But she needed to know what was happening at the place she used to call home. A huge rock alongside the mountain gave her the perfect viewing spot. Charlotte aimed for the cliff and landed on the large boulder. From up here, she could see everything; the lake she first floated across, the large trees she first soared over, and the castle—or what was left of the castle. As the flames roared higher into the air, the tears ran down her face. She thought of the good people who cared for her. Charlotte hoped they would be okay and maybe they were not in the house when it blew up.

The sounds of sirens filled the cool afternoon's air and the different colors of flashing lights told Charlotte ambulances were already parked at the old castle. It didn't look good. Charlotte lowered her head and said goodbye to her old life. She had seen enough and needed to be safe. She glided back toward her waiting grandparents. Charlie scolded her. But her grandfather scooped her up in his arms and gave her a big kiss.

"You're getting stronger, my tiny one," he said with a sparkle in his eyes. "I have something you should see."

"What?" Charlotte asked.

"A picture of your mother when she was about your age. You look so much like her," he said planting a soft kiss on her cheek.

"Grandpa?" Charlotte asked.

"Yes, my sweet," he replied.

"Can we leave tonight?" she whispered.

"Leave?" he asked.

Charlotte cried and between sobs said, "I'm afraid... if someone wants everyone dead, won't they come after me next?"

Chapter 86

LEE STEPPED OFF the plane happy to finally be home. Her flight was delayed at two different airports, one in London and the other in New York. But all in all, she was glad to be away from those creepy men and their odd behavior. She wasn't sure why she was sent there in the first place. But she had thirty days of leave and she was going to enjoy every second of it.

"Lee!" Tabatha yelled as she grabbed hold almost knocking her over.

"My God, just kill me all ready. It's good to be back in the states," Lee said dropping her luggage at Tabatha's feet to give her a hug. "I'm sorry I gave you such a fright."

"It's okay, as long as you're fine. But don't do it again."

"I guess I'm fine. My side still hurts. That was the worst bug I've ever had... must have been a foreign one."

"Very funny. All you need to worry about is getting some long overdue rest."

As they left the airport, Lee couldn't help but notice the man watching them from across the terminal. An eerie feeling ran up her spine, and for some unknown reason she felt personally violated.

"Let's get out of here and get some dinner," Lee protested. "Where did you park the car?

* * * * * *

Lee and Tabatha munched on their dinner and only every once in a while did they glance up at each other. Both had bad thoughts running through their minds not knowing if they should share them with each other.

"These pork chops are pretty good and you didn't fry them?" Lee asked. "Really?"

"No, just broiled with heavy seasoning," Tabatha replied, picking up her glass of milk. "Was the hotel nice?"

"It was beautiful. Too bad I was sick most of the time. I couldn't really enjoy it," Lee replied. "So how's your case?"

"You won't believe what I have to tell you. Even if I painted you a picture. I just have to tell someone."

"Spill," Lee said taking a bite of her baked potato.

"We're analyzing skeletal remains of what might be a true cross-breed between an animal and human. We believe it was part feline."

"Get real," Lee sighed, rolling her eyes.

"No, honest," Tabatha replied leaning closer to Lee in order to whisper.

"We had to go to a site where some strange bones were buried. But there was nothing left. We do have some samples that were taken before the whole skeleton was stolen."

"Stolen?" Lee asked surprised. "Who'd steal a thing like that? Grave-robbing lost its appeal years ago."

"Perhaps," Tabatha whispered. "But they had pictures of the thing. The head looks like a cat and the body looks like a human, except it didn't have any feet or hands."

"Paws?" Lee giggled.

"We're not sure what they were, too deformed to really tell," Tabatha said, ignoring the mocking. "But the DNA results so far have come back positive for both animal and human mixed together."

"That's impossible," Lee stated.

"Well obviously it's not, because someone succeeded."

"Succeeded in what?" Lee asked. "In having sex with a cat?"

"No, silly. Someone took animal DNA and implanted it in a human. Then brought the egg to full term."

"You're joking right?"

"I've never been more serious in my life. This whole case scares the crap out of me. I mean, do you know the implications of their success?"

"Scary thought," Lee sighed.

"Did I mention the skeleton had clothes on when they found it?"

* * * * * *

"I'm not feeling so good," Lee said rolling onto her stomach.

Tabatha sat next to her friend. "What's wrong?"

"I don't know. I hurt."

Tabatha placed her hand on Lee's forehead. Fear gripped her body. "My God, Lee, you're burning up."

Lee jumped from the bed and ran into the bathroom. Tabatha knew Lee was very ill. She grabbed her phone and Dr. Loomsbury picked up after the first ring.

"Looms!" Tabatha yelled. "Lee's sick, I mean really sick. She's puking all over the place. She's been sick since she got off that plane."

"Can you get her to me?" Loomsbury asked.

"We'll be right there," Tabatha replied, as she threw her cell onto the bed.

* * * * * *

Tabatha paced the floor at The Agency waiting for Loomsbury to give her any news on her friend. After what seemed like forever, the door opened and Loomsbury stared at her.

"Looms... how is she?" Tabatha asked.

"She's alive. Very sick... but alive."

"What's wrong with her? Is it food poisoning?"

"Although I would agree eating your dinners could be dangerous," Loomsbury said with a grin. "It was not food poisoning. She's pregnant."

"Pregnant?" Tabatha yelled. "That's not possible."

"Well she is."

"You don't understand," she replied. "Lee doesn't date men."

* * * * * *

Lee was asleep when Tabatha entered her room. She sat next to her friend and took her hand. Tears ran down Tabatha's face as she contemplated the facts. Did Lee cheat on her... was she unfaithful? She loved Lee and refused to jump to conclusions. There had to be a logical explanation as to how Lee got pregnant. But until she could talk to her, she knew nothing good would come from speculations.

"She has a serious infection," Loomsbury said standing at the foot of Lee's bed.

"She said she had an appendicitis attack," Tabatha explained. "They took out her appendix."

"No," Loomsbury replied with a frown. "I don't know what the surgery was for, but it was *not* to remove her appendix."

"But the scar," Tabatha added.

"She has a new scar," Loomsbury said. "But I'm not sure why."

"Could they have made her pregnant?" Tabatha asked.

Loomsbury thought for a moment before answering. "Perhaps. But whatever they did caused the infection she's now fighting. And this infection just might kill her. Oh my!"

"Oh my what?" Tabatha asked now more worried than ever.

"I just thought of something." Loomsbury grabbed the phone and yelled, "We need to schedule General Longhorn for emergency surgery. I believe she's carrying a device."

* * * * * *

"Lee?" Tabatha whispered between sobs. "Lee, how are you feeling?"

"Like shit," she moaned. "What happened to me?"

"You just had surgery," Tabatha replied, holding Lee's hand.

"Where am I? I feel like someone's sitting on my stomach."

"Lee," Tabatha whispered. "I have something to tell you. Something terrible."

"Am I going to die?"

"No," Tabatha replied.

"Then it's not that terrible. So tell me already."

"You're pregnant."

"What do you mean I'm pregnant?" Lee said laughing. "How can I be pregnant? I haven't been with anyone but you."

Tabatha wasn't sure how much she should reveal to her friend... her lover... her life. Could she handle the news? What would it do to her in her delicate condition?

"When you were overseas," she whispered. "Remember how you were so sick?"

"Yes. So what? People have appendicitis all the time."

"Well..."

"Well what? Speak up, Tabatha," Lee demanded. "What are you not telling me about my surgery?"

Tabatha sighed and decided to just say it. "They took your eggs... fertilized them... and put them back inside you. There I said it."

"They did what? Why?" Lee screamed as tears ran down her cheeks.

"We don't know why," Tabatha said trying to console her friend. "But there's more."

"More?" Lee asked not sure if she wanted the answer.

"When they ran tests on the fluid around the baby... well..."

"Well what, Tabatha?"

"Well... the DNA results came back funny."

Holding her breath, Lee asked, "Funny *ha-ha* or funny weird?"

"Funny weird."

"Weird how?" Lee whispered.

"The DNA of your baby also includes DNA of an animal."

"An animal? Really?" Lee yelled. "And what kind of an animal?"

"A lizard," Tabatha whispered with her eyes squinting to shut out the view. "Actually a chameleon."

"I'm carrying a chameleon?" Lee cried. "A reptile?"

"Not exactly," Tabatha tried to explain. "You see, there's only some chameleon DNA in the baby. But we're not sure what it's for. They're running tests now."

"Oh great," Lee screamed. "This is just great. I'm having a baby that's going to hang from the trees and change color. Do you know how hard it will be to find a kid in a room if he looks like a couch?"

"On a good note," Tabatha said with a smile. "It has one head, two arms and two legs. All the important parts are there."

"Like that makes me feel a lot better," Lee snorted as she slapped the mattress.

Chapter 87

NATE'S STOMACH GROWLED from the aroma of cooking pizza. He wondered if he had time to order and eat before they arrived. But no sooner did he have the thought than the *womp womp* echoed through the parking lot. The four Forest Rangers wearing freshly ironed uniforms ran into the field and stood at attention.

"Ah man," Nate yelled running to get them out of the way. "Hey guys. Back up or they can't land."

Nate yelled several times before the men finally ran back to the parking lot. The helicopter descended and several men in black uniforms jumped out. They found strategic places to stand guard and stared into the sky. The Rangers looked at Nate as if needing direction.

"Why don't you make sure the cars keep moving through the lot," Nate said pointing to the line of cars that had stopped to watch.

Nate pulled out his badge and the Rangers nodded. They almost looked relieved. One of the men in black approached and when he was satisfied with Nate's credentials waved at the helicopter. Jeff Lewis was followed out by Allen Greghardt. Strickland, the president, stepped out last. Nate smiled as Lewis got closer.

"How was the ride?" Nate asked, shaking Lewis's hand.

"Not bad," he replied. "Let me introduce you. Viv, this is Nate, one of our top agents."

"Nice to meet you, sir," she replied.

"My pleasure to meet you, Madam President," Nate said.

Strickland held out her hand.

Nate shook Strickland's hand and said, "My car's over here."

The helicopter left as quickly as it arrived and soon all four were heading down East Galena Street toward Tyler's house.

* * * * * *

"You have a very nice home, Miss Brighten," Strickland said as she was introduced to Tyler.

"I'm honored to have you in my home," Tyler said motioning for Strickland to take a seat on her couch. "Please make yourself comfortable. And you can call me Tyler"

"Wow, our manners are just too much for me right now," Maddie said, walking into the room.

"Mad!" Strickland yelled jumping up to give her a hug. "It's so great to see you again. How's the leg?"

"Oh, it's a leg," Maddie said hitting her prosthetic limb.

"I keep forgetting your leg is fake, Aunt Mad," Tyler said.

"I hate to intrude on such a tender homecoming," Greghardt interrupted. "But we do have business to discuss."

"Fine," Strickland said sitting on the couch. "So where do we go from here?"

The sound of the doorbell made everyone jump. Nate opened the door and laughed. Skyler smiled and waved as she walked in.

"Evening, Uncle Nate," Skyler said, giving him a hug. "This is Gabe."

* * * * * *

The results were printed in black on the stark white paper. Caiden pulled the sheet from the printer himself. But neither could believe what they were reading. What he was seeing was impossible, completely impossible. Tyler read the report next, praying the words would magically change.

"Now what do we do?" Tyler asked staring at him.

Caiden shook his head. He was just as bewildered. "I have no idea? Quit?"

"And who'd pay our bills? Huh?" Tyler asked.

Caiden folded the paper and slipped it into his pocket. "Let's get to work on the real stuff."

"This is real stuff," Tyler said as a tear ran down her cheek. "That's why I'm so scared."

"Someone is doing something they shouldn't," he said, trying to calm her. "That's all this is... nothing more."

"But what if these people's DNA should mix with everyone else?" she asked. "What happens to humanity when that happens? Do weird things start popping out of our kids?"

"Tyler... it's okay. Usually when people play God, the hybrids can't reproduce... like the male mule for instance."

"Thanks," Tyler said shaking her head. "I'll try to remember that when I see someone glowing in the dark."

"We'll give the results to your aunt and uncle tonight," he said. "Your aunt invited me over for dinner again."

Tyler smiled.

Chapter 88

TINA SAW THE red light blinking on her phone. She wasn't sure if she wanted to answer it. The number was from NIH. Vernon Geeshmore was not checked off her list yet and she wasn't sure if he'd been cleared. But if she didn't answer, ignoring his call could cause problems.

"Madam President's Office, Tina speaking."

"Where is she?" Geeshmore demanded.

"I'm sorry?"

"Ears clogged, Tina? Where is she?"

"Excuse me?" Tina was stalling for time. She waved for an agent. "I'm sorry?"

The agent clicked on his earpiece so he could listen. He nodded to Tina who tried to keep the man talking.

"Tina... where's the president?" Geeshmore demanded again.

"She's in conference sir," Tina replied. "May I take a message for her?"

"NO!" he yelled. "Go get her."

"I'm sorry?"

"What the hell is going on over there?" Geeshmore yelled. "Get me the goddamn president."

The agent smiled and slapped his hand over his mouth. It took all of Tina's strength not to laugh.

"Excuse me, sir? Madam President is in conference and cannot be disturbed. May I take a message please?"

"Tina," Geeshmore yelled. "Put Viv on the damn phone right now."

"I'm sorry, sir," Tina replied. "Madam President is in conference and cannot be disturbed. May I transfer you to the vice president perhaps?"

"Tina!" Geeshmore screamed. "If you don't put her on right now..."

"You'll what exactly, sir?" Tina replied glancing up at the agent. The agent nodded and pointed his finger to the phone. Tina knew they had a lock. The agent wrote a short note and dropped it on her desk before running from the room. The note said... *keep him talking.*

* * * * * *

The smoke floated through the air as the aroma of sizzling meat aroused their anticipation of the coming meal. Vivian was enjoying herself. It'd been a long time since she'd been with a group of people in a family setting, and this felt like a family. She slept soundly through the night and woke full of energy. With their meetings behind them and a beautiful summer day ahead, Strickland was ready to relax and visit.

"Hmmm," Strickland hummed. "Those look good."

"Who wants cheese on their hamburger?" Nate hollered flipping them one by one.

"Who in the world is asleep on my bed?" Tyler asked handing a plate of cheese to Nate. "That's the question I have."

"Ah man," Nate moaned. "I forgot all about the damn lawyer. Is he still asleep?"

"Yes and who is he?" Tyler asked with her hands on her hips.

"You've got a strange man in your bedroom?" Skyler said laughing, opening a jar of pickles.

"Do I know him?" Caiden asked hugging Tyler and kissing her on the cheek.

"I forgot you ran to the store, sweetheart. I brought him in early this morning," Nate explained. Tyler stared so he added, "It's a long story. Hey Mad, can you wake the lawyer?"

"Certainly," Maddie said walking into the house laughing.

"Who's the lawyer," Strickland asked.

"The strange guy sleeping on my bed," Tyler replied.

It was so comfortable being around Strickland, everyone was forgetting she was the president. But they were all having a good time joking on Tyler about the stranger in her room.

"Actually, that's Early's guy," Lewis replied. "He's a little upset over losing his client so I thought he should rest."

"He lost his client?" Strickland asked. "How do you lose a client? You mean she fired him and hired another?"

"No," Greghardt replied taking a sip from his beer. "He actually lost her. We don't know where she is."

"Okay," Strickland said surprised. "Where was she last seen?"

"In jail," Nate answered chuckling while stacking the hamburgers onto a plate.

"In jail?" she repeated. "He lost her while she was in jail?"

"Actually," Lewis added. "She was taken from her cell and we don't know who took her."

"I see," Strickland said. "Is there anything I can do to help?"

"Yes," Nate replied laughing. "Go find her; we need her."

Everyone was laughing when Maddie and Drake walked outside.

"You look like shit," Nate said to Drake.

"I feel like shit," Drake replied. "Any news on my client?"

"Yes," Strickland said giggling. "She's missing."

"Can I have a hamburger?" Gabe asked.

"By the way," Greghardt added with a smirk, "That missing client is our little murder lady. Remember?"

"Oh my," Strickland replied.

"Are you the president?" Drake asked, and everyone laughed.

Chapter 89

CARRIE WATCHED AS Marty ate with one hand and held the other close to her chest. *How long is she going to pretend*?

"When do you plan on feeding your baby?" Carrie asked staring at Marty.

Marty looked at Carrie and frowned.

"You're obviously protecting something very special and precious," Carrie explained. "Your jacket is moving. It's either a small animal or a baby and I'll bet on the baby."

"It's our little sister Lizzie," Eliza said with a mouth full of crackers.

"I'll bet she's hungry," Lacey interjected. "Where's her bottle and formula... I'll make one for you."

"I have it," Macie offered handing Lacey her pack. "She has to have a special bottle in order to drink."

Lacey stared at the huge nipple and shrugged her shoulders. "Mix the formula as it says on the container?"

Marty nodded but didn't release her strong grip on Lizzie.

"May I?" Carrie asked holding out her hands for the baby. "Please, I promise not to hurt her."

"She needs to be changed," Marty replied.

"May I change her?" Carrie asked. "Please?"

Marty reluctantly released her grip on little Lizzie and allowed Carrie to take her. Carrie gasped as the beautiful fuzzy little girl with the extra long jaw squealed in her arms.

"She is one of us," Seith screamed when he saw the little girl.

"She has fur like me."

"Wow," Carrie whispered examining the little girl. "She's adorable."

Carrie's eyes looked down at the baby who was a little over thirty inches long. Soft white and golden hair covered her body and shimmered in the light. As Carrie changed her diaper, she could see Lizzie was a human, except for her feet. She had no toes, just soft stubs... almost like hoofs. Her long tail was interesting and Carrie wasn't sure what to do with it until she saw Marty had already cut a hole in the diapers. Her hands were normal. Lizzie's eyes were a dark green and her thick lips were beautiful. Her jaw and nose protruded a little more than normal, but it wasn't enough to take away from her beauty. In fact, it added to it. Lizzie smiled and Carrie's heart melted for this little baby girl.

"What kind of a defect is this?" Carrie asked glancing up at Marty.

"The doctors couldn't give us an explanation," Marty said.

Lacey handed the warm bottle to Carrie. Lizzie reached for it and guided it into her mouth.

"Well," Carrie soothed. "You must feel better now with a dry diaper and some food in your tummy."

"She reminds me of the babies we saw in the laboratory," Lacey said playing with Lizzie's feet, making her giggle.

"What babies?" Marty asked.

"There's a laboratory down here," Carrie explained. "It's no longer used, but some of the experiments are still there."

"May I see?" Marty asked.

Carrie stared into nothing trying to decide if it was a good idea to show anyone else that nasty room.

Marty saw the concern on Carrie's face and added, "Please?"

"I can feed the baby," Learl said holding out her arms. "I promise I'll take care of her."

"We can stay too," Macie added with a smile glancing over at Eliza.

"I don't want to stay away long," Marty said.

Her eyes were sincere which played deeply on Carrie's heart. She couldn't refuse.

"Fine," Carrie said at last handing the baby to Learl. "Now

don't move from *this* couch with *this* baby. Understand?"

Learl nodded. Her eyes were wide with the anticipation of caring for the baby. She kissed Lizzie on the head and watched every move she made.

"Well," Lacey said. "Looks like she's in good hands."

"I go with you," Seith volunteered. "I know this place."

The hall was dark and eerie. Carrie sighed with relief when they entered the laboratory. With only two flashlights, the group had to walk in pairs to see. Marty was especially interested in the babies floating in the jars with deformities similar to her daughter. She was also interested in Seith. When they returned, Marty was quiet.

"What are you thinking?" Carrie asked.

"I'm trying to put everything together," Marty explained. "Those jars hold real babies?"

Carrie and Lacey nodded.

"And Seith's skin looks like my Lizzie's," she surmised. "So does his face... Seith, do you have toes?"

"No," he replied. "My feet like hers."

"May I see?" Marty asked.

Seith sat on the couch and removed his shoes. When he pulled off his socks, Marty gasped. Seith's foot looked like one giant toe with a huge nail wrapped around it. She couldn't tell where it started or where it ended.

"We have to file it down all the time," Learl explained. "If we don't it cracks and bleeds."

"A hoof?" Marty whispered.

"What's a hoof?" Seith asked.

"It's not important," Marty replied with a smile.

Chapter 90

"YES, TINA?" STRICKLAND said into her cell. "I see, well put him through. It's Geeshmore," she whispered to Greghardt and Lewis. She held up her hand to let them know he was on the line. "Vernon? What's so important you just had to track me down... I see, and you need me to do what exactly... All right, Vernon, I'll look into it. Thank you for being so concerned about one of my generals—yes, one of mine, I am the Commander in Chief. Good day to you too, sir." Strickland sighed and glanced up at the ceiling as though saying a private prayer.

"What was that all about?" Lewis asked as Strickland dropped her phone into her pocket.

"That was Vernon Geeshmore. He had a fit on Tina yesterday—demanded I talk to him. How rude."

"And?" Greghardt prodded.

"Oh," Strickland replied. "Seems he can't locate General Longhorn and he's worried."

Lewis' phone chirped. He was surprised to see Loomsbury's name on the screen.

"Lewis," he answered. "Really? Well that's good... really good... oh no... that's bad... really bad... now that's interesting... very interesting... yes please do... thank you, doctor."

"And?" Strickland inquired.

"Seems your general is at The Agency with an infection from a botched operation while in Scotland," Lewis explained. "Agent Schuster brought her in."

"Really?" Strickland replied. "Will she be okay?"

"Yes," Lewis added. "But she's pregnant. Loomsbury ran some tests and the fetus is not exactly human."

"Excuse me?" Strickland asked.

Greghardt's phone rang and he looked surprised when he saw the name.

"Greghardt," he said as his face lit up with a smile. "Excellent... where exactly? Great, great... yes send me the details right away... thank you and good work."

"And?" Strickland and Lewis asked together.

"When the implant was removed from Early, seems Loomsbury also implanted a tracking device. And it's working," Greghardt replied. "She's here, in Washington."

"Really?" Strickland said raising an eyebrow. "I wonder what's so special about this state?"

Chapter 91

DR. SPANGLEHOLTZ WIPED his forehead with his kerchief and peeked at Geeshmore. They were in trouble and no matter how he looked at it, their lives were in jeopardy. Geeshmore played with a broken nail on his finger and Dr. Nestle stared at them as though they were some of the FBI's most wanted.

"Any explanation as to what went wrong?" Nestle asked starting the conversation.

Geeshmore and Spangleholtz shook their heads not saying a word. They knew whatever they said would be used against them.

"I want that general found," Nestle added, glancing around the dim office. "How can a US general just disappear?"

"You run the CDC," Geeshmore said lowering his eyes. He knew he was treading in dangerous waters but had to say something. "Can't you call her in with a fake epidemic or something?"

"Yeah, put out an all-points bulletin?" Spangleholtz asked.

"Of course," Nestle replied shaking his head. "I'm going to post a notice about a general who just happens to have a highly contagious disease. Now, where exactly did she contract this disease and how do we know so much about it? She just returned from Scotland, you idiots, not some third world country. I can't believe I'm actually trying to have a conversation with you two. Get out of my office. You make me sick."

Geeshmore and Spangleholtz stood outside Dr. Nestle's office and stared at each other. Neither had any idea how to find the missing general.

"Is there anything I can get for you?" the young assistant asked when they didn't move.

"A new life," Geeshmore said as they left the office together.

Chapter 92

CHARLOTTE SMILED AS they sped down the highway. Charlie was reading her a book, and she felt wanted. Behind them the mountains beckoned her, but she knew she was safe with her new family. The farther they drove from castle the better off she was. Charlotte was still confused as to what a mother and father were, but at least she had her grandparents and older brother. She watched through her window as she snuggled in her blankets. She didn't know where they were going, but she was happy.

A sign announced the small town of Sumas. The US border was only a few more miles and Miracle Valley was just beyond.

"Not much farther," Grandfather said as they crossed into Canada.

Charlie glanced up from the book and smiled. "We're almost home?"

"Almost," his grandmother replied. "Almost."

Charlie read to Charlotte until they parked outside a beautiful ranch house. Several barns and sheds were scattered around the property. A young man approached the vehicle and smiled.

"You the Wentlies?" he asked.

"Yes," Grandfather replied getting out of the car.

"House is stocked just as requested," the young man said. "Everything is turned on and ready for yah."

"This is for your troubles," Grandfather replied handing the young man some money.

"Thanks, let me know if I can ever do anything else for yah."

"I will," Grandfather said looking into the backseat. "We're home, kids."

Charlotte loved the house. It wasn't as big as the castle but that was okay. Trees were everywhere and she loved trees. Snuggled between two mountain peaks was a small lake, just big enough for her. Grandfather said they own over three hundred acres so no one should ever bother them. No trespassing signs had been posted all along the fence he built just for her. Charlotte stood at the top of a huge tree and admired the view. In the distance she could see the snow-covered mountaintops.

It felt good to spread her wings in the sunlight. With a little hop, Charlotte soared through the heavens and toward the lake. Several birds glided next to her as if welcoming her to her new home. As she drifted to the water, she allowed her feet to slide across the surface. It felt like skating on a cloud. Her grandparents and Charlie watched as their little angel explored her new surroundings.

"Are we safe here?" Charlie asked.

"As safe as we'll ever be," his Grandfather answered.

Chapter 93

CARRIE AND LACEY stopped to eat and rest. It'd been several hours since they left the tunnel. They were there for a purpose and not to play. Lacey used her GPS to determine their exact location. But without cell phones, they couldn't call anyone. They lost their phones when they slid into the hole.

"It's getting dark, we'll need to make camp soon," Carrie replied tapping her on the arm.

They hiked until it got too dark to see. Carrie had the tent up and a fire burning before the stars came out. They ate wild duck with wild potatoes and mushrooms for dinner. It was delicious. Carrie had just buried the bones when it started to pour. With everything tucked away inside their tent, the two settled down to rest and listen to the rain.

* * * * * *

Gabe pulled his jacket tighter around his neck. The water was seeping onto his sweatshirt and he was cold and hungry. Three agents tried to keep up with him but were having trouble. The owl DNA added to Gabe's human DNA not only enhanced his vision, but also gave him more strength and vigor. The smell of smoke told him Carrie and Lacey were near but, with the wind blowing and the rain pouring, he wasn't sure which direction to go.

Gabe waited under a tree to see how long it would take for them to reach him. "Why don't you wait here," he suggested when the agents finally caught up.

"We're fine," one of the men said. But to Gabe he didn't look fine.

"Really?" Gabe asked. "I can cover more ground if you just wait here. You can set up camp and I'll bring back something to eat."

"Fine." The agents finally agreed.

Before they could change their minds, Gabe took off at a slow jog up the steep incline. Leaves and twigs were everywhere, but he didn't care. The smoke was stronger here and he knew they were close. The rain slowed and he could see better through the trees. Unlike West Virginia, these mountains were not covered in vines or brush. He liked it better this way. Not as cluttered.

He finally saw their tent. It was high atop the next ridge. A large ravine separated them. He searched for a way across. But there was nothing. He would have to hike down then back up to reach them.

He needed to eat. Water, he could smell water. Far below a rushing river ran between the two mountains. He would find food there. Gabe scampered down the mountain to the flowing water. It was calm here, but to his right and his left he could see the white foam that meant rocks.

With a large stick, he snagged several fish. Between several boulders, he found a secluded spot and ate. All he needed was for a bear to find him. He knew bears loved fish. The fish was good. Even raw it tasted almost sweet. With all the bones, he had to carefully pick out the tasty meat. When he finished, he tossed the remains back into the water and rinsed off his hands. He felt better with his stomach full.

A line of boulders and fallen logs made the perfect bridge. Climbing up the next mountain was not as easy. The morning sun was just cresting over the ridge when he reached the top. Their tent was only a few yards away.

"Carrie!" he yelled. "Lacey, it's me, Gabe."

"Gabe?" Carrie asked sitting up in her sleeping bag. "Am I dreaming?"

"If you are then so am I," Lacey said struggling to get to her feet. "I heard him too."

"Over here, Gabe," Carrie yelled.

Before they could free themselves from their bags, Gabe's head poked into their tent with a big smile.

"What in the world are you doing here?" Lacey asked.

"Nice to see you too," Gabe said, laughing.

CHAPTER 94

THE WORLD WAS spinning around her faster than she could keep up.

"What?" Carrie screamed into the agent's cell phone. "Blow up what? Where?"

"Carrie," Maddie said trying to calm her, "just come back and everything will be fine."

"No!" Carrie screamed. The phone cracked when it hit a rock after she threw it. Carrie ran up the mountain as the agents stared at her.

"What's going on?" one of the agents asked Lacey.

"We left people up there," Lacey said. "We have to get them out before it blows."

Lacey ran after Carrie yelling for her to slow down. Gabe shrugged and ran after the girls. The three agents stared at each other confused as to what to do next.

"Hello?" Maddie yelled into the receiver. "Carrie? Anyone?"

* * * * * *

The chopper landed in a firebreak not far from the summit. Several agents dressed in black jumpsuits were the first to exit. Nate and Lewis hopped out last. They couldn't track the girls, but they could track Gabe. The men followed the device over the first ridge when Lewis spotted them.

"Carrie... Lacey... Gabe!" Lewis yelled.

"Wait for us," Nate hollered.

Carrie ran ahead but Gabe and Lacey waited. When the men arrived, Lacey tried to fill them in the best she could as they hurried toward the tunnel. Lacey darted in without warning them of the strong odor.

"Oh my God!" Lewis shouted slapping his hand over his nose and mouth.

Nate gagged.

"Sorry," Lacey replied not slowing down. The stench didn't seem to bother her anymore. "This is how they make sure no one escapes."

"What are you talking about?" Lewis yelled trying not to breathe.

"The people who live here," Lacey explained as she slowed her pace. "There's something inside them that explodes if they try to leave."

"Perhaps to a freedom they were not counting on?" Nate ran not looking at the bloody walls.

Lacey gave Nate a strange stare but continued down the tunnel.

"What is this place?" Lewis asked, trying to catch up.

"We're not sure," Lacey replied. "Some kind of laboratory maybe?"

"Up here in the mountains?" Nate asked from behind. "This is a strange way to get to it."

"I'd be happy to take you in another way," she said as she pushed on the door. "But we're in a hurry."

"Excuse me?" Lewis added.

"Long story," Lacey replied walking into the small office.

Carrie was holding a bundle of blankets in her arms when the three entered. Tears filled her eyes.

"I'm going to take the family out first," Carrie stated. "You need to find a way to get the others out. Maybe with a rope through the hole."

"Might work," Lacey replied. "When you get out, tell the agents where the hole is and we'll wait for them there."

"How much time do we have?" Carrie asked staring at Lewis.

"We're not sure," Lewis replied staring at the strange creatures blinking at him.

"Gabe, come with me," Carrie said as she darted through the

office with the family and Gabe following.

The small group ran through the tunnel and Carrie prayed everyone would make it out alive. She had no idea how long before it would be blown up.

"Gabe," Carrie yelled, holding the baby close to her chest. "When we get outside I'm going to point you in the direction of where a ceiling caved in. I need you to direct the agents to that hole so the others can get out. We can't bring them out this way. If they go out another way, maybe their devices won't go off."

"Or what? They'll blow?" Gabe added running behind the small group.

* * * * * *

Gabe stood on the ridge and examined the mountain side. The fallen leaves were thick with brush and small saplings. He couldn't see an opening. The men stood behind him scanning the area with their binoculars attached to their helmets. The sun was setting and the red and orange horizon cast an eerie glow.

"I have to get higher," Gabe said staring down the mountain.

No one answered the boy. They just looked at him. Gabe shook his head and laughed. A tall pine with scarce branches was just what he needed. With little effort, Gabe scaled the tall trunk as if it were a ladder. The men in black scratched their heads as the boy scurried up the tree and disappeared into the thick canopy.

Gabe could see the whole mountain side from here. He felt free and at home high in the sky. If he could, this is where he would build a house. The sun was almost gone and with the darkness came the boy's amazing eyesight. He concentrated and allowed his vision to adjust to the darkening shadows. With little effort, his eye muscles tightened and the forest floor expanded through his mind. It was as if he were only a few feet above the sloping side. A mile, in Gabe's eyes, was easily transformed into just a few feet. His eyes scanned every inch of the fallen leaves until he saw it. About halfway down the slop was a jagged black hole.

"Got it," he yelled from above the trees.

The men stared at each other. But not a word was spoken. The walk down the slope was tricky and they used their rifles to slow their descent. The leaves flew in rivers past their feet and caused their minds to whirl.

Being the first to arrive, Gabe yelled into the dark hole. "Hello?" As his eyes adjusted he could see everyone standing in the dark. "They're here."

"I can't see a damn thing," one of the agents said kneeling next to the hole.

"They're right there," Gabe said pointing.

A fallen tree was the perfect anchor, the rope ladder was dropped into the hole. Lacey was the first out and hugged Gabe.

"Thanks, friend," she said with a smile. "Okay guys, your boss is down there, recommend you hop to it."

Two agents climbed down to help the others. A couple of the hybrids couldn't climb and needed to be pulled out. But with a little patience and a few soothing words, everyone was soon walking across the mountaintop to a waiting helicopter. The creatures had never seen such a thing before and were frightened. As they walked, Gabe explained he too was a hybrid. He told them everything the scientists told him. Gabe's fascinating story seemed to do the trick, because the strange group was soon being whisked to a nearby Air Force base.

* * * * * *

Maddie and Vivian waited for everyone to arrive. The room was sterile and made her jumpy. Lacey and Gabe were the first to burst into the room. Strickland stared as the two ran in with several unusual individuals at their sides.

"We made it," Nate exclaimed giving Maddie a hug and kiss on the cheek. "Let's get out of this place."

"Oh my." Vivian Strickland smiled at the small unusual group of individuals who were staring at her.

* * * * * *

Vivian smiled at the baby. She was something with her long blonde hair and green eyes. The child won her heart.

"What are we going to do with you?" she whispered into the baby's ear.

Strickland eyes widened and she gasped as a soft voice echoed through her mind.

"She spoke to you?" Marty asked smiling.

"Yes," Strickland replied staring into the baby's eyes. "You *are* very special and I promise to take good care of you."

The others sat quietly on a couch and as she studied their faces, she said softly, "And I promise I will protect all of you with my life."

"Any ideas what to do with them?" Lewis asked as Greghardt paced the room.

"Loomsbury said they can't reproduce," he replied. "So we don't have that to worry about."

"I don't believe they'll be the problem," Nate replied. "It's the normal wackos who'll hunt them down."

"What if?" Lewis said mostly to himself. "What if?"

Chapter 95

THE KNOCK ON the door made everyone jump. Alex stared at Early and concern flooded his eyes. She could see he was scared and it made her stomach tighten. Obviously, she was not supposed to be there. The girls refused to leave her lap since they woke. Daren sat as close refusing to let go of her hand.

"Now what?" Alex stated staring at the door.

"You'll have to answer it sometime," she whispered kissing the girls on their heads and squeezing Daren's hand.

The pounding continued but with more force.

"Who is it?" Alex yelled.

"This is the FBI," a stern voice answered. "Back away from the door."

Before Alex could take a step, the door burst open and several men ran into the room with their guns drawn. Lights flashed everywhere and Early grabbed hold of her children. The girls started to cry as Daren jumped in front of them. No one was ever taking his mother away again.

"Early!" Drake yelled running to the small family huddling on the sofa. "Early, are you okay?"

Tears fell down Early's face as she stared proudly into her attorney's eyes. "I told you they were alive," she cried. "I told you."

"You told me," he said as tears rolled down his cheeks. "You told me."

Alex's arms were yanked behind him and someone read him his rights. Early flinched. Her love still burned for him but the pain of deceit was too strong. She wasn't sure if she should cry or feel sorry.

"Come, sweetheart," Drake said to Early. "We need to get you out of here."

"Where are we going?" she asked. "I don't have a home anymore."

"Mrs. Sutton," a warm voice said from behind Drake. "I'm Dr. Loomsbury and I'm here to take you and your family into protective custody."

"You're going into a protection program sweetheart," Drake explained. "You're safe now."

"Do I have to go back to jail?" she asked between tears.

"No," Loomsbury replied. "It is all over Mrs. Sutton. But we must hurry."

Chapter 96

NESTLE STRAIGHTENED HIS tie and studied himself in the mirror. He was proud of his accomplishments thus far. His decision to remove Spangleholtz from the position as director at the Washington hospital gave him the most comfort. Although the recent deaths of the women were still fresh in his mind, Nestle smiled. Marty Starling, Early Sutton and the other women were now just a horrible nightmare he could soon forget. From this day forward, Nestle knew he could focus all his efforts on a more important matter—changing the human genome to eradicate disease and illness forever.

His research proved that with a little tweaking, the human RNA could be stabilized. Then, he, Dr. Ronald Nestle, would be revered as a god. Ever since he was inducted into the society and learned of their secrets, Nestle realized their goals matched his. After all, the overall bases of their theories were not that different. But, no matter how much he argued his stance, those stupid idiots just wouldn't listen to him. He had no other choice but to finish his important project himself.

Nestle glanced down at the bound manuscript. He read the title out loud, *Retyping of Heritable Mutations*.

"Who are you talking to now, Roland," Dr. Crystal Derrier asked as she stood in the darkness.

Nestle didn't respond but sighed, "And who let you in?"

Derrier swayed her hips as she strolled into the dim light. "It's always so dark in here, Roland. Are you afraid the light might show off your imperfections?"

"Again Crystal, why are you here?"

"So touchy, Ro," Derrier sneered looking down at his desk. *"Retyping of Heritable Mutations,* huh? That sounds like interesting reading. How long do you have this checked out for?"

"It's mine," he stated lifting his chin with an air of pride.

"You mean you bought it?" she asked as she picked it up.

"No, I wrote it."

"You write?" she smirked skimming through the pages. "Let's see... *chromosome abnormalities involves the loss or gain of chromosomes or breakage and rejoining of chromatids...*" She read it out loud. "Sounds boring." Derrier tossed the manuscript back onto the table.

"My theories will change the world for the better," he stated with a strangeness reflecting in his eyes.

"Really?" she mused. "And how do you figure that, Ro? Does this mean you've finally decided to kill yourself and rid our planet of one less varmint?"

Derrier took a seat and crossed her legs. She stared at him as though expecting an honest answer. When none came, she laughed.

"What's so funny?"

"You," she replied. Her face scrunched as though experiencing a foul order.

"What do you want, doctor?" He sat in his chair. Nestle studied the woman who sat on the other side of his desk. He never really understood who hired her. But then again, when it came to the society no one really knows who's running the show. It was important for him to tread lightly. Otherwise, he wouldn't be around long enough to apply his theories and become a god, which was his true destiny.

"I'm here," Derrier began, "because you've been a naughty boy, Roland." Without giving the man a chance to respond, she stood and straightened her skirt. She took in a deep breath and adjusted her jacket. Her long dark hair rolled in gentle waves as she turned to leave. But one quick glance over her shoulder gave Nestle a chill that iced his soul.

"Be a good boy, Roland," she whispered, then after an ominous grin she was gone.

"I hate that woman." He glanced through his manuscript. "I need to fix this section," he whispered grabbing a pen.

Chapter 97

LOOMSBURY LOOKED PALE in the dim light of the darkened room. He glanced over at Greghardt and shook his head.

"Does he ever get out much?" Lewis whispered.

"What?" Greghardt asked.

"The man's as white as a sheet. Tell him to go outside once in awhile? He looks like death."

"Excuse me," Loomsbury coughed clearing his throat clicking to advance to the next slide. "After reading the manuscript we obtained thanks to our Agent Derrier, I believe I have a better understanding of how our new friends came to be."

Loomsbury clicked on the screen again and a copy of the manuscript's first page revealed the title and author. *Retyping of Heritable Mutations by Dr Roland Nestle, Director, Centers for Disease Control and Prevention.*

"We found this on Dr. Nestle's office computer," Lewis spoke up.

Loomsbury ignored the outburst and continued. "The document describes the insertion of DNA and RNA from other species to correct a human deficiency."

"Deficiency?" Lewis asked.

"Yes," Loomsbury replied. "Our DNA is remarkable, capable of making billions of healthy individuals. But, at the same time, our DNA is also capable of making people ill. Currently, we have identified and categorized over eight thousand genetic disorders that are passed down to our children. Many are fatal or debilitating, and all are due to a DNA replication error. Many of these errors are detected early and the pregnancy can be terminated, but again, just as many are not discovered until it is too late. DNA degeneration can also cause the human body to be more susceptible to viral infections, those illnesses caused by contagious random strands of RNA that come into contact with the human host."

"So how does he do it?" Lewis asked. "How do you create an Elizabeth Starling?"

"It depends," Loomsbury replied scratching his head. "According to the manuscript there are two ways. One is through genetic splicing. Select which rungs of the DNA you want to fix, so to speak, and splice in the foreign DNA into that rung. Another method is to create an RNA virus and implant that virus into a fertilized egg... or person. Elizabeth Starling was created by genetic splicing. The boy, Gabe, was created with a virus. Only slight variations can be made with an RNA virus. Massive changes can be accomplished by splicing."

"Are there any others?" Lewis asked.

"Selection of parents I suppose," Loomsbury surmised. "But no, these are the only two methods covered in this document. However, his theory does discuss mass distribution of an RNA virus into the populous. With the right virus, his ideas could cause dramatic changes overnight. Changes that would occur over and over again forever—mutation."

"What kind of changes are you talking about?" Lewis asked rubbing the back of his head. For some reason, he had a very good idea of where this discussion was leading and he didn't like it.

"Millions could die," Loomsbury said lowering his eyes. "A virus is not a living entity as is a bacterium. A virus is just a tiny particle of an RNA strand with a coat of protein." Loomsbury used his hands to try and explain. "It's coated in a lipid membrane for protection from the elements. Most are shaped like a ball, but some look like exotic spiders. Viruses don't contain the enzymes needed to carry out the chemical reactions for life. Instead, viruses carry only one or two enzymes that are used to decode their genetic instructions. A virus must have a host—a plant or an animal. Outside a host, viruses cannot function or reproduce. Therefore, we say viruses are nonliving. It is our own cells that reproduce a virus, our own cells that betray us. And we get sick, or change."

"Change?" Lewis repeated.

"According to his manuscript, Dr. Nestle theorizes his viruses would strengthen the human to be able to withstand the common cold, or under the right condition, die. Dr. Nestle has already classified the human genome into categories from desirable to less desirable. His virus would target the less desirable to eliminate them; burden gone."

"And what traits do his less desirable have?" Lewis asked now wondering about the possibilities this manuscript would have on the world if released.

Loomsbury clicked his screen and a chart displayed with several columns of various colors. He cleared his throat before continuing. "According to Dr. Nestle the human population is categorized into races and then sub-races." Loomsbury clicked off the screen and turned to the small audience of two men. "I have to be honest. This makes me very nervous. What Dr. Nestle tried to do, but failed, was to put a genetic coding on the poor and undereducated—the underlings of the world. And anyone who truly studies the poor or needy will find they are of the same genome types as all the others. No genetic typing can categorize people into a *less* desirable." Loomsbury used his two fingers to create quotations around the word *less*.

"I see," Lewis replied and Greghardt nodded.

"I've studied the data since the start of the human genome project and all we can conclude is that humans are 99.9 percent the same everywhere. It's only when the DNA degrades for whatever the reason—hereditary, environmental, chemical, emotional," Loomsbury flung his arms over his head, "just pick a reason and the final DNA result is different. You cannot use genetic testing to determine if a person will end up rich, poor, educated, married; it just doesn't work that way. We can tell if there's a genetic flaw such as Down Syndrome or Mitochondrial Disease or Wilson Disease, or the color of the hair, or their eyes," Loomsbury sat down and rested his head on his hands and cried. "But... but..."

Lewis walked over to the young doctor. He knelt and

whispered into his ear. "My friend, there will always be a Dr. Frankenstein and a Dr. Jeckle in this world. But that is why we have you."

Loomsbury dried his eyes on the back of his hands and wiped his nose on his sleeve. After a deep breath he looked into Lewis's eyes. Tears ran down his face and Lewis could see the fear was real.

"But you don't understand," Loomsbury cried.

"Unfortunately," Lewis whispered, "we do."

"And," he begged.

"And I need you to be strong my friend," Greghardt added. "We need *you* to read and re-read that manuscript until you know it by heart. Then go through that crazy man's electronic files again and again until you can figure out what he's planning."

"Can't you just arrest him?" Loomsbury cried. "Lock him away?"

"It is not illegal to be crazy in America," Lewis replied.

"That's never stopped us before," Loomsbury yelled.

"No, but we need to know who he's working with," Lewis explained. "And if we eliminate Mr. Nutcase too soon, we may lose the ties of those who are pulling his strings.

Chapter 98

"YOU WANT TO do what?" Geeshmore stared at Dr. Nestle with pure hatred. "You are in my office now, Roland, and we're back in DC, so don't try and pull any society rank here."

"Ranking has nothing to do with it," Nestle replied sitting in front of the director of the National Institute of Health.

"You had Dr. Spangleholtz removed as one of your problems, then the mothers, and now you want to release a... a virus... to... to cleanse the world... of what you call undesirables? Have you totally lost your mind?"

"Actually Vernon," Nestle replied brushing his hair from his face. "I believe my mind is actually starting to clear up. I'm seeing things all too clearly now."

* * * * * *

"Dr. Nestle?" a young man in a gray pinstriped suit with a pink tie said smiling and holding out his hand. "We're so excited to have you here, sir. I'm Mr. Williamson, Ryan Williamson and I'm the Director."

Another brown-noser. Nestle snickered shaking the man's hand. "Yes, we've been meaning to get out here and see your facilities for some time. But just haven't had the opportunity. I do apologize."

"Nothing to apologize for," Williamson replied. "The Barker Institute is happy you chose us to service your needs. And we have assigned our two best scientists to your new project. Oh here they are now."

A young man and young woman walked toward them wearing white lab coats and holding clipboards. They didn't smile, but they didn't frown either. Nestle watched how they walked and instantly liked them.

"Let me introduce you to our top geneticists, Dr. Brighten and Dr. Harding. Doctors, this is Dr. Roland Nestle of the CDC. He's in charge of your new project."

Tyler held out her hand and Nestle shook it. "Please, call me Tyler."

"And you can call me Caiden." Caiden held out his hand.

"Nice to meet you Tyler and Caiden," Nestle replied. "I understand you've read the reports? And you're aware of the urgency and the need of confidentiality in regards to our new project."

"Yes sir, we are," Caiden replied winking at Tyler.

The group entered a conference room to discuss the urgency as Tyler fumbled with the pen that held the small recording device. As the doors closed, Tyler wondered how in the world she ever got herself into this mess.

* * * * * *

Nate and Maddie sat listening to Nestle give his instructions to the scientists and couldn't believe what they were hearing. In order to safeguard the human population, they would need the help of every nation on Earth. It was many years ago when people won their class-action lawsuits against their governments. For years, the authorities denied the spraying of toxic gases into the upper atmosphere in order to slow the pace of global warming. However, the scientists never considered the negative implications. They accidently changed the normal rainfall around the world. But it wasn't until the second- and third-generation babies were born with strange life-threatening abnormalities did the people take action.

The spraying stopped, and after a time the people and the land healed. But what others didn't understand was the concept of being able to distribute chemicals, or viruses, over a mass area and how easily, cheaply and secretly it could be achieved. And this is what Nestle wrote in his manuscript.

Now, he was talking to two geneticists about methods on how to make large quantities of a virus and how to keep that virus contagious in different environments. In other words, Tyler and Caiden are being paid to research the lipid membrane. To determine how the outer coating of a virus can be strengthened to protect it in all types of weather and conditions. But the most horrifying requirement that sent panic through the listeners was his request the virus be protected from all chemicals including chloride and sunlight—the last two remaining defenses the human population have in their arsenal against the RNA killer. If successful, other viruses would eventually mutate and there would be no way to eliminate even the most common of illnesses, including a common cold. No surface could be sanitized—a countertop, a door handle, a medical instrument, not even a human hand. All viruses would be free to run rampant throughout the planet killing both animals and plants, and causing mass extinction of all life on Earth.

Nestle would get his wish; he would become a god. But not a god of life.

Chapter 99

TYLER PACED THE room and wondered if her carpet would last through this crazy ordeal she was thrown into. Maddie and Nate sat on the couch reading though their notes. Caiden stood by the window and watched as Prince chased a small squirrel out of the yard. Everything seemed normal enough, but life was suddenly anything but.

"Aunt Mad," Tyler said sitting on the floor in front of her aunt and uncle. "I never wanted to do what you two do. That's why I went into science. This is Skyler's thing, not mine."

"Sweetie," Maddie said leaning over to run her fingers through her niece's hair. "We could have switched you with your sister. But she just doesn't have the knowledge to pull it off. Dr. Nestle would have seen right through her. You and Caiden are the best at what you do. You can give him what he needs even though it won't work. You two can write the reports so if others review your findings, you can make it look like it will work."

"You're never alone sweetheart," Nate added. "We have agents all through your company. The receptionist, the new director, most of security, the janitors; Tyler, you are not alone. If anyone tried to do anything to hurt you or Caiden, there are enough of us to protect you. We even placed agents in the towns of Granite Falls, Lochsloy, Jordan, and Marysville. They're at the police departments, fire departments, health departments, stores, food courts. Honey, they're everywhere."

"And Mr. Nutcase," Maddie added, "is never alone. The Agency has a remarkable way of sliding people into the right places at the right times. With every success and with every failure, we've learned. There was a case not too long ago that involved an army sergeant. It was believed he was using the military women for personal pleasures. Within two weeks, everyone who worked around this man was one of ours. Every area this man visited was under surveillance. Each time he thought he was sexually abusing one of his female troops he was actually digging himself a deeper grave. Our female agents are well trained and are not afraid to use their bodies in any way necessary to complete their missions. Sex with strangers does not frighten or bother us. We turn those strong desires of our enemies against them, but also do not allow them to enter us here." Maddie patted her chest. "We think of it as simply shaking someone's hand. It means nothing to us."

"So what happened to the guy," Tyler asked with tears running down her face. Her aunt never validated her suspicions before. She had an idea of what Maddie did for The Agency. But never spoke to her about it. Now, her aunt was freely confiding to her and it touched her deeply.

"When we had enough evidence," Maddie answered, "One of our agents helped him to have an early heart attack. He died serving his country, which allowed his wife and children to live out their lives in comfort. A win-win solution for all, the world is rid of a major useless individual and his family can go on living without shame."

"But that makes you judge and jury, Aunt Mad," Tyler said wiping her eyes. "Almost playing God."

"But what you don't understand," Nate explained sitting down his notes, "is behind the scenes, The Agency has a panel of judges who hears each case. It's this panel that passes down the sentencing. Each case has a set of lawyers who represent all the players. Dr. Nestle has legal representation, he just doesn't know it. His lawyer continuously fights for his life. The only difference is there's no appeal process. Once the sentence has been set, it's carried out within twelve hours. The Agency is thorough and the rules are absolute. There is no hiding of evidence and everything is admissible. If a person is found guilty, you can rest assured they're guilty. If there is any doubt, any at all, the individual is allowed to live. Their lives may forever be changed, but they will not die."

"So The Agency is more than just an agency?" Tyler asked feeling a little better.

"The Agency is woven throughout the world's governments including the United Nations," Nate explained. "It's very powerful and was created to stop those who would use the established laws against mankind. Corporations have gotten so rich and so powerful, today's governments have no way to fight them. Corruption is everywhere and people are so hungry for power and money they'll do anything to get it. Anything."

"Even kill our planet," Tyler whispered.

"Even that," Maddie added.

"Then I'm doing a good thing," Tyler suggested.

"Sweetheart," Caiden replied hugging Tyler around her shoulders. "You are doing a brave and powerful thing. In some ways, you are more powerful than the largest corporations of the world right now."

"Tyler," Nate added. "We are not here to push our wants or ideas on anyone. We are here to ensure the laws established to protect people's rights are carried out. That's all. Those who have the need to break those laws are the ones subjected to The Agency's punishments. We can accomplish things most governments are prohibited from doing. That's why The Agency was founded by all nations."

"And probably why dictatorship has all but left our world," Maddie said laughing.

"What do you mean?" Tyler asked.

"Shortly after the establishment of The Agency, all countries ruled by a dictator suddenly changed to a republic or democratic system. It was quite interesting. Some remained in power as presidents while others retired."

"Weird," Caiden stated.

"It's human nature mostly," Nate replied. "Intelligent people are more concerned about their own welfare and know when they've lost. It's the crazies, like Mr. Nutcase, who are the most dangerous. He doesn't even realize if he puts his plan into action he will not only kill off his undesirables, but he will also kill himself."

Chapter 100

EARLY AND ALEX stared at each other. Neither said a word. They didn't have to for their eyes spoke for them. Early's eyes showed anger and hopelessness, perhaps with a touch of abandonment. Alex's eyes showed regret and sadness. Tears fell as he stared at the love of his life. He rubbed his face with his hands smearing his tears.

Early stood firm. She thought it odd the sheen from the large table could grab her attention and pull her from her anger. But for some reason, it seemed to sooth her. Her eyes followed the reflection of the window and trees outside. A small cloud was passing and created a beautiful picture just a few feet away. If only she could hold on to her babies and jump into that reflection, then maybe her life would be happy again.

"My name's Dr. Leonora Priddleton," a young girl of about twelve said walking into the room. "I'm Dr. Loomsbury's assistant." Her braided pony tails swished as she walked. She used her finger to push her dark-rimmed glasses up on her nose which enhanced her dark eyes. The white coat floated just inches above the floor. Early had to smile as the young girl placed several stacks of paper on the table.

"Good afternoon," a fresh and friendly voice echoed from behind the young girl. "My name's Adrian Whitetower and I'm representing Daren, Dakota and Nevada, your children."

"What?" Alex stated raising his head. "Why?"

"We will discuss that in a few minutes," Adrian replied sitting across from Alex. "Please, Early, take a seat. The table is large, wherever you feel the most comfortable."

Suddenly the room exploded with people entering from several doors. Lewis and Greghardt entered with Strickland trailing behind looking lost and bewildered. Early studied her and knew instantly she was about to lose her grip on reality, because she had been there once herself. Without giving it a second thought, Early sat next to Strickland and took her hand. She smiled at her and Strickland gave Early's hand a gentle squeeze.

Several other people entered Early had never seen before. They carried folders with pictures and documents. She was scared, but also knew the president would not let anything happen to her children or her. It was on the plane ride from Washington to Oklahoma when she personally promised both Early and Marty she would protect them and their children with her life. Early felt safe for the first time in many months.

Lewis cleared his throat and spoke, "Dr. Priddleton, Agent Whitetower, this meeting is yours."

"Thank you, Dr. Lewis," Adrian began. "The reason we called you here is because it's important the parents of my clients have full knowledge of the happenings surrounding their creation and their faked deaths. First, let me say I am not here to remove your children from your custody. They are yours. However, their best welfare is my top priority."

Alex and Early nodded.

"Early," Adrian continued. "Do you know the story of what happened the last night you were with your family?"

"Yes," Early stated. "I made love to Alex and then I woke up in a courtroom accused of murdering them." Early tensed as she spoke the words. But Strickland's grip on her hand tightened and gave her something real to cling to.

"And Alex," Adrian said looking over at him. "What do you remember?"

"I woke up in a strange house with no wife and my children asleep in the next room. My head was spinning and later I was told my wife had killed herself. It took me months to find out the truth, but when I did I called in all my resources to help me rescue her."

"But..." Early started to say and was cut off by Adrian.

"Wait, Early, let me give you all the details as The Agency understands them," Adrian added holding up her hand. "We have all the evidence here and I brought in those agents assigned to gather that evidence. You'll be able to ask all the questions you want."

Early nodded and glanced over at Alex who was crying. She could see the pain in his eyes but wasn't sure if she could ever trust him again. He was supposed to protect her from terrible things, not be a part of it.

"Earlier that day you bought some wine," Adrian said. "Do you remember?"

"Kind of," Early answered.

"You entered a wine store and pick out a red chardonnay," Adrian replied. "You purchased it from this cashier." Adrian slid a colored picture toward Early. "This woman is an agent of the Philips Institute. The woman substituted your bottle for another. She had several under the counter. No matter what wine you picked, she had another laced with a strong sedative. Both you and your husband didn't wake up that evening or the following morning."

"What?" Early cried.

"Alex," the young Dr. Priddleton said pulling everyone from their thoughts. "Would you please stand?"

Alex rose from his chair.

"Now, would you raise your shirt so we can see your abdomen?"

As Alex pulled his shirt, Early saw a small scar just above his bellybutton. The scar was very similar to hers. Alex had been implanted with the same drug inducing system that was implanted in her. But was this truth or were they trying to deceive her? Her mind twirled with all the implications.

The main door opened and Drake entered carrying his briefcase and a huge smile. He nodded to Lewis and Greghardt taking a seat next to Dr. Leonora Priddleton.

"Nice you could make it, Drake," Lewis said with a grin.

Drake tugged on one of the doctor's braids before speaking. "Thank you, sir. A little more traffic at the airport than expected."

"Drake!" Early yelled. Seeing Drake suddenly made things a

whole lot better.

Drake placed his finger over his mouth to quiet her. But his wink brought a smile to her face.

"The boy, Daren, has no abnormal DNA sequencing," Priddleton explained thumbing through her notes and ignoring the short intruption. "Alex is his father and Early is his mother. However, the twins, Dakota and Nevada, are a different story. Again, Alex is the father and Early is the mother. However, their DNA sequence has been spliced with Dolphin DNA. Dolphins and humans share many of the same chromosomes. Humans have forty-six where dolphins have forty-four. However, when compared, our chromosomes are basically the same. Therefore, it's understandable the first attempts at genetic splicing between separate species would be with those we share the most similarities, our friends the dolphins."

When no one responded, Leonora continued. "We analyzed the twin's DNA and discovered the splicing was done in the area of lungs and breathing."

"What that means Early," Drake interrupted. "Both you and your husband were used as guinea pigs."

"But..." Early said then stopped herself.

"Go on," Agent Whitetower added trying to encourage Early. "Please ask your questions. Both of you."

"How did they splice my eggs without me knowing?"

"Alex was working for the Philips Institute," Agent Adrian Whitetower explained. "They saw an opportunity. The clinic that performed your invetro fertilization was also part of the Philips Institute. Once they decided on using you, it wasn't hard to set the wheels in motion."

"But then why take Early away from us?" Alex cried.

"You Alex," Drake explained, "are a medical doctor. You specialize in fetal bone abnormalities. You would be easier to convince about what they were doing than your wife. Therefore, they tried to remove *her* from the equation."

"But ruin her in the public's eye!" he screamed. "Put her on trial, have her killed? Who are these sick people anyway?"

"I can answer that question," a woman at the end of the table said standing up. "I'm Agent Carrie Clarke and I was assigned to the case from early on. And this is my partner Agent Skyler

Brighten."

Skyler stood, nodded then sat back down.

"During our investigation we ran into this symbol," Carrie said sliding a photo across the table. "The Skull and Bones Society is a Yale University alumni funded and backed by the Philips Institute. The society began in 1832 and was established for the betterment of the human race. This society has been responsible for the placement of prominent people in important positions around the world. A lot of good has come from this society, but also a lot of bad. Within the Philips Institute are many individuals who believe our world is overpopulated. And if allowed, they would *first* fix the human DNA by expanding our lives by many years. And *second*, rid our world of the less fortunate.

"As our investigation progressed, we were able to match past Bonesmen with individuals within our government. Bonesmens are what that society calls their graduates." When Early cringed, Carrie added, "Kind of sick, I know. Anyway, we were able to connect the dots and two major players jumped to the top of our list, the Director of the National Institutes of Health, Dr. Vernon Geeshmore, and the Director of the Centers for Disease Control, Dr. Roland Nestle. Dr. Nestle was also recognized by General Longhorn at an overseas conference where he never registered. That was my first clue." Carrie sighed and again shrugged her shoulders.

"We found Dr. Eugene Spangleholtz deceased in a New York hotel about a month ago," Skyler added standing to face the crowd. "It was cited as a brain aneurysm, however, after analyz-ing his blood, we determined it was drug induced. The man was murdered."

"That was our second clue," Carrie exclaimed with a huge smile. "So my partner and I put the two together and did a little more digging. And with the discovery of the old laboratory..."

"What old laboratory?" Alex asked.

"Oh," Carrie replied. "I guess I left that part out. Lacey found it, or more like it, fell into it, an old Skull and Bones laboratory hidden in the mountains of Washington. We found huge jars with body parts."

"And whole deformed babies," Skyler stated shocking Early and Alex.

"How long had these experiments been going on?" Early asked.

"Tests on some of the fetuses date to the 1950s, give or take a decade," Dr. Leonora Priddleton interjected, her long and braided ponytails danced around her.

"The 1950s?" Early yelled. "I thought this stuff was illegal or something."

"It has been illegal in the United States for some time. Our government amended our constitution to prohibit human and animal hybrids. However, in other countries such as the United Kingdom, it's not illegal. However, the Human Fertilization Embryology Act was amended in the 1990s to allow for hybrids of all kinds for medical research," Leonora added. "However, the Act does provide for the prohibition of allowing the... the..." Leonora paused before continuing. "Hybrids from maturing."

"So they broke the law," Early yelled. "Go arrest them."

"The Agency doesn't arrest people, Early," Carrie replied lowering her head. "We either confiscate them... or..."

"Kill them!" Early screamed jumping to her feet. "Then kill them! Kill them all! Look what they did to my girls, and to little Lizzie, and Gabe. It was WRONG!" Early sat down and cried into her hands.

Alex leaped to his feet knocking his chair to the floor. He knelt beside Early and placed his hand on her shoulder. Early hesitated only slightly before falling into his arms. She screamed and cried inside her husband's tight embrace.

"We'll go away, Early," he said crying on her shoulder. "I'll be more careful and I'll never let anything like this happen again. I was told you were all over the news. But we were forbidden to watch TV. They secluded us from the world."

"How did you find out about me then?"

"An employee named Hope. She dropped me a note and inside was a newspaper clipping. It was of your trial," he cried. "I was so angry and scared. I didn't know where to start or what to do. I started making phone calls. At first I wasn't sure who to trust so I wrote down everything I could remember."

"His notes are now a valuable piece of evidence," Carrie added patting Early on the back. "It helped us to piece the rest of the story together."

"Early," Drake said standing next to Carrie. "From what I can tell, Alex knew as much as you did. He is innocent of any wrong-doing sweetheart."

Early dried her eyes and stared at Drake. Her eyes were red and swollen, but she looked happy. "You see, Drake," Early said between tears. "I told you my family was alive. I told you."

"You told me sweetheart, and you taught me a valuable lesson," Drake replied as a tear rolled down his cheek. "I will always listen and hear what my clients are telling me. I never doubted you Early... never."

"I know," Early cried. "I know."

Chapter 101

"I WANT TO speak to the pilots myself," Nestle ordered to the frightened man standing in front of him.

"But sir," he stuttered. "Our pilots are all over the world."

"Then put me through on a mass conference call, you idiot," Nestle yelled. "It's not difficult."

"Yes sir," the man said stumbling on his words.

Nestle sighed. "This project's not happening as easily as I'd hoped. I requested the two genetic scientists be present for the mass spraying, but of course they've been assigned to another project. I'll have to have that Ryan Williamson removed as Director before the day's over. But at the moment, I've more important things to tend to."

"You're going through with this I see," Geeshmore said. "You've actually lost your mind."

"Come here," Nestle demanded as Geeshmore entered.

"What?" Geeshmore asked standing in front of the man.

Nestle grabbed Geeshmore's shirt and pulled him in. "Don't you ever say that to me again. I'm the one who's saving mankind. It will be *ME* they will be paying their respects to... and DON'T YOU FORGET IT!"

Geeshmore pushed Nestle away and adjusted his shirt and tie. His face was red with anger. He'd had just about enough of this crazy lunatic. He stared at him for just a moment before he left the room with his hands in a fist.

"Stupid asshole," Geeshmore said pushing the elevator button for the lobby.

"Who's an asshole?" Derrier asked as the elevator started to move.

Geeshmore was so angry he didn't look to see who else was riding down before speaking. He jumped and gasped at the same time. "Damn it, Crystal. You scared the shit out of me."

"You didn't answer my question, Vernon," she said gliding her lip gloss over her thick lips. "Who's an asshole?"

"No one," Geeshmore said turning to face the doors.

"Could you possibly be talking about dear sweet Ro?" she asked placing her arm through his and grabbing on firmly. "Not my precious Ro?"

The doors opened and they exited the elevator into the lobby together, arm in arm toward the waiting black cars parked along the curb.

* * * * * *

The screens blinked on and the airmen watched as Dr. Roland Nestle's face appeared before them. From Nestle's side, there were many screens each only a few inches in diameter. To him, everyone looked different, but in reality it was the same group of men. If Nestle had taken the time to look at the uniforms, he would have seen they were all the same. But today, Nestle was too busying becoming a god and he wasn't paying attention to the trivial details.

"Men," Nestle said with his back firm and his chin held high. "Today's assignment will be the most important of your life. Stay on your flight paths; do not deviate. It's critical you release your load at the coordinates given. Do not waste your precious cargo. But do not spray sparingly either. I wish you Godspeed as you propel us into the future."

The screens went blank and the men stared at each other with surprise on their faces. Then the laughter stared. They continued laughing as they stood and retrieved their trash carts from the side of the room. The Agency janitors continued to laugh as they headed to their floors to begin their daily cleaning.

* * * * * *

Nestle wiped his forehead with his handkerchief. He prayed

he didn't look too afraid to the military pilots around the world. It was the first time he'd ever delivered such an important speech, but he also knew it would not be his last. He left the small conference room and walked down the hallway to his office. The large CDC complex in Fairfax, Virginia offered him the privacy he required for this special project. His room was small but comfortable. He knew the spraying would be over before he sat down for his dinner. Nestle was so excited he couldn't wait to get home to the six o'clock news.

Throughout the day, progress reports dropped on his desk by his assistant, Amelia, included location of military planes and amounts of cargo released, as well as current weather conditions for those areas. Nestle was more than excited when he read not one storm dared to dampen his goals today. Obviously, Mother Nature was on his side.

He watched the clock as the minutes ticked away. As the little hand got closer to five, Nestle's anticipation increased to a level about to explode. At exactly a quarter to five, Nestle bid good night to Amelia and ran from his office.

Amelia watched as the elevator closed behind her boss. She picked up the phone and dialed the number given to her earlier that morning.

"Amelia Anderson speaking, I'm reporting Dr. Roland Nestle has left the building," she said as clearly as she could. "Good night." The dial tone echoed in her ear as she studied the phone. That was the weirdest call she ever had to make.

* * * * * *

Nestle's dinner consisted of a granola bar and a cup of coffee. He was not about to waste time stopping to pick something up and he had no spare minutes to stand in front of a microwave. With his wife at their home in Atlanta, Georgia, Nestle sat contently alone and hungry in front of his TV with a small snack and a cup of hot caffeine. He watched and listened through the local news, political views and daily accomplishments of those in the sports arenas. But not one word was mentioned about the jets or the intense spraying. It had been years since the citizens had seen the white streaks in the sky. Any signs of new spraying would have brought immediate attention and complaints.

Ranting and raving, Nestle called his contact at the Department of Defense and tapped his foot waiting anxiously for the man to answer. After several rings, a voice echoed through his ear.

"Extension 7742," the voice said. "May I help you?"

"Yes, this is Dr. Nestle of the CDC, I need to speak with Special Agent Fallon."

"Yes sir," Nate replied covering the mouthpiece to hide a laugh. "Please hold."

Nate sat the receiver on the table and chuckled heading into the bathroom.

"Maddie," he yelled. "Are you finished with your bath, sweetheart?"

"Not really," she replied, "what's up?"

"The call came in earlier than expected. Special Agent Fallon is being requested."

"Damn," she said dripping with water. "Can you grab my robe and another towel please?"

Maddie ran to the living room laughing all the way. She paused for a few moments to steady herself before sitting in the chair. Calmly she picked up the receiver and placed it next to her ear. "This is Special Agent Fallon."

Water dripped from her hair and into her eyes. She dried her face with the corner of her towel. Her job is one of the best ever.

Nestle hesitated. He was expecting a man not a woman to be his contact. But he decided it didn't matter as long as the spraying took place.

"I saw nothing on the news this afternoon," Nestle stated.

Maddie rolled her eyes and grinned. She waited a few seconds before speaking. It was important to intensify his apprehension. Taking in a deep breath, Maddie spoke slowly. "Project Hygeia was completed at twenty-three twelve GMT."

"Damn it woman," he yelled. "What time would that be here... in Virginia?"

Maddie had to hold the phone away as she tried hard not to laugh. When she regained her composure, she replied, "That would be eighteen twelve eastern standard time, or twelve minutes after six this afternoon. It is now nine thirty in Virginia. Or approximately three hours ago. Is there anything else I can help you with?"

"I don't see any lines in the sky!" he yelled.

"Well," Maddie replied as professionally as possible. "Since the sun has all ready set, I don't see how you can see much of anything other than stars right now. Is there anything else I can help you with?"

"Yes," Nestle screamed. "Go fuck yourself."

Nestle slammed the phone down so hard Maddie had to hold it away from her ear. Her laughter was loud and Nate could hear it echoing down the hallway as he tossed the wet towel onto the side of the tub.

"My God I love my job," Maddie shouted at Nate. "This is just too much fun and we get paid for it."

* * * * * *

Nestle sat in his office the next morning steaming. He spent most of the evening pacing his room. Sleep finally caught him a little past two in the morning, and after a restless night of fighting his blankets, Nestle could probably count a total of three hours of sleep. His coffee cup was empty again, and he didn't feel like walking down the hall.

"Amelia!" he yelled.

"What?" she hollered from her desk.

Nestle had to bite his tongue. The woman was new. She was assigned to him only a few months ago, and he hated her. She couldn't type, couldn't file and had terrible phone manners. But her ass was nice and her boobs bounced when she walked. So at least she had a few good secretarial qualities.

"Get your sweet ass in here please," he yelled.

Amelia stood at his door and stared at him with her hip swayed to one side. "You rang?"

Nestle held out his empty cup and wiggled it.

"Honestly?" Amelia whined. "What am I your wife or something?"

"Just go get the fucking coffee," he sneered. "*Please*?"

"Well. Since you said *please*, how can I refuse." Amelia yanked the cup from his hand and the few remaining drops splashed him in the face. "Oops," she said as she left his office.

Nestle wiped the coffee from his chin and growled. Not only

did he need to get rid of Ryan Williamson, but now he needed to figure out how to get rid of this bitch of a secretary. The phone rang, which startled him. Excitement ran through him as he thought of the possibilities. This could only be good news.

"Dr. Nestle," he said into his phone.

"This is the office of the president. Dr. Nestle, this is Tina Killian, Senior Advisor. Please hold for Madam President."

What in the hell could she possibly want? Nestle waited for the woman to come to the phone. She was always calling at the wrong time.

"Nestle," Strickland stated with a staunch professionalism that frightened him. "A car is waiting for you downstairs. I need you in my office immediately."

"Yes ma'am," he said replacing his receiver.

"Your coffee, sir," Amelia said sitting his cup on his desk.

"Not now. I've just been summoned to the White House." Nestle grabbed his jacket and ran from his office.

* * * * * *

Amelia watched as the elevator doors closed. She grabbed her purse and her two personal items, a picture of her and her husband and a small clock. The door clicked as she pulled it behind her. Another assignment completed and she was ready to check out.

In the parking lot, her cell phone rang twice before a sweet voice answered. "Dr. Lewis's office, Connie speaking."

* * * * * *

Nestle stood in front of Tina tapping his foot. His anger was rising because he really didn't have time for this shit. He had important things to do.

"Tina," he snapped. "You called *me* remember?"

"Yes sir," she replied.

Tina was irritating him, but to explode on a Senior Advisor to the president probably wouldn't be a good idea. He had to maintain his composure if his project was to be successful.

"Tina?" he asked. "How much longer?"

"I have no idea sir," Tina replied. "Please have a seat. Madam President will be with you shortly."

With nothing else to do, Nestle plopped into the nearest chair. He pulled out his cell to check his emails, nothing new. Obviously the virus hadn't reached its full effectiveness yet. The genetic scientists did tell him it could be days before any symptoms appeared in the general population. After shoving his phone back into his pocket, Nestle was surprised to see Geeshmore enter the waiting room.

"What are you doing here?" he asked with a growl.

"I was summoned."

"Summoned?" Nestle repeated. "What are you a witness or something?"

"No," Geeshmore answered. "I received a call a car was waiting for me and to get into it. What are you doing here?"

"Please gentlemen," Tina urged. "Voices carry from this room. I must ask you to be quiet."

"Sorry, Tina," Geeshmore said taking a seat next to Nestle and crossing his legs.

The phone on Tina's desk beeped twice and she smiled. "The president will see you now."

"Thank you, Tina," Geeshmore replied and opened the door leading to the oval office. "Good morning, Madam President."

"Good morning," Strickland replied taking a seat on a couch. "Please join me, you too Roland."

The men sat on the opposite couch and tried to relax. Nestle kept pulling out his phone and checking for messages. Geeshmore crossed his legs, then adjusted himself, switched his legs, and adjusted himself again.

"You two remind me of little boys sitting in a principal's office," Strickland stated. "What have you done now?"

"Excuse me?" Geeshmore asked.

"Neither of you can sit still," she explained. "So tell me, what have you done?"

"Nothing," Nestle stated so quickly he didn't even convince himself.

"I see, well then," Strickland said but was cut off when Tina rushed into the room and turned on her TV.

"Madam President!" Tina stated with eyes opened so wide Nestle believed they would fall onto the floor at any moment. "You have to see this for yourself."

Tina turned on the TV and pointed to the screen. People were running madly through the street as an announcer explained the situation. But the sound was off. Strickland grabbed the remote and turned up the volume. The announcer looked terrified. Medical and rescue personnel were scrambling from victim to victim checking for any signs of life. Police were directing foot traffic and more medical personnel were arriving every second. Screams and pleas for help echoed throughout the room.

"My God!" Strickland yelled. "What in the world is going on now?"

...are trying to do everything they can to help those affected. We're still not sure if this is a terrorist attack or something else. We've been warned about the overuse of antibiotics and perhaps this is the day we've all feared. People have been dropping like flies all morning. For those of you just turning in, this is Margaret Walsh, with Fox News coming to you live from Atlanta. Shortly after rush hour, people started showing signs of being ill... coughing, vomiting, fainting or screaming. Those still in their vehicles crashed into buildings or other cars. It is chaos here and we still don't have any idea what is causing this sudden illness. So far the death toll has reached over a hundred and more are dying as the minutes pass...

Strickland muted the TV and stared at Tina. "Do you know if this is a local event?"

"No," Tina stated. "It's happening in cities all over our country. Could this be a terrorist attack, Madam President?"

Greghardt burst into the room tossing a newspaper at Strickland. "Madam President. We have a deadly epidemic on our hands! Ah! The CDC and NIH have arrived. Thank God, men, we need your help."

Greghardt took a seat between Nestle and Geeshmore and stared at them.

"So," Strickland said crossing her arms and legs. "What should we do, Dr. Nestle, Dr. Geeshmore? Please advise."

The two men sat quietly. It seemed that neither wanted to speak. Geeshmore adjusted himself again by crossing his legs, and Nestle pulled out his phone to check for messages. But again, neither spoke.

"Okay men," Strickland added. "I need the advice from my

two health officials. What should we do?"

The men remain quiet. Geeshmore leaned forward and looked over at Nestle for guidance but when none came, he sat back.

"Vernon?" Strickland asked. "You don't look so good. Are you coming down with a virus?"

Geeshmore coughed to clear his throat, "No, I don't believe so."

"Maybe we should go outside and check for ourselves," Strickland stated.

Geeshmore leaned forward and glanced at Nestle. "Um... no?"

"And why not?" Strickland asked. "Is there some reason we shouldn't go outside and take in a deep breath?"

"No? Not really. Not sure what we'd find." Geeshmore's face was now whiter than newly fallen snow. He looked like he was about to have a heart attack. "Why don't you ask Roland?"

"Ah come on," Strickland urged. "Let's take a walk. Roland, would you walk with me, Vernon? You too. I have a rose garden yah know. It's quite beautiful this time of year."

Neither man moved and neither man spoke.

"Okay," Strickland said standing. "Will you please tell me what you have done now?"

"Nothing, Madam President," Nestle stated.

"Well, I've had just about enough of this little party." Strickland walked to the small door leading to her private conference room and opened it. "Will you join us please?"

The men couldn't see who she was talking to. They turn around in their seats and cocked their heads. As people entered, their eyes widened. Several adults and many young children stood in a line in front of the president's desk. Little Lizzie cried in her mother's arms as Macie dug out a bottle of milk from the diaper bag. Dakota and Nevada jumped up and down in front of their mother and Gabe talked to Daren. Learl reached for her friend Seith's hand and smiled at the men sitting on the couch.

"Hi Dr. Nestle," Learl said with a grin. "I didn't know you were here. It's nice to see you again."

"I think I will ask you one last time," Strickland said standing in front of the frightened men sitting on the couch. "What did you *two* do now?"

* * * * * *

The meeting was held at the prestigious Sea Island hotel along the Georgia coast. Strickland stared at her hands wondering if she was sick. Not a drop of sweat anywhere. Her hands should be soaked by now, but they were dry.

"What's wrong?" Lewis asked taking the seat next to her.

"Yes sir," the bartender said waiting for the man's order.

"Bourbon," Lewis stated with a forced smile. The bartender nodded and handed Lewis a small glass with the glittering golden liquid.

"Is something bothering you, Madam President?" he asked.

"Not really," she replied taking a sip of her iced coffee. Strickland squinted her eyes trying to see deeper into her palms. But everything seemed just as normal as ever.

"Time to go," Greghardt said approaching the pair sipping on their drinks. "Ready?"

Strickland nodded and followed Greghardt down the decorated hallway. The polished wood floor echoed their footsteps as they entered the small meeting room. Strickland admired the intricately carved woodwork that lined the walls. An oriental rug covered the floor under the large table. For such a small room, the overall ambience was comforting. Three men stood at the table's end patiently awaiting their arrival. Their hands were clasped and they stood as rigid as three oak trees. Strickland had to smile. All three wore a light gray suit with dark red ties. Only one wore glasses, but all had graying goatees.

The man in the middle spoke first, "I'm Dr. Jonathan Russel, president and CEO of the Philips Institute. To my right is Dr. Fraymont Van Duyn, vice president of Internal Affairs, and to my left is Mr. Robert Collins, our legal counsel."

The two men nodded as they were introduced, but no one offered their hand as a gesture of trust. Greghardt snickered before he introduced his small clan.

"We are pleased you could join us today, gentlemen. I'm Dr. Allen Greghardt, executive liaison to The Agency. This is Dr. Jeffery Lewis, president and CEO. I'd like to personally introduce you to my friend and the president of the United States, Madam

Vivian Strickland."

"We are honored to meet you, Madam President," Russel stated. He nodded his head and smiled slightly.

"Thank you," Strickland said as she studied the three men. "Exactly how can we be of assistance?"

Russel cleared his throat before speaking. "I'm sorry," he coughed, "but I must stress this is a very delicate situation. Normally we take care of our own, but unfortunately this time we must ask for the help of The Agency and the US Government."

"I see," Strickland replied. "But what can be of such urgency you need our help?"

"We've known of the accomplishments of The Agency for quite some time. I must say your work is very impressive. Very thorough and clean."

"Again, Mr. Russel," Strickland said with a slight frown, "how exactly can we help you today?"

"We share two mutual friends," he replied lowering his head. "And I must state we are very disappointed in their recent behavior."

"I see," Strickland said now interested in who they could possibly be talking about. "Who are these two mutual friends? Do they have names?"

"Vernon Geeshmore and Roland Nestle," Russel replied lowering his head.

"I see," Strickland said but as she spoke she couldn't hold back her amusement. For some reason, hearing such an important individual state he was ashamed of her two knuckheads not only caught her off guard, but was the funniest thing she'd heard in many months.

Strickland's eyes started to tear as cries of delight filled her with happiness. Her laughs echoed through the room, and one by one the men started to smile. Lewis was first to follow Strickland's cries of joy, followed by Greghardt and the attorney Collins. It was only a few seconds before the other two joined in. Everyone was laughing so hard they had to hold their stomachs. It took several minutes before they regained control. Strickland pulled a small packet of tissues from her purse. After keeping several for herself, she passed the small packet to Lewis to share with the others.

"Thank you," Russel said as his chuckles filled the room. "I needed that."

"You're quite welcome," Strickland said wiping her eyes. "Let's be honest here. We know you're some of the richest men in the world. So you have us at a disadvantage. Vernon and Roland are *my* problem, but how are they also yours?" It was a wonderful release to laugh so hard.

"We've been following the two for a long time," Russel said at last. "We had an idea as to what they were up to, but wasn't sure how we were going to prove it or how far they had progressed. We needed to know all the players. But it seems it was just a few."

"We wish to turn this over to you," Fraymont said passing a large bound folder to Strickland. "All of our evidence is in there. You will have no problems convicting them."

"It's important the Philips Institute and the society remain clean of any accusations," Russel added with a frown.

"Society?" Greghardt asked.

"Skull and Cross Bones," Russel replied. "It's our men's society at Yale. For some reason, anything... out of the ordinary is always blamed on them."

"I see," Greghardt added.

"The Philips Institute is very interested in the welfare of this planet and all the people who live on it. We do groom selected men and teach them our ways of the society. But we do not condone the experimentations our mutual friends were conducting."

"I find that hard to believe," Lewis stated.

The three men looked sternly at him and frowned.

"Why do you say that, Dr. Lewis?" Russel replied.

"We found the laboratory," Lewis answered.

"We did too," Fraymont interjected, "and we shut it down. It was buried. We were disgusted by what happened there."

"And are you responsible for the explosion in West Virginia?" Lewis asked.

"Yes," Russel said with frown. "We discovered one of the doctors, a Dr. Eugene Spangleholtz, was trying to create human crossbreeds and succeeded. The creations that could not function were euthanized. Others were transferred to assisted-living centers. We'll ensure they're properly cared for. They will want for nothing. No one was killed in the explosion."

"It's all in the report you have in front of you, Madam President," Fraymont replied. "Dr. Spangleholtz was murdered and our investigation and conclusions are all there too."

"I see," Strickland said.

"The addresses of their concealed offices are also in that report. We'll help in any way we can to remove our mutual friends from society. We like the way you guided them to your scientist in Washington. Very impressive." Russel chuckled and shook his head. "Next time I need help, I'm contacting The Agency."

"We wish to compensate you for your troubles," Fraymont said handing Greghardt a sealed envelope. "The Philips Institute apologizes and we are embarrassed two of our own decided they didn't need to follow our rules anymore. What they did is strictly prohibited."

The three men stood and nodded to the three still sitting.

"Please stay and enjoy the facilities," Russel said before leaving. "We must return, but your rooms are paid for until Monday at noon. We've also covered your meals and a few little treats to help you relax. Please, stay and allow us to show you how sorry we are all this happened."

"Thank you," Strickland added. "But honestly we can't..."

"No," Russel interrupted. "It's all taken care of and no one will be able to trace who paid for what. Everything is on a cash basis with us. Enjoy your weekend. Good day to you all."

Strickland watched as the three left the room and shut the door behind them.

"That was weird," Strickland said looking at the large envelope in Greghardt's hand. "What's in it?"

Greghardt shrugged his shoulders and opened the envelope. "Well, there's a check here for The Agency in the sum of one billion, two hundred million dollars to begin with."

"Nice," Lewis said pulling the check from Greghardt's grip. "That will just about pay to take care of our mutual friends, and then some."

"What else?" Strickland asked.

"A letter of apology to Early and Alex Sutton with a check of two million, four hundred thousand. There's another apology letter for Marty Starling and the others with a check for the same amount. And another for Gabe's mom. Our letter asks for us to care for the hybrids we have in our custody." Greghardt shook his head and smiled.

"What's so funny?" Lewis asked.

"I guess with so much money you can buy your apologies."

"I looked up the Philips Institute before we came in here," Strickland added. "They're worth over nineteen trillion dollars."

"Well then," Greghardt said. "These payments are just a drop in the bucket to them... chunk change."

"I think it's a nice gesture for Early and Marty and the others," Strickland said. "But how do you put a price tag on what happened to them?"

"Beats me, but as for me," Lewis said staring at the pretty check, "I'm going to consider the Philips Institute as a good client."

Chapter 102

MARTY AND EARLY read and re-read their letters.

"Do we have to pay taxes on this?" Marty asked.

"Don't know," Lewis replied. "But we've set up appointments with our accountants for you. Also our investment department will help. Don't worry, you're in good hands."

"I can't believe this," Early said staring at the check. "Why?"

"They felt responsible," Lewis explained.

"But..." Marty started.

"Hey, never question fate," Lewis said with a grin. "Just enjoy your families. Your kids will be grown before you know it. Go... enjoy your lives."

"Thank you," Early cried as she hugged Lewis. "Thank you for giving me my life back."

"You are welcome," Lewis said with a tear running down his cheek. "You are very welcome. But thank your lawyer. He did all the work."

"I have," Early replied. "Trust me I have."

"Oh, and we paid for his services for you," Lewis said. "You owe him nothing. We also offered him a job... and his secretary. So just go and have a good life, Early. You both, keep in touch."

When the women left Lewis's office, Carrie entered.

"Well," she said. "I guess we did it again."

"We always do," Lewis said staring out at the sunset.

"Will it ever end?" Carrie asked joining Lewis at the window.

"Doubt it."

* * * * * *

Early and Marty watched as the older children played in the pool. Although the area was enclosed, the sun still filtered through and was enough to brighten their spirits.

"Your daughter is so cute," Early said.

"Would you like to hold her?"

"I'd love to," Early replied reaching for the baby. "I especially love her little feet."

"They are a challenge," Marty replied. "But with the correct shoes she should be fine as she grows. Has anything special shown up in your girls yet?"

"Nothing," Early replied as she bounced the giggling Lizzie on her knees.

"She used to have fur," Marty added. "But it's all gone now. I just love her long golden hair."

"It's much thicker than normal. She'll love it when she gets older. Her face seems to be shaping up nicely too."

"Yes," Marty said looking out at the children jumping into the water trying to place her view on Early's twins. "I was worried at first. But with the face plate she sleeps with, it's helping to reshape her skull. I think she'll look normal when she's older."

"Normal?" Early replied. "Yes... but much more beautiful than the average."

"What have you decided about your husband?" Marty asked holding out a towel for Eliza.

"Can I get a drink, mommy?" Eliza asked with water dripping onto her mother. "I'm thirsty."

"Honestly, Eliza?" Marty snapped jumping from her chair. "Yes, I'll go get you a drink. Excuse me, Early, while I get something for these kids. I'll grab us some drinks too."

"Thanks Marty," Early said smiling at Eliza and bouncing Lizzie on her knee. "Are you enjoying the water?"

"Yes ma'am," Eliza said wiping her face. "And I like the way Dakota and Nevada can stay underwater for so long. It's pretty cool."

"What do you mean?" Early asked.

"They don't have to come up for air if they don't want to," Eliza replied. "We counted to four hundred and they're still sitting on the bottom."

"Dakota... Nevada...." Early yelled. "Come here please."

Chapter 103

THE WEEKS PASSED and the winter months covered the city in a light blanket of snow. Three administrative judges sat patiently waiting for the others. It had been a long deliberation, but their decisions were final. Each judge wore a black robe and sat pompously behind the bench. The room looked like any other courtroom, in any city across America. But unlike other courtrooms, the rulings set down here were final... no appeals... no stays... no pardons.

Vernon Geeshmore and Roland Nestle were escorted into the room by two armed guards. Their attorneys were at their sides. Normally, most verdicts and sentences were carried out in closed sessions. But special cases deserved special accommodations, and this was an extraordinary case. Lewis and Greghardt sat in the back of the room eating popcorn and sipping soda through a straw.

Nestle could smell the popcorn as soon as he entered. He scrunched his nose turning toward the odor. When their eyes met, Lewis and Greghardt smiled and waved. With a frown and growl, Nestle took his seat. He looked up at the three administrative judges. But not one of them noticed who was seated in the room, they were too busy reading the material in front of them.

With it all quiet except for the occasional munching of popcorn from the back of the room, the bailiff stood and asked everyone to stand.

"This is going to be such an exciting event," Lewis said jumping to his feet.

"I can't wait for the ending," Greghardt added, "I bet it has a great twist."

Nestle could hear every word they said, and they could tell his anger would soon engulf him. After introducing the judges, the bailiff asked everyone to take their seats.

"Would Vernon Geeshmore please stand?" One of the judges said.

Geeshmore hesitated for only a second before his attorney grabbed his arm and pulled him into a standing position. Sweat rolled from his temples.

The female judge in the middle spoke softly, "Vernon Geeshmore, you have been charged with twenty-four counts of murder in the first degree, two counts of terrorism against the United States, sixteen counts of kidnapping, thirty-two counts of committing and initiating hate crimes, three counts of Government fraud, and four counts of bank fraud. Mr. Geeshmore, how do you plead?"

Geeshmore didn't know how to answer. He stood quiet and dumbfounded. His attorney shook his head and answered for his client. "We plead guilty your honors."

"Very well," she replied. "This court hereby finds you guilty on all counts. Hereafter, you are stripped of all honors of doctorate. Hence forth, you are not permitted to use the title of *doctor*. Your license to practice has been suspended indefinitely. Your position as Director of the National Institutes of Health is hereby terminated effective immediately. For your crimes against the people of the United States, you are hereby fined seven million, two hundred thousand dollars. We sentence you to eight hundred years in a high security federal penitentiary without the possibility of parole. Do you have anything to say to this court?"

"No ma'am," Geeshmore said as tears ran down his face.

"I must add, Mr. Geeshmore, you make me sick," the female judge stated. "I don't know what you were thinking, or if you were thinking at all, but the sight of you makes me ill. Bailiff, remove this scum from my sight."

As the armed guard escorted him from the room, Geeshmore turned one last time to look upon the man he used to call his friend. Nestle looked away as Geeshmore shook his head. The door banged loudly as it closed behind the guilty man and the sound reverberated around the room.

"Well," Lewis laughed. "I wasn't expecting all of *that*, were you?"

"Not at *all*," Greghardt chucked. "This is better than I expected."

Again the aroma of popcorn filled the air as the pair in the back munched and sipped loudly.

"Would Roland Nestle please rise and face the court," the same judge announced.

Nestle jumped to his feet. He stood firm and proud glaring into the eyes of the three clowns sitting in front of him. Nestle didn't know who they thought they were, but this was a lynching if there ever was, not to mention a major farce. One day he'd make them all pay.

"Roland Nestle," the female judge said from a few feet up. "You have been charged with eighty-six counts of murder in the first degree, one hundred and forty-two counts of murder in the second degree, seven counts of terrorism against the United States, eighty-four counts of kidnapping, seventy-nine counts of committing and initiating hate crimes, twelve counts of Government fraud, and sixteen counts of bank fraud. Mr. Nestle, how do you plead?"

"Not guilty... Not anything! I refuse to acknowledge these proceedings," Nestle said firmly. "And I want to say this whole ploy is a ridiculous display on how some people can waste taxpayers' money." Nestle turned and stared at the two men eating the popcorn. He scowled. "This is a farce and a mockery of our legal system."

The female judge ignored his statement and said, "Very well. This court hereby finds you guilty on all counts. Hereafter, you are stripped of all honors of doctorate. Hence forth, you are not permitted to use the title of *doctor*. Your license to practice has been suspended indefinitely. Your position as Director at the Centers of Disease Control is hereby terminated effective immediately. For your crimes against the people of the United States, you are hereby fined one hundred million dollars. You are ordered to spend one hour with each of the victims for restitution.

It is this court's determination you are dangerous not only to yourself, but to society and the world at large. Therefore, this court sentences you to death which is to be carried out by gas inhalation if it does not occur earlier. Do you have anything to say to this court?"

"Yes," Nestle said frozen with anger. "Go fuck yourselves... all of you!"

* * * * *

Nestle found himself strapped to a wall inside a small room with no windows. He was stripped naked except for a short towel wrapped around his waist. A table with a baseball bat, some knives, and other odd items was in front of him. Two arm guards stood at attention at his sides.

"What kind of bullshit is this supposed to be?" Nestle screamed. "I have rights!"

The two guards ignored his shouts. With his wrists and ankles strapped to the wall, the only things he could move were his hips or his head.

"You fucking bastards," he yelled. "Let me go!"

EPILOGUE

THE SNOW WAS just starting to melt as the new spring flowers broke through the surface of the thawing ground. The aroma of fresh green grass filled the air with a newness that brightened everyone's spirits. Maddie took in a deep breath of the clean damp air and smiled. Only a few puffy clouds floated in the early morning sky, which meant it was going to be a beautiful day.

Carrie's car screeched to a stop near the curb in front of Maddie's house. She waved as she jumped from the car. Something had excited her and Maddie knew she'd hear all about it in just a few minutes. After a long embrace, they entered the house and sat at the kitchen table. With hot fresh coffee in hand, Maddie couldn't wait any longer.

"Spill," Maddie urged.

"What?" Carrie asked.

"What? I know something's up. Now spill."

"Okay," Carrie replied holding out her left hand.

"Wow," Maddie exclaimed. "It's beautiful."

"Devon proposed last night," Carrie said proudly displaying her diamond ring. "It was so romantic. It was just us two sitting by the fire. He was telling me about the new case he's assigned to and I was telling him about mine. Then he left the room to get us some water. When he returned, he was smiling. He got down on one knee, which isn't easy for him. He's so big and clumsy, and then he proposed. I cried."

"That's so sweet," Maddie said releasing Carrie's hand. "I remember when Nate proposed to me. It was the happiest day of my life, other than the birth of my babies."

"Did you hear what happened to Dr. Nestle?" Carrie asked.

"Yes, I did," Maddie replied. "I also heard when word reached Vernon he had a heart attack. But he's still alive from what I understand."

"I wished I could have seen his face when Marty or Early walked in," Carrie said laughing. "Can you imagine?"

"No I cannot," Maddie replied rubbing her arms.

"Kind of ironic, don't you think?" Carrie asked.

"What do you mean?"

"Well, he thought he had it all—money, power, a great job, and then *poof*, all gone," Carrie laughed.

The doorbell pulled the two from their thoughts.

"I'll get it," Nate yelled from the other room.

The sound of children's voices echoed through the house and Maddie smiled. "I guess Early and Marty are here."

"Did you hide the eggs and baskets?" Carrie asked.

"Yep," Maddie said with a grin. "Let's go see the pretty Easter dresses."

"Hey Mad," Carrie said, taking hold of Maddie's hand.

"Yes?"

"I love you."

"And I love you too, Carrie Clarke, soon to be Carrie Clarke-Arvol, and happy Easter, my sweet."